Primo Levi was born in Turin in 1919 and trained as a chemist. Arrested as a member of the anti-fascist resistance during the war, he was deported to Auschwitz. His experiences there are described in two classic autobiographical works, *If This Is A Man* and *The Truce*. He also wrote a number of universally highly-acclaimed novels and essay collections, including *If Not Now, When?*, *Moments of Reprieve* and *The Wrench*. *The Drowned and the Saved*, Levi's impassioned attempt to understand the 'rationale' behind the concentration camps, was completed shortly before his tragic death in Turin in 1987.

'Beautifully scripted flights of scientific fantasy . . . provoking, amusing and masterfully crafted' *Vogue*

'Marvellously inventive' *Glasgow Herald*

'Sinewy and compelling' *Jewish Chronicle*

'Levi's beautifully crafted stories always provoke and challenge, yet do so with crafty originality' *Sunday Tribune*

Also by Primo Levi in Abacus:

Other People's Trades
The Drowned and the Saved
If This Is A Man/The Truce
The Wrench
The Periodic Table
Moments of Reprieve
If Not Now, When?

The Sixth Day and Other Tales

PRIMO LEVI

Translated by Raymond Rosenthal

Storie naturali was originally published under the
pseudonym Damiano Malabila

An *Abacus* Book

First published in Great Britain by Michael Joseph Ltd, 1990
Published in Abacus by Sphere Books Ltd, 1991

Originally published in Italy as *Storie naturali* and *Vizio di forma*.

Printed and bound in Great Britain by
BPCC Hazell Books
Aylesbury, Bucks, England
Member of BPCC Ltd.

ISBN 0 349 10186 8

Sphere Books Ltd
A Division of
Macdonald & Co (Publishers) Ltd
165 Great Dover Street
London SE1 4YA

A member of Maxwell Macmillan Publishing Corporation

CONTENTS

There were one hundred men in arms.
And when the sun rose in the sky,
They all took a step forward.
Hours passed, without a sound:
Their eyelashes did not flicker.
But when the bells tolled,
They all moved a step forward.
So the day passed, and it was evening,
But when the first star flowered in the sky,
Then all of them together took a step forward.
'Get back, get out of here, filthy ghosts,
Return to your old night':
But no one replied, and instead
All in a circle took a step forward.

– PRIMO LEVI

The Mnemogogues

Dr Morandi (but he was not yet accustomed to hearing himself addressed as doctor) had gotten off the bus with the intention of remaining incognito for at least two days, but he soon realized that he would not be able to do so. The owner of the Café Alpino had offered him a neutral welcome (evidently she wasn't sufficiently curious or sufficiently sharp); but from the tobacconist's smile, at once deferential and maternal and slightly mocking, he'd understood that he was already the 'new doctor' and no postponing it. I must have my degree written on my face, he thought: – '*Tu es medicus in aeternum*,' and, what is worse, everyone will be aware of it. Morandi had no taste at all for irrevocable things, and, at least for the moment, he felt inclined to see in this whole business nothing but a huge and everlasting nuisance. Something along the lines of the birth trauma, he concluded without too much coherence.

And in the meantime, as a first consequence of the lost incognito, he must go and look for Montesanto, without delay. He returned to the café to take the letter of introduction from his suitcase, and he began to search through the deserted village and beneath the relentless sun for the nameplate.

He managed to find it after many pointless turns; he hadn't wanted to ask anyone for directions, for on the faces of the few people he had encountered he thought he read a far from benevolent curiosity.

He had expected the nameplate to be old, but he found it older than all possible expectation, covered with verdigris, the name almost illegible. All the shutters of the house were closed, the low façade peeling and faded. At his arrival there was a rapid and silent scampering of lizards.

Montesanto himself came down to open the door. He was a tall, corpulent old man, with myopic yet vivacious eyes in a face with heavy, tired features: he moved with the silent massive assurance of a bear. He was in shirtsleeves, without a collar; the shirt was crumpled and of dubious cleanliness.

Along the stairs, and then above in the office, it was cool and almost dark. Montesanto sat down, and asked Morandi to sit on a particularly uncomfortable chair. Twenty-two years in here, Morandi thought with a mental shiver, while the other man unhurriedly read the letter of introduction. He looked around as his eyes became accustomed to the dusky light.

On the desk, letters, magazines, prescriptions and other papers of a by now indefinable nature had yellowed and attained a staggering thickness. From the ceiling hung a spider's long thread, rendered visible by the dust adhering to it, and it languidly followed the imperceptible breath of the noonday air. A glassed-in cupboard with a few antiquated instruments and a few small vials in which the liquids had corroded the glass, marking the level they had remained at for too long a time. On the wall, strangely familiar, the large framed photograph of the Medical Graduates of 1911 that he knew so well: there was the square forehead and the strong chin of his father, Morandi Senior; and right next to him (alas, how hard to recognize!) the now present Ignazio Montesanto, slim, neat, and frightfully young, with that air of an intellectual hero and martyr so favored by the graduates of that period.

Having finished reading, Montesanto deposited the letter on the pile of papers on the desk, where it became perfectly camouflaged.

'Fine,' he said then. 'I'm glad that destiny, luck, . . .' and the sentence ended in an indistinct murmur which was followed by a long silence. The old physician leaned back, resting the chair on its hind legs, and turned his eyes to the ceiling. Morandi waited for him to resume speaking; the silence was starting to become burdensome when Montesanto unpredictably began.

He talked at length, first with many pauses, then more rapidly; his physiognomy became animated, his eyes glittered mobile and alive in his ravaged face. Morandi, to his surprise, realized that he was experiencing a precise and gradually growing liking for the old man. This was evidently a soliloquy, a great vacation that Montesanto was granting himself. For him the opportunity to talk (and you sensed that he knew how to talk, knew the importance of it) must be rare, brief returns to a bygone vigor of thought perhaps lost by now.

Montesanto told the story: about his cruel professional initiation on the battlefields and in the trenches of the previous war; about his attempt at a university career, undertaken with enthusiasm, continued with apathy and abandoned amid the indifference of his colleagues, who had discouraged all his initiatives; about his voluntary exile in this post as municipal doctor in this forsaken town, searching for something too indefinable to ever be found; and then about his present life as a lonely man, a stranger in the midst of a community of small lighthearted people, good and bad, but irretrievably distant from him; about the definitive prevalence of the past over the present, and the final shipwreck of every passion, except for his faith in the dignity of thought and the supremacy of the things of the spirit.

What a strange old man, Morandi thought; he had noticed that for almost an hour now the doctor had spoken without looking at him in the face. At first he had made various attempts to lead him back to a more concrete plane, to ask him about the sanitary conditions of the surgery, about the equipment that must be replaced, about the pharmaceutical cabinet, and perhaps even about his own personal situation; but he had not succeeded, because of his own timidity and a more calculated reserve.

Now Montesanto was silent, his face turned toward the ceiling and his gaze adjusted to the infinite. Evidently the soliloquy continued within him. Morandi was embarrassed; he asked himself whether or not a reply was expected from him, and what it should be, and whether the doctor was still aware that he was not alone in the office.

He was aware. He abruptly let the chair settle its four legs on the floor, and in a strange hoarse voice said:

'Morandi, you're young, very young. I know that you're a good doctor, or rather that you'll become one; I think that you're also a good man. In case you're not good enough to understand what I have told you and what I will now tell you, I hope that you will be good enough not to laugh at it. And should you laugh at it, it will be no great misfortune: as you know, it is unlikely that we shall meet again; and in any event, it is in the nature of things that the young should laugh at the old. I merely beg you not to forget that you will be the first to know these things about me. I mean no flattery in telling you that you seem to me particularly worthy of my confidence. I'm sincere: you represent the first opportunity I've had in years, and probably you will also be the last.'

'Tell me,' Morandi said, quite simply.

'Morandi, did you ever notice how powerfully certain smells evoke certain memories?'

The blow was unexpected. Morandi swallowed with an effort; he said that he had noticed and also that he had made an effort to explain it.

He could not explain the change in subject. Within himself he concluded that, at bottom, this must be only some sort of fixation, such as all doctors have after reaching a certain age. Like Andriani: at sixty-five, rich in fame, money and patients, he had just barely enough time to cover himself with ridicule because of that business of the neural field.

Montesanto had gripped the corners of his desk with both hands and was staring into the void, wrinkling his brow. Then he went on:

'I will show you something unusual. During the years of my work as an associate in pharmacology I studied rather thoroughly the action of adrenaline absorbed through the nose. From this I did not glean anything useful for humanity except for a single, as you will see, rather indirect result.

'Also in the years that followed I devoted a good deal of my time to the problem of olfactory sensations, and their relation to molecular structure. This, in my opinion, is a most fruitful field, as well as one open to researchers equipped with modest means. Even recently I've been pleased to see that some people take an interest in it, and I am also up-to-date on your electronic theories; but by now the one aspect of the problem that interests me is something else. Today I possess what I believe no one else in the world possesses.

'There are those who take no interest in the past and let the dead bury the dead. However, there are also those who care about the past and are saddened by its continuous fading away. Furthermore, there are those who are diligent enough to keep a diary, day by day, so as to save everything of theirs from oblivion, and preserve their materialized memories in their home and on their person: a dedication in a book, a dried flower, a lock of hair, photographs, old letters.

'I by my nature can only think with horror of the eventuality that even a single one of my memories should be erased, and I have adopted all those methods, but I've also created a new one.

'No, what is involved is not a scientific discovery: I simply have used to best advantage my experience as a pharmacologist and have reconstructed, with exactitude and in preservable form, a number of sensations that mean something to me.

'I call them – but I repeat, don't think that I often speak of them – I call them mnemogogues:

"arousers of memories." Would you mind coming with me?'

He rose and headed down the hallway. Halfway along he turned and added, 'As you can well imagine, they must be used parsimoniously, if you don't want their evocative power to weaken; what's more, I don't have to tell you that they are unavoidably personal. Absolutely. One might actually say that they are my very person, since I, at least in part, am formed out of them.'

He opened a cupboard. Inside there were about fifty small bottles with ground stoppers, all numbered.

'Please, pick one.'

Morandi looked at him perplexed; he extended a hesitant hand and chose a small bottle.

'Open it and sniff it. What do you smell?'

Morandi inhaled deeply several times, first keeping his eyes on Montesanto, then tilting back his head in the posture of someone searching his memory.

'This would seem to be the smell of a barracks.'

Montesanto in his turn sniffed. 'Not exactly,' he answered. 'Or at least not so for me. It is the odor of elementary school rooms; in fact, of my room in my school. I won't expatiate on its composition; it contains volatile fatty acids and an unsaturated ketone. I understand that for you it's nothing: for me it's my childhood.

'I'm also preserving the photograph of my thirty-seven classmates in the first grade, but the scent from this small bottle is enormously quicker in recalling to my mind the interminable hours of tedium spent over the spelling primer; the particular state of mind of children (and of the child!) during the terrifying suspense before the first dictation test. When I sniff it – not now: obviously a certain degree of concentration is necessary – when, as I was saying, I sniff it, my innards are convulsed in just the way they were at the age of seven as I waited to be called up to be interrogated. Would you like to pick another one?'

'I think I remember . . . wait . . . In my grandfather's villa, in the country, there was a small room where fruit was stored to ripen . . .'

'Perfect,' Montesanto said with sincere satisfaction. 'Exactly as the treatises state. I'm so pleased that you hit on a professional odor; this is the breath of a diabetic in the acetonemia phase. With a few more years of practice you would have certainly figured it out yourself. As you well know, an ominous clinical sign, the prelude of things to come.

'My father died from diabetes fifteen years ago; it was neither a brief nor a merciful death. My father meant much to me. I sat up with him for many, many nights, impotently watching the progressive obliteration of his personality; those hours of vigil were not sterile. Many of my beliefs were shaken by them, much of my world changed. So for me it is neither a matter of apples nor diabetes, but the solemn, purifying travail, unique in life, of a religious crisis.'

'. . . This can only be carbolic acid!' Morandi exclaimed, sniffing the third bottle.

'Exactly. I thought that this odor would mean something to you too; but, come to think of it, it isn't a year yet that you finished your shifts in hospital, the memory has not yet matured. For I'm sure that you have noticed, haven't you? that the evocative mechanism of which we are speaking requires that the stimuli, after having acted repeatedly in connection with a certain environment or a certain state of mind, then cease to operate for rather a long period of time. In any event, it is a matter of common observation that memories, in order to be suggestive, must have an antique flavor.

'I too worked shifts in the hospital and have filled my lungs with carbolic acid. But this happened a quarter of a century ago, and in any case since then carbolic acid has ceased to represent the foundation of antisepsis. But in my time it was: so that even to this day I cannot smell it (not chemically pure carbolic acid, but this sort, to which I've added traces of other substances that make it specific for me) without a complex picture arising in my mind, a picture that includes a tune fashionable at that time, my youthful enthusiasm for Biagio Pascal, a certain springlike languor in my loins and knees, and a female classmate who, so I've heard, has recently become a grandmother.'

This time he himself had chosen a small bottle; he handed it to Morandi. 'I must confess to you that I'm still rather proud of this preparation. Even though I never published its results, I consider this to be my true scientific success. I would like to hear your opinion.'

Morandi sniffed with the greatest care. It certainly was not a new smell: one might call it scorched, dry, warm . . .

'. . . When you strike together two flint stones?'

'Yes, that too. I congratulate you on your olfactory prowess. One often smells this odor high in the mountains when the rocks warm under the sun, especially when there is a scree of stones. I assure you that it wasn't easy to reproduce in vitro and to stabilize the substances that constitute it without altering the sensible properties.

'There was a time when I often went up into the mountains, mostly alone. After reaching the peak I would lie down beneath the sun in the still and silent air, and it seemed to me that I had attained a goal. At those moments, and only if I set my mind to it, I would perceive this slight odor that one rarely smells elsewhere. As far as I'm concerned, I ought to call it the odor of peace achieved.'

Having overcome his initial uneasiness, Morandi was taking an interest in the game. At random he unstoppered a fifth bottle and handed it to Montesanto. 'And what about this?'

From it emanated a light airy smell of clean skin, powder and summer. Montesanto sniffed, put back the small bottle and said curtly, 'This is neither a place nor a time, it is a person.'

He closed the cupboard; he had spoken in a definitive tone. Morandi had mentally prepared some expressions of interest and admiration, but he was unable to overcome a strange inner barrier and gave up on articulating them. He hastily look his leave with a vague promise of another visit, rushed down the stairs and out into the sun. He sensed that he had blushed deeply.

Within five minutes he was amid the pine trees furiously climbing up the steepest slope, trampling on the soft underbrush, far from any path. It was very pleasant to feel his muscles, lungs and heart working at their full power, just like that, naturally, without having to help them along. It was quite wonderful to be twenty-four years old.

He accelerated the rhythm of his climb as much as he could until he felt the blood throbbing loudly in his ears. Then he stretched out on the grass, with his eyes closed, contemplating the red glimmer of the sun through his eyelids. Then he felt washed clean.

So that was Montesanto. . . . No, there was no need to flee, he would not become like that, he would not let himself become like that. He would not speak about it to anyone, not even to Lucia, not even to Giovanni. No, that would be ungenerous.

Although, actually . . . only to Giovanni . . . and in completely theoretical terms . . . was there anything one couldn't speak about to Giovanni? Yes, he would write about it to Giovanni, tomorrow. Or rather (he checked the time) right away; the letter could perhaps still leave with the evening mail. Immediately.

Angelic Butterfly

They sat in the jeep, stiff and silent: they'd been living together for two months, but there was not much familiarity among them. That day it was the Frenchman's turn to drive. They went down the Kurfürstendamm, jolting over the pocked asphalt, turned into the Glockenstrasse barely skirting a drift of rubble, and continued along it up to the Magdalene: there a bomb crater full of slimy water blocked the street; from a submerged pipeline gas gurgled in large viscous bubbles.

'It's farther down, number twenty-six,' the Englishman said. 'Let's continue on foot.'

The house at number twenty-six appeared intact, but was almost isolated. It was surrounded by abandoned plots from which the rubble had been removed; grass was already growing on them and here and there they had been turned into anemic vegetable gardens.

The bell didn't work; they knocked at length in vain, then forced the door, which gave way at the first push. Inside there were dust, cobwebs and a penetrating odor of mold. 'On the second floor,' the Englishman said. On the second floor they found the nameplate: LEEB; there were two locks and the door was sturdy – it withstood their efforts for a long time.

When they entered they found themselves in the dark. The Russian switched on a flashlight, then he threw open a window; they heard a rapid scamper of mice, but they did not see the animals. The room was empty: not one piece of furniture. There was only a crude scaffolding, and two thick parallel poles which ran horizontally from wall to wall at a height of two meters from the floor. The American snapped three photographs from different angles, and drew a quick sketch.

On the floor was a layer of foul rags, wastepaper, bones, feathers and fruit peels; there were large reddish brown stains, which the American scraped carefully with a blade, collecting their dust in a glass vial. In one corner, a small heap of an indefinable material, dry, white and gray: it smelled of ammonia and rotten eggs and swarmed with worms. 'Herrenvolk!' the Russian said with contempt (they spoke German to each other); the American gathered a sample of that substance as well.

The Englishman picked up a bone, carried it to the window and examined it attentively. 'From what sort of animal is it?' the Frenchman asked. 'I don't know,' the Englishman replied. 'Never saw a bone like this. You would say that it's from a prehistoric bird: but this ridge is only found . . . well, it'll be necessary to cut a thin section of it.' In his voice could be heard revulsion, hatred and curiosity.

They gathered together all the bones and took them to the jeep. There was a small crowd of curious onlookers. A child had climbed into it and was rummaging under the seats. When they saw the four soldiers, they scattered quickly. The soldiers were able to get hold of only three of them: two oldish men and a girl. They questioned them; they knew nothing. Professor Leeb? Never heard of him. Frau Spengler? from the first floor? Died in the bombings.

They climbed into the jeep and started the motor, but the girl, who had already turned to leave, came back and asked, 'Do you have cigarettes?' They did. The girl said, 'When they did in Professor Leeb's nasty beasts, I was there too.' They hoisted her into the jeep and took her to the Allied headquarters.

'So that story was really true?' the Frenchman said.

'Apparently,' the Englishman answered.

'A nice little job for the experts,' the Frenchman said, patting the small bag of bones. 'But for us too: now we have to write up a report, they won't spare us that. Filthy job!'

Hilbert was in a fury. 'Guano,' he said, 'what else do you want to know? The kind of bird? Go to a fortune-teller, not a chemist. For four days I've been racking my brains over your disgusting findings: I'll be hanged if the devil himself can make more out of it. Bring me other samples: albatross guano, guano from penguins, from gulls; then I'll be able to make comparisons, and perhaps, with a bit of luck, we'll be able to talk about it again. I'm not a guano specialist. As for the stains on the floor, I've found some hemoglobin in them. If anyone asks me where from I'll end up in the guardhouse.'

'Why in the guardhouse?' the commissioner asked.

'In the guardhouse, yessir: because if anyone asked me I'd tell him he's an imbecile, I don't care if he outranks me. There's everything in there: blood, cement, cat piss and mouse piss, sauerkraut, beer – in short, the quintessence of Germany.'

The colonel rose ponderously. 'Enough for today,' he said. 'You're invited for tomorrow night. I've found a place that's not at all bad, in the Grunewald, on the shore of the lake. We'll talk about it again, when all of us will be a little less nervous.'

It was a requisitioned beer hall and you could find everything there. Next to the colonel sat Hilbert and Smirnov, the biologist. The four men from the jeep sat at the two longer sides; at the end of the table were a journalist and Leduc, from the military tribunal.

'This Leeb,' the colonel said, 'was a strange person. The time he lived in was conducive to theories, as you well know. And if the theory was in harmony with the environment, not a whole lot of documentation was necessary for it to be launched and received also in the highest places. But in his way Leeb was a serious scientist: he searched for facts, not for success.

'Now, don't expect me to present Leeb's theories with great accuracy: in the first place, because I have understood them only to the extent that a colonel can understand them; and in the second, because, well, since I'm a member of the Presbyterian church . . . in short, I believe in the immortal soul and I'm concerned about mine.'

'Listen, colonel,' Hilbert of the obstinate brow broke in, 'listen. Tell us what you know, please. For no other reason but that since three months yesterday all of us have been busy with nothing else . . . after all, it seems to me the time has come for us to know what game we're playing. Also so that we can work a bit more intelligently, you understand.'

'That's more than right, and besides we're here this evening for just that purpose. But don't be surprised if I go the long way round, and you, Smirnov, must correct me if I stray too far afield.

'So then. In certain Mexican lakes there lives a small animal with an impossible name, shaped a bit like a salamander. It's been living quite blithely for I don't know how many millions of years, and yet it has title to and is responsible for a sort of biological scandal: because it reproduces itself at the larval stage. Now, as far as I have been given to understand, this is an extremely grave matter, an intolerable heresy, a low blow by nature at the expense of its scholars and lawmakers. In short, it is as if a caterpillar, actually a she-caterpillar, in short a female, mated with another caterpillar, was fertilized and deposited its eggs before becoming a butterfly, and naturally other caterpillars were born from the eggs. So what's the point of becoming a butterfly? What's the point of becoming a 'perfect insect'? You might just as well do without it.

'In fact, the axolotl does without it (that's the name of the little monster, I'd forgotten to tell you). He almost always does without it: only one individual out of a hundred or a thousand, perhaps particularly long-lived and quite a while after having reproduced itself, is transformed into a different animal. Don't make those grimaces, Smirnov, or else you talk. We all express ourselves as best we can and know how.'

He paused. 'Neoteny, that's what this mix-up is called, when an animal reproduces itself at the larval stage.'

Dinner had ended, and the time had come to light up their pipes. The nine men moved to the terrace and the Frenchman said, 'Fine, all this is very interesting, but I don't see what it has to do with . . .'

'We're getting there. All that remains to be said is that for a few decades now they apparently (and he waved his hand in the direction of Smirnov) have been able to get their hands on these phenomena, and to some extent guide them. That, by administering to the axolotl's hormone extracts . . .'

'Thyroid extract,' Smirnov clarified grudgingly.

'Thanks. Thyroid extract . . . the molting must always take place. Take place, that is, before the death of the animal. Now, this is what Leeb had got into his head. That this condition is not as exceptional as it might seem: that other animals, many perhaps, all perhaps, perhaps also man, have something in reserve, a potentiality. A further capacity for development. That unquestionably they are in a preliminary stage, a tentative drafting stage, and can become 'other,' and don't do so only because death intervenes beforehand. That, in short, we too are neotenic.'

'On what experimental basis?' a voice asked from the dark.

'None, or very little. A long manuscript of his is on file: certainly a very curious mixture of acute observations, reckless generalizations, extravagant and foggy theories, literary and mythological divagations, polemical suggestions saturated with malice, rampant adulation for the Very Important Persons of the period. I'm not surprised that it remained unpublished. There is a chapter on the third teething of hundred-year-olds which also contains a curious case study of bald people whose hair grew again in extreme old age. Another deals with the iconography of angels and devils, from the Sumerians to Melozzo da Forli and from Cimabue to Roualt; this contains a passage that seems fundamental to me, in which in his at once apodictic and confused manner, with maniacal insistence, Leeb formulates the hypothesis that . . . in brief, that angels are not a fantastic invention nor supernatural beings nor a poetic dream but our future, what we will become, what we might become if we lived long enough, or subjected ourselves to his manipulations. And in fact the next chapter, which is the longest in the treatise and of which I've understood very little, is entitled *Physiological Foundations of Metempsychosis*. Still another chapter contains a program of experiments on human alimentation: a program of such great scope that a hundred lives would not be sufficient to realize it. It proposes to subject entire villages for generations to crazy diets based on fermented milk, or fish eggs, or barley sprouts, or puree of algae; with the rigorous exclusion of exogamy, sacrifice (that's exactly what is written: *opferung*) of all individuals at the age of sixty and their autopsy, may God forgive him if he can. There also is, as an epigraph, a quotation from *The Divine Comedy*, in Italian, which deals with worms, insects far removed from perfection and 'angelic butterflies.' I almost forgot: the manuscript is preceded by a dedicatory epistle addressed to guess who? To Alfred Rosenberg, the fellow of *The Myth of the Twentieth Century*, and it is followed by an appendix in which Leeb mentions experimental activity 'of a more modest character' undertaken by him in the March of 1943: a cycle of ground-breaking and preliminary experiments so that (with due caution for the sake of secrecy) it can be carried out in an ordinary civilian dwelling. The civilian dwelling granted to him for the purpose was located at 26 Glockenstrasse.'

'My name is Gertrude Enk,' the girl said. 'I'm nineteen years old, and I was sixteen when Professor Leeb set up his laboratory on the Glockenstrasse. We lived opposite, and from the window it was possible to see all sorts of things. In 1943 there arrived a small military truck: four men in uniform and four in civilian clothes got out of it. The civilians were very thin and did not lift their heads; two were men and two were women.

'Then a number of cases arrived with the words 'war materiel' written on them. We were very cautious and would look only when we were certain that no one noticed, because we had understood that there was something rather murky underneath all this. For many months nothing else happened, the professor would come only once or twice a month: alone, or with military men and party members. I was very curious, but my father always kept saying, 'Leave it alone, don't bother with what's going on in there. For us Germans the less we know, the better.' Then came the bombings; the house at number twenty-six remained standing, but the air blasts shattered the windows. The first time, in the room on the second story we saw the four people lying on the floor on pallets. They were covered as though it were winter, while actually during those days it was exceptionally hot. They seemed to be dead or asleep: but they couldn't be dead because the male nurse right alongside them was quietly reading a paper and smoking his pipe; but if they were asleep, wouldn't they have been awakened by the sirens sounding the all-clear?'

'The second time, though, there no longer were pallets and the people were gone. There were four poles placed across the room halfway up and on them roosted four ugly beasts.'

'What do you mean, four beasts?' the colonel asked.

'Four birds: they looked like vultures, although I've only seen vultures at the cinema. They were frightened, and they let out terrifying cries. They seemed to want to jump down from the poles, but they must have been chained, because they never raised their feet from the perch. They seemed to make an attempt to fly, but with those wings . . .'

'What kind of wings did they have?'

'Sort of wings, with a few sparse feathers. They looked like . . . they looked like the wings of roasted chickens, that's it. We couldn't see the heads very well because our windows were too far up, but they were anything but beautiful and very scary. They resembled the mummy heads you see in the museums. But then the nurse came in immediately and pulled the blanket in such a way that we couldn't look inside. The next day the windows were already repaired.'

'And then?'

'And then nothing else. The bombings were more and more frequent, two, three a day; our house collapsed, everyone died except for my father and myself. Yet, as I already said, the house at number twenty-six remained standing; only the widow Spengler died, but out in the street, caught by a low-level strafing.

'The Russians came, the end of the war came, and everyone was hungry. We had built ourselves a shack nearby, and I got along some way or other. One night we saw a lot of people talking in the street, in front of number twenty-six. Then one of them opened the door and they all went inside, jostling each other. So I said to my father, 'Let me go see what's happening'; he made the usual remarks but I was hungry and so I went. When I got upstairs it was almost over.'

'What was over?'

'They'd slaughtered them with clubs and knives and had already cut them up into pieces. The leader must have been the male nurse, I thought I recognized him; besides, he was the one who had the keys. Actually, I remember that when they were through, he went to the trouble of locking all the doors – who knows why, for there was nothing left inside.'

'What became of the professor?' Hilbert asked.

'No one knows for sure,' the colonel answered. 'According to the official version, he's dead. He hanged himself when the Russians arrived. But I'm convinced that is not true: because men like him give up only when faced by failure, whereas he, no matter how one may judge this dirty business, was not a failure. I believe that if we were to search thoroughly, we would find him, and perhaps not all that far away; I believe that we haven't heard the last of Professor Leeb.'

Order On The Cheap

I am always pleased to see Mr Simpson. He's not one of your usual salesmen, who remind me of public defenders: he's truly in love with the NATCA machines, believes in them with innocent faith, torments himself over their flaws and breakdowns, triumphs with their triumphs. Or at least, that's how he seems to be, even if he is not – which, to all intents and purposes, amounts to the same thing.

Even leaving aside our business relations, we're almost friends; nevertheless, I had lost sight of him in 1960, after he sold me the Versifier: he was terribly busy, filling the demands for that very successful model, working every day until midnight. Then, toward the middle of August, he had phoned to ask me whether I was interested in a Turbo confessor: a fast, portable model very much in demand in America and approved by Cardinal Spellman. I wasn't interested and I told him so quite bluntly.

A few months ago Mr Simpson rang my doorbell unannounced. He was radiant and in his arms, with the fondness of a nanny, he carried a box of corrugated cardboard. He wasted no time on conventionalities: 'Here it is,' he said triumphantly. 'It's the Mimer: the duplicator we've all dreamt about.'

'A duplicator?' I said, barely able to conceal a gesture of disappointment. 'Sorry, Simpson, I never dreamt about duplicators. How could anything be better than the ones we've got? Look here, for example. Five cents and in a few seconds a copy, and they are irreproachable copies; dry processing, no reactive agents, not even a single breakdown in two years.'

But Mr Simpson wasn't easy to deflate. 'If you'll forgive me, anyone can reproduce a surface. This reproduces not just the surface but also in depth'; and with a politely hurt expression he added, 'The Mimer is a *true* duplicator.' From his attaché case he cautiously drew two stenciled sheets with colored headings and placed them on the table. 'Which is the original?'

I examined them attentively; yes, they were the same, but weren't two copies of the same newspaper, two prints from the same negative, equally the same?

'No, look more closely. You see, for this demonstration material we've deliberately chosen a coarse paper, with many extraneous elements in the pulp. Furthermore, we tore this corner deliberately before duplication. Get a magnifying glass and take your time examining it. I'm in no hurry – this afternoon is devoted to you.'

At one spot on one of the copies there was a fleck, and next to it a yellow grain; at the same position on the second copy there was a fleck and a yellow grain. The two tears were identical, down to the last tiny speck that could be distinguished through the glass. My skepticism was being transformed into curiosity.

Meanwhile Mr Simpson had pulled from his case an entire file. 'This is my ammunition,' he said to me smiling, with his pleasant foreign accent. 'It's my support group of twins.' There were handwritten letters, underlined at random in various colors; envelopes with stamps; complicated technical drawings; varicolored childish doodlings. Of each specimen Mr Simpson showed me the exact replica, both front and back.

I carefully examined the demonstration material: it was in truth totally satisfactory. The grain of the paper, every mark, every shading of color, were reproduced with absolute fidelity. I noticed that the same rough spots found on the originals were to be found on the copies: the greasiness of the crayon lines, the chalky dryness of the highlights in the tempera background, the embossment of the stamps. Meanwhile Mr Simpson continued his pitch. 'This is not an improvement on a previous model: the very principle on which the Mimer is based is revolutionary, extremely interesting not only from a practical point of view but also conceptually. It does not imitate, it does not simulate, but rather it reproduces the model, re-creates it identically, so to speak, from nothing. . . .'

I gave a start: my chemist's viscera protested violently against such an enormity. 'Really! How from nothing?'

'Forgive me if I've let myself be carried away. Not just from nothing, obviously. I meant to say from chaos, from absolute disorder. There, that's what the Mimer does: it creates order from disorder.'

He went out to the street and from the trunk of his car took a small metal cylinder, not unlike a container of liquid gas. He showed me how, by means of a flexible tube, it should be connected with the Mimer's cell.

'This is the fuel tank. It contains a rather complex blend, the so-called pabulum whose nature for the time being is under wraps; based on what I think I understood from the technicians at NATCA during the training course at Fort Kiddiwanee, it is likely that the pabulum is made up of not very stable composites of carbon and of other principal vital elements. . . . The procedure is elementary: between you, me and the lamppost I really haven't understood why it was necessary to call all of us to America from the four corners of the world. Now look, you put the model to be reproduced in this compartment and in this other compartment, which is identical in shape and volume, you introduce the pabulum at a controlled velocity. During the duplication process, in the exact position of every single atom of the model is fixed an analogous atom extracted from the alimentation mixture: carbon where there was carbon, nitrogen where there was nitrogen, and so on. Naturally, we salesmen have been told almost nothing about the mechanism of this long-distance reconstruction, nor have we been told in what way the enormous bulk of information at stake is transmitted from cell to cell. Nevertheless we are authorized to report that a recently discovered genetic process is repeated in the Mimer and that the model 'is linked to the copy by the same relationship that links the seed to the tree.' I hope that all this has some meaning for you, and I beg you to excuse my company's reticence. You'll understand: not all the details of the apparatus are as yet covered by a patent.'

Contrary to all normal business procedures, I was unable to disguise my admiration. This was truly a revolutionary technique: organic synthesis at low temperature and pressure, order from disorder silently, rapidly, and inexpensively – the dream of four generations of chemists.

'You know, they didn't achieve this easily: as the story goes, the forty technicians assigned to Project Mimer, who had already brilliantly solved the fundamental problem, that is, the problem of oriented synthesis, for two years obtained only mirrorlike copies, I mean reversed and therefore unusable. The NATCA management was already about to begin producing the device anyway, even though it would have to be activated twice for each duplication, entailing twice the expense and twice the time; then the first direct reproduction specimen was supposedly realized by chance, thanks to a providential assembling error.'

'All this leaves me perplexed,' I said. 'Every invention is usually accompanied by a story, probably bruited about by its less ingenious competitors, a story that explains the discovery by the felicitous intervention of chance.'

'Maybe,' Simpson said. 'At any rate, there is still a long way to go. You should know right from the start that the Mimer is not a rapid duplicator. For a model of approximately one hundred grams it takes no less than an hour. Furthermore there exists another limitation, obvious in itself: it cannot reproduce, or it does so only imperfectly, models that contain elements not present in the available pabulum. Other special, more complete pabula have already been realized for specific needs, but apparently they've run into difficulties with a number of elements, mainly with the heavy metals. For example (and he showed me a delightful page of an illuminated Codex), till now it is impossible to reproduce the gilding, which in fact is absent in the copy. And for all the more reason it is impossible to reproduce a coin.'

At this point I was startled once more, but this time it wasn't my chemist's viscera that reacted, but rather the coexistent and closely commingled viscera of the practical man. Not a coin, but what about a bank note? a rare stamp? or more decently and elegantly, a diamond? Does the law perhaps punish 'fabricators and vendors of fake diamonds'? Do there exist fake diamonds? Who could prevent me from putting a few grams of carbon atoms into the Mimer and rearranging them in an honest tetrahedic order, and then selling the result? Nobody: not the law, and not even my conscience.

In such matters, the essential thing is to get there first, because no imagination is more industrious than that of men greedy for gain. So I set aside all hesitation, bargained moderately over the Mimer's price (which in any case was not excessive), obtained a 5 percent discount and payment terms for a period of 120 days, and ordered the apparatus.

The Mimer, together with fifty pounds of pabulum, was delivered to me two months later. Christmas was coming; my family was in the mountains, and I had remained alone in town, devoting myself intensely to study and work. To begin with, I read the instructions several times, until I almost knew them by heart; then I took the first object at hand (it was a common gambling die) and prepared to reproduce it.

I placed it in the cell, brought the machine to the prescribed temperature, opened the small graduated valve for the pabulum and waited. There was a slight hum and from the discharge tube of the reproduction cell issued a weak gaseous spurt: it had a curious odor, similar to that of not very clean newborn babies. After an hour, I opened the cell: it contained a die exactly identical with the model in shape, color and weight. It was lukewarm, but it soon acquired the temperature of the room. From the second die I made a third, and from the third a fourth, easily and without the slightest hitch.

I became more and more curious about the Mimer's inner mechanism, which Simpson had not been able (or not wanted?) to explain to me with satisfactory precision, and about which there was no mention in the instructions. I detached the hermetic cover of cell B, opened a small window in it with a saw, attached to it a small glass slide, sealed it firmly and put the cover back in place. Then I again introduced the die into cell A, and through the window I attentively observed what was happening in cell B during the duplication. Something extremely interesting took place: The die formed gradually, starting from below, in extremely thin superimposed layers, as though it were growing from the base of the cell. Halfway through the duplication, half of the die was perfectly formed, and you could clearly distinguish the section of the wood with all of its veins. It seemed permissible to deduce that in cell A some analyzing device 'explored' by lines or by planes the body to be reproduced, and transmitted to cell B the instructions for the fixing of the single particle, perhaps of the very atoms, drawn from the pabulum.

I was satisfied with the preliminary test. The next day I bought a small diamond and made a reproduction of it which proved to be perfect. From the first two diamonds I made another two; from the four another four, and so on in geometric progression until the cell of the Mimer was full. At the end of the operation, it was impossible to pick out the original diamond. In twelve hours of work I had produced $2^{12} - 1$ pieces, that is, 4,095 new diamonds; the initial investment for the equipment was amply amortized, and I felt authorized to go on to further experiments of greater or lesser interest.

The following day I duplicated without difficulty a sugar cube, a handkerchief, a railroad timetable and a pack of playing cards. The third day I tried it on a hardboiled egg: the shell turned out thin and insubstantial (for lack of calcium, I suppose), but albumen and yolk were completely normal in appearance and taste. Then I obtained a satisfactory replica of a pack of cigarettes; a box of safety matches was perfect-looking but the matches didn't light. A white and black photograph gave an extremely faded copy due to lack of silver in the pabulum. Of my wristwatch I was able to reproduce only the band, and the watch itself from then on proved useless, for reasons that I'm unable to explain.

The fourth day I duplicated a number of fresh beans and peas and a tulip bulb, whose germinating power I promised myself to check on. Besides these, I duplicated a quarter pound of cheese, a sausage, a round of bread and a pear, and ate it all for lunch without perceiving any difference from the respective originals. I realized that it was also possible to reproduce liquids, placing in cell B a container identical to or larger than the one containing the model in cell A.

The fifth day I went up into the attic and searched until I found a live spider. It must certainly be impossible to reproduce moving objects with precision; therefore I kept the spider in the cold on the balcony until it was numb. Then I introduced it in the Mimer; an hour later I had an impeccable replica. I marked the original with a drop of ink, put the two twins in a glass jar on the radiator, and began to wait. After half an hour the two spiders began to move simultaneously, and immediately started to fight. Their strength and skill were identical, and they fought for more than an hour without either one being able to prevail. At that I put them in two different boxes. The next day both had woven a circular web with fourteen spokes.

The sixth day I took apart the small garden wall stone by stone and found a hibernating lizard. Its double was externally normal, but when I brought it back to room temperature I noticed that it moved with great difficulty. It died within a few hours, and I was able to ascertain that its skeleton was very weak: in particular, the long bones of its small paws were flexible as rubber.

On the seventh day I rested. I phoned Mr Simpson and asked him to call on me right away; I told him about the experiments I had performed (not about the experiment with the diamonds, naturally), and, with the most insouciant facial expression and tone of voice I could muster, I asked a number of questions and made some proposals. What exactly was the Mimer's patent status? Was it possible to obtain a more complete pabulum from NATCA containing, even in small quantities, all the elements necessary for life? Was there available a larger Mimer with a five-liter capacity, able to reproduce a cat? or a two-hundred-liter capacity, able to duplicate . . .

I saw Mr Simpson turn pale. 'Good lord,' he said to me, 'I . . . I am not willing to follow you along this path. I sell automated poets, calculators, confessors, translators and duplicators. But I believe in the immortal soul, I believe I possess one and I do not wish to lose it. And neither do I wish to collaborate in creating one with the methods you have in mind. The Mimer is what it is: an ingenious machine for copying documents, and what you propose is . . . I'm sorry, but it's disgusting.'

I was not prepared for such an impetuous reaction on the part of mild Mr Simpson, and I tried to bring him to his senses: I pointed out to him that the Mimer was something, was much more than an office duplicator, and the fact that its very creators were not aware of it could mean a fortune for me and for him. I insisted on the twofold aspect of its virtues: the economical aspect as creator of order and thus of wealth, and the – how shall I put it? – Promethean aspect of a new and refined instrument for the advancement of our knowledge concerning vital mechanisms. In the end, rather obliquely, I also hinted at the experiment with the diamonds.

But it was all useless: Mr Simpson was disturbed, and he seemed incapable of understanding what I was saying. In obvious contradiction to his interest as a salesman and corporation man, he said that it was 'a bunch of nonsense,' that he only believed the information printed in the presentation pamphlet, that he was not interested in adventures of thought nor tremendous profits, and that in any event he didn't want to be involved in this business. I had the impression that he wished to add something else; but then he said an abrupt good-bye and left.

It is always painful to break off a friendship. I had the firm intention of getting in touch with Mr Simpson again and I was convinced that a basis for agreement, or even collaboration, could be found. I certainly meant to telephone him or write to him; yet, as unfortunately happens during periods of intense work, I put it off from one day to the next until the beginning of February, when among my mail I found a circular letter from NATCA, accompanied by a frosty note from the Milan agency signed personally by Mr Simpson: 'We hereby bring to your attention the NATCA circular, of which we attach a copy and translation.'

No one will shake my conviction that it was Mr Simpson himself, moved by his foolish moralistic scruples, who caused it to be distributed by the company. I do not repeat the entire text, too long for these notes, but the essential clause runs as follows:

> The Mimer, as is true of all NATCA duplicators in existence or yet to be fabricated, is put on the market for the sole purpose of reproducing office documents. NATCA agencies are authorized to sell them only to legally constituted commercial or industrial firms, and *not to private persons*. In each case the sale of this equipment will take place only upon the purchaser's releasing a declaration in which he states and promises that he will not use the apparatus for:
>
> the reproduction of paper money, checks, IOUs, stamps, or other analogous objects that correspond to a definite monetary value;
>
> the reproduction of paintings, drawings, etchings, sculptures, or other works of figurative art;

> the reproduction of plants, animals, *human beings*, be they living or defunct, or parts thereof. NATCA will not be responsible for the actions of its customers or users of its machines, which conflict with their signed declarations.

It is my opinion that these limitations will not contribute much to the Mimer's commercial success, and I will certainly point this out to Mr Simpson if, as I hope, I shall once more have the opportunity to meet with him. It is incredible how reputably reasonable people will do things that are in such obvious conflict with their own interests.

Man's Friend

The first observation concerning the arrangement of the epithelial cells of the tapeworm go back to 1905 (Serriurier). It was, however, Flory who first sensed their importance and meaning, and described them in a long paper dated 1927, accompanied by extremely clear photographs in which for the first time the so-called Flory mosaic was made visible also to the layman. As is well known, they are flattened cellules, of an irregularly polygonal shape, set out in long parallel lines, and characterized by the repetition of similar elements numbering a few hundred, at variable intervals. Their significance was discovered under singular circumstances: the merit for this goes not to a histologist nor a zoologist but to an Orientalist.

Bernard W. Losurdo, professor of Assyriology at Michigan State University, in a period of forced inactivity due in fact to the presence of the irksome parasite, and thus moved by a purely circumstantial interest, happened by chance to see Flory's photograph. Nevertheless, a number of singularities that no one had noticed until then, did not escape his professional eye: the lines of the mosaic are constituted by a number of cellules that varies within not very large margins (approximately, from twenty-five to sixty); there exist groups of cellules that are repeated with a very high frequency, almost as though these were obligatory associations; and finally (and this was the key to the enigma), the terminal cellules of each line are at times arranged according to a schema that could be described as rhythmical.

It was undoubtedly a fortunate circumstance that the first photograph which Losurdo examined should present a particularly simple schema: the last four cellules of the first line were identical with the last four of the third; the last three of the second line were identical with the last three of the fourth and sixth; and so on, according to the well-known schema of terza rima. Yet great intellectual courage was required to take the next step – that is, to hypothesize that the entire mosaic was not rhymed in a purely metaphorical sense but constituted nothing less than a poetic composition and conveyed a meaning.

Losurdo had such courage. His deciphering work was long and patient and confirmed his original intuition. The conclusions at which the scholar arrived can be briefly summarized as follows:

Approximately 15 percent of the adult individuals of the tenia solium are bearers of a Flory mosaic. The mosaic, when it exists, is repeated identically in all the mature proglotids and is congenital: it is therefore a specific characteristic of a single individual, comparable (the observation is made by Losurdo himself) to a man's fingerprints or the lines of his hand. It is formed by a number of 'verses' which can vary from about ten to two hundred, and what's more, at times rhymed, at other times best defined as rhythmic prose. Despite appearances, this is not a matter of alphabetic writing; or, more precisely (and here we can do no better than quote Losurdo himself): 'It is a both highly complex and primitive form of expression, in which alphabetic writing and acrophonetics, ideography and syllabism interweave in the same mosaic and sometimes in the same verse, without apparent regularity, as though the extremely ancient familiarity of the parasite with the culture of his host in his diverse guises were reflected in it in a compendiary and confused form; almost as though together with the fluids of man's organism the worm had drawn also a small part of his knowledge.'

Not many mosaics have been deciphered by Losurdo and his collaborators. Some are rudimentary and fragmentary, barely articulated, what Losurdo calls 'interjectory.' They are the most difficult to interpret, and mainly express satisfaction with the quality or quantity of the food, or disgust with some less pleasing component of the chyme. Others are limited to a brief sententious phrase. The following, already more complex but of doubtful interpretation, is understood as the lament of an individual in a condition of suffering, who feels close to expulsion:

'Farewell, sweet repose and sweet abode. No longer sweet for me, for my time has come. There is so much weariness on my (. . .): please, leave me thus, forgotten in a corner, in this good warmth. But lo, that which was food is poison, where there was peace is anger. Do not tarry, because you're no longer welcome: detach your (. . .) and descend into the hostile universe.'

Some mosaics seem to allude to the reproductive process and to the worms' mysterious hermaphroditic loves:

'You I. Who will separate us, since we are one flesh? You I. I mirror myself in you and see myself. One and manifold: light is death, darkness is immortal. Come, contiguous spouse, hold me close when the hour tolls. I'm coming, and my every (. . .) sings to heaven.

'I have broken the (membrane?) and I've dreamt the sun and the moon. I've twisted upon myself, and the firmament has welcomed me. The past emptied, an instant's virtue, innumerable progeny.'

But far more interesting are certain mosaics of a manifestly more elevated level, in which is adumbrated the new and perturbing horizon of affective relationships between parasite and host. We'll quote some of the most significant:

'Be benign with me, oh powerful one, and remember me in your sleep. Your food is my food, your hunger is my hunger: reject, I beg you, the acrid garlic and the detestable (cinnamon?). Everything proceeds from you: the suave humors that give me life and the warmth in which I lie and praise the world. May I never lose you, oh my generous host, oh my universe. Just as the air you breathe and the light you enjoy are for you, so are you for me. May you live long and in good health.

'Speak, and I shall listen. Go, and I shall follow. Meditate, and I shall understand you. Who is more faithful than I? Who knows you better than I? Lo, I lie trustingly in your dark bowels, and mock the light of day. Listen all of you: everything is vanity, except for a full belly. Everything is mystery except for the (. . .).

'Your strength penetrates me, your joy descends into me, and your anger (crimps?) me, your weariness mortifies, your wine exalts me. I love you, oh sacred man. Forgive me my sins, and do not turn your benevolence away from me.'

The motif of sin, which is here barely hinted at, surfaces instead with curious insistence in several of the more evolved mosaics. It is remarkable, Losurdo affirms, that the latter belong almost exclusively to individuals of considerable size and age, who have tenaciously resisted one or more expulsive therapies. We will cite the best-known example, which has by now crossed the limits of specialized scientific literature and was recently welcomed into an anthology of foreign literature, arousing the critical interest of a much vaster audience.

'. . . Should I therefore call you ungrateful? No, for I have transcended and crazily I have led myself to shatter the limitations imposed on us by Nature. By recondite and marvelous paths I have come to you; for years, in religious worship, I had drawn from your founts life and wisdom. I should not have made myself manifest: this is our sad destiny. Manifest and infested; hence your righteous anger, oh master. Alas, why have I not desisted? Why have I rejected the wise inertia of my ancestors?

'But lo: just as your wrath is righteous, so my admittedly impious audacity is quite just. Who did not know it? Our silent words are not heard by you, proud demigods. We, a population without eyes or ears, receive no mercy from you.

'And now I shall go away, because you wish it. I shall go in silence, as is our custom, to meet my destiny of death or foul transfiguration, I ask for only one gift: that this message of mine will reach you and be meditated upon and understood by you. By you, o hypocritical man, my similar and my brother.'

The text is undoubtedly remarkable, by any criterion. Just for curiosity's sake, we must report that the author's final wish went unfulfilled. In fact his involuntary host, an obscure bank clerk in Dampier (Illinois), decisively refused to look at it.

Some Applications of the Mimer

Gilberto is the last person in the world into whose hands a three-dimensional duplicator should have fallen; and instead the Mimer fell into his hands immediately, one month after it was launched on the market and three months before the well-known decree forbade its construction and use; that is to say, in ample time for Gilberto to get into trouble. It fell into his hands without my being able to do anything about it: I was in San Vittore prison, doing time for my pioneering work, and far from imagining who was continuing it and in what way.

Gilberto is a child of the century. He's thirty-four, a good employee, my friend for many years. He doesn't drink, doesn't smoke, and cultivates a single passion: that of tormenting inanimate matter. He has a tiny cubicle which he calls a workshop, and there he files, saws, solders, glues and sands. He repairs watches, refrigerators, electric razors; he builds devices to turn on the radiators in the morning, photoelectric locks, flying models, acoustic probes to play with at the seaside. As for automobiles, they last him only a few months: he disassembles and assembles them continually; polishes, lubricates, modifies them; attaches futile accessories to them; then gets fed up and sells them. Emma, his wife (an enchanting girl), endures his manias with admirable patience.

I had barely returned home from prison when the phone rang. It was Gilberto, and he was enthusiastic as usual: he had owned a Mimer for twenty days now, and had devoted twenty days and twenty nights to it.

Without stopping to catch his breath he told me about the marvelous experiments he had performed, and about those he meant to perform: he had bought Peltier's book, *Theorie Generale de l'Imitazione*, and the treatise by Zechmeister and Eisenlohr, *The Mimer and other Duplicating Devices*; he had registered for an accelerated course in cybernetics and electronics. The experiments he had performed sadly resembled mine, which had cost me quite dearly. I tried to tell him so, but to no avail: it is difficult to interrupt someone on the telephone, and especially Gilberto. In the end, I brutally broke off the connection, left the receiver off the hook, and devoted myself to my own affairs.

Two days later the telephone rang again: Gilberto's voice was charged with emotion, but contained an unmistakable note of pride.

'I must see you immediately.'

'Why? What happened?'

'I've duplicated my wife,' he replied.

He arrived two hours later, and told me about his foolish enterprise. He had received the Mimer, had performed the usual beginner's games (the egg, the pack of cigarettes, the book, etc.); then he'd become bored, had taken the Mimer to his workshop and disassembled it down to the final nut. He had thought about it all night long, had consulted his treatises, and had concluded that transforming the one-liter model into a larger one should not be impossible, and not all that difficult either. No sooner said than done: he had gotten NATCA to send him, I don't know on what pretext, two hundred pounds of special pabulum; he had bought metal sheeting, strips and gaskets; and seven days later the job was completed. He had built a sort of artificial lung, had manipulated the Mimer's timer, accelerating it by about forty times, and connected the two parts to one another and to the pabulum tank. That is Gilberto, a dangerous man, a small noxious Prometheus: he is ingenious and irresponsible, arrogant and foolish. He is a child of the century, as I said before. Indeed, he is a symbol of our century. I've always thought that, if the occasion arose, he would have been able to build an atom bomb and drop it on Milan 'to see the effect it would have.'

As it had occurred to me from the start, Gilberto had no precise notion when he decided to upgrade his duplicator except perhaps one that was typical of him, of 'fabricating' a larger duplicator with his own hands and at little cost, because he is extremely skillful at making the debit column in his private account book disappear by some sort of mental legerdemain. The detestable idea of duplicating his wife, he told me, had come to him only later, when seeing Emma in a deep sleep. Apparently it was not particularly difficult: Gilberto, who is robust and patient, slipped the mattress with Emma on top of it off the bed and all the way into the drum of the duplicator; it took him more than one hour, but Emma did not wake up.

It is not at all clear to me what motive incited Gilberto to create for himself a second wife, and thus violate a considerable number of divine and human laws. He told me, as though as it were the most natural thing, that he was in love with Emma, that Emma was indispensable to him, and that therefore it had seemed to him a good thing to have two of her. Perhaps he told me this in good faith (Gilberto is always in good faith), and he certainly was and is in love with Emma, in his own fashion, childishly, and so to speak from below up; but I'm convinced that he decided to duplicate her for quite different reasons, out of a mistaken spirit of adventure, out of a morbid Herostratos-like desire; in fact 'to see what effect it might have.'

I asked him whether it hadn't occurred to him to discuss the matter with Emma, to ask her permission before using her in so unusual a manner. He turned beet red: he had done worse; Emma's deep sleep had been induced, he had given her a sleeping potion.

'And now where do you stand, with your two wives?'

'I don't know, I've yet to decide. They're both still

sleeping. Tomorrow we shall see.'

Tomorrow we weren't going to see anything, or at least I wasn't. After a month of enforced inertia, I had to leave on a long trip which kept me away from Milan for two weeks. I already knew what was waiting for me on my return: I would have to help Gilberto out of his trouble, just as I had when he had built a steam-driven vacuum cleaner and made a present of it to the wife of his office manager.

In fact, I had barely returned when I was peremptorily summoned to a family council: Gilberto, I and the two Emmas. The latter had been tactful enough to mark themselves off: the second, counterfeit Emma wore a simple white ribbon in her hair, which gave her a vaguely nunlike air. Aside from this, she wore Emma's clothes with nonchalance; obviously she was identical to the original in every aspect – face, teeth, hair, voice, accent, a small scar on the forehead, the permanent, the gait, the tan from the recent holidays. I noticed, however, that she had a bad cold.

Against all my expectations, the three of them seemed in excellent spirits. Gilberto proved to be stupidly proud, not so much of the feat he had accomplished as of the fact (for which he could claim no credit) that the two women got along well. As for them, they really filled me with sincere admiration. Emma the first displayed toward her new 'sister' a maternal solicitude; Emma the second responded with a dignified and affectionate filial deference. Gilberto's experiment, abominable from so many points of view, nevertheless constituted a valuable confirmation of imitation theory: the new Emma, twenty-eight years old when born, had inherited not only the identical mortal form of the prototype, but also her entire mental endowment. With admirable simplicity, Emma the second told me that only two or three days after her birth she had become convinced that she was the first, so to speak, synthetic woman in the history of mankind; or perhaps the second, if one took into consideration the vaguely analogous instance of Eve. She had been born asleep, because the Mimer had also duplicated the sleeping potion that ran through the veins of Emma the first, and she had awakened 'knowing' that she was Emma Gatti, née Perosa, the sole wife of the accountant Gilberto Gatti, born in Mantua on March 7, 1936. She remembered very well everything that Emma the first remembered well, and badly everything that Emma the first remembered badly. She remembered to perfection the honeymoon trip, the names of 'her' schoolmates, the childish and intimate details of a religious crisis Emma the first had gone through at the age of thirteen and had never confessed to a living soul. But she also remembered very well the arrival of the Mimer in the house, Gilberto's enthusiasm, his tales and his attempts, and therefore she had not been excessively astonished when she had been informed of the arbitrary creative act to which she owed her existence.

The fact that Emma had a cold made me think that their identity, originally perfect, was destined not to last: even if Gilberto were to prove the most evenhanded of bigamists, if he were to institute rigorous turns, if he were to abstain from any manifestation of preference for one of the two women (and this was an absurd hypothesis, because Gilberto is a bungler and a botcher), even in that case a divergence would in the end certainly become manifest. One had only to consider that the two Emmas did not materially occupy the same portion of space: they would not have been able to pass through a narrow door simultaneously, show up together at a ticket window, occupy the same place at the table; therefore they were exposed to diverse incidents (the cold), to diverse experiences. They would inevitably become differentiated, spiritually and corporeally – and once differentiated, would Gilberto have been able to remain equidistant? Certainly not; and in the face of a preference, even though minuscule, the fragile equilibrium à trois was destined to shipwreck.

I presented these considerations of mine to Gilberto, and tried to get him to understand that they were not a gratuitous pessimistic hypothesis, but rather a prediction solidly based on common sense, almost a theorem. I furthermore pointed out to him that his legal position was, to say the least, dubious, and that I had ended up in prison for much less: he was wedded to Emma Perosa, also Emma the second was Emma Perosa, but this did not erase the fact that there were two Emma Perosas.

But Gilberto proved inaccessible: he was stupidly euphoric, in the state of mind of a newlywed husband, and as I spoke I could see that he had other things on his mind. Instead of looking at me, he was lost in contemplation of the two women, who precisely at that moment were pretending to fight over which of the two should sit on the armchair that they both preferred. Instead of answering my arguments, he announced that he'd had a wonderful idea: the three of them would leave on a trip to Spain. 'I've figured out everything: Emma the first will report that she's lost her passport, she will have a duplicate issued and we will get through with that. Actually no, how silly of me! I will make the duplicate this very evening with the Mimer.' He was very proud of this stroke of genius, and I suspect that he had chosen Spain precisely because passport control is rather strict at the Spanish border.

When they returned two months later, things were coming to a head. Anyone would have noticed: relationships among the three remained at a level of urbanity and formal politeness, but the tension was obvious. And Gilberto did not invite me to his house; he came to mine, and he was no longer in the least euphoric.

He told me what had happened. He told it to me in a very clumsy manner, because Gilberto, who has an undeniable talent for sketching the pattern of a differential on a cigarette pack, is by contrast desperately inept when it comes to expressing his feelings.

The trip to Spain had been both amusing and fatiguing. In Seville, after a very full day, a discussion had arisen in an atmosphere of irritation and weariness. It had arisen between the two women over the one subject on which their opinions could diverge, and in fact did diverge. Had Gilberto's exploit been opportune or not, legitimate or illegitimate? Emma the second had said yes; Emma the first had said nothing. Her silence had been all that was needed to tip the balance: from that instant Gilberto's choice was made. In regard to Emma the first he experienced an increasing embarrassment, a feeling of guilt that became heavier day by day; at the same time his affection for the new wife increased and devoured apace his affection for the legitimate wife. The break had not yet taken place, but Gilberto sensed that it was soon to come.

Also, the temper and personality of the two women were becoming increasingly different. Emma the second became more and more young, attentive, responsive and open; Emma the first progressively withdrew into a negative attitude of injured renunciation, of rejection. What was he to do? I advised Gilberto not to do anything rash, and I promised him, as is my habit, that I would concern myself with his problem; but privately, I was quite determined to give a wide berth to that melancholy mess, and I could not repress a sense of malicious, sad satisfaction at the fact that my facile prophecy had come true.

I would never have expected to see a radiant Gilberto drop into my office two months later. He was in top form, garrulous, loud, perceptibly fatter. He got to the subject without hesitation, with his typical egocentricity: for Gilberto, when things go well for him, they go well for the entire world; he is organically incapable of being concerned about his fellow man, and on the contrary is offended and astonished when his fellow man does not concern himself with him.

'Gilberto is a champ,' he said. 'He has settled everything in the blink of an eye.'

'I'm pleased to hear that and I praise you for your modesty; on the other hand it was about time that you straightened things out.'

'No, look, you didn't understand me. I'm not talking about myself; I'm talking about Gilberto the first. He's the one who's a champ. I, not to boast, resemble him a lot, but I don't deserve much credit in this business: I've only existed since last Sunday. But now everything has fallen into place; all I must do now is settle the situation between myself and Emma the second at the city clerk's office. I can't exclude the possibility that we may need to have recourse to some small deception, for example get married, Emma the second and I, and then distribute ourselves each with the spouse he or she wants. And then, naturally, I'll have to look for a job; but I'm convinced that NATCA would gladly welcome me as a publicist for the Mimer and their other office machines.'

Versamina

There are trades that destroy and trades that preserve. Among those that preserve, the better ones, by their very nature, are precisely those that consist in preserving something: documents, books, works of art, institutions, traditions. It is common knowledge that librarians, museum guards, sacristans, beadles and archivists not only are long-lived but are preserved for decades without visible alteration.

Jacob Dessauer, limping slightly, climbed the eight wide steps and after twelve years of absence entered the lobby of the Institute. He asked for Haarbaus, for Keeber, for Wincke: none of them were there anymore, they were either dead or transferred; the only known face was that of old Dybowski. Dybowski had not changed: the same bald skull, the same dense, deeply scored wrinkles, the badly shaved beard, the bony hands with their multicolored spots. Also the gray, patched, too short smock.

'Ah yes,' he said, 'when the hurricane blows it's the taller trees that fall. I'm still here; obviously I didn't bother anyone, neither the Russians, nor the Americans, nor those others, before.'

Dessauer looked around: many panes were still missing from the windows, many books from the shelves, there was little heat, but the Institute lived on; students, men and women, passed through the corridors, dressed in threadbare and worn-out clothes, and in the air the typical acrid smells that he knew so well. He asked Dybowski for news about those who were absent: almost all of them had died during the war, at the front or in the bombings; also

Kleber, his friend, had died, but not because of the war. Kleber, Wunder Kleber, as they called him, Kleber of the miracles.

'Yes, him: haven't you heard talk about his story?'

'I've been away for many years,' Dessauer replied.

'That's true: I wasn't thinking,' Dybowski said, without asking any questions. 'Do you have half an hour? Come with me, I'll tell you all about it.'

He led Dessauer to his cubicle. Through the window entered the gray light of a misty afternoon: the rain fell in gusts onto the weeds that had invaded the flower beds, so well kept at one time. They sat on two stools, before a rusted and corroded technical scale. The air was heavily laden with the smell of phenol and bromine; the old man lit his pipe and pulled a brown bottle out from under the workbench.

'We've never lacked for alcohol,' he said, and poured some into two beaked retorts. They drank, then Dybowski began talking.

'You know, these aren't things one tells to just anyone. I tell them to you because I remember that you were friends and so you will be better able to understand. After you left us, it's not that Kleber changed a lot: he was obstinate, serious, attached to his work, educated, extremely skillful. He did not even lack that touch of madness which in our laboratory is hardly a disadvantage. He was also very shy: with you gone, he did not make other friends; instead many curious little manias seized hold of him, as will happen with those who live alone. You remember that for years he had been following a line of research of his own on benzoyl derivatives: as you know, he had been exempted from military service because of his eyes. They didn't call him up for the army even later on, when they drafted everyone; we never found out why – maybe he knew people in high places. So he continued to study his benzoyl derivatives; I don't know, perhaps they were of interest to those others because of the war. He fell upon the versaminas by chance.'

'What are the versaminas?'

'Wait, you'll find out later. He tested his preparations on rabbits; he had already tested about forty of them when he noticed that one of the rabbits behaved in a strange way. It refused food, and instead it chewed the wood, bit the wires of the cage, until it bled at the mouth. It died a few days later from an infection. Now, another person wouldn't have paid much attention, but not Kleber: he belonged to the old school, he believed more in facts than statistics. He had the B/41 (it was the forty-first benzoyl derivative) administered to three more rabbits, and obtained very similar results. Here I too almost came into the story.'

He paused, waiting for a question, and Dessauer did not disappoint him.

'You? In what way?'

Dybowski lowered his voice a bit. 'You know, meat was scarce, and my wife thought it was a pity to throw all the experimental animals into the incinerator. So every so often we ate some of them: many guinea pigs, a few rabbits; dogs and monkeys never. We chose the ones that seemed less dangerous, and we happened precisely to pick one of the three rabbits I told you about; but we only realized it later. You see, I like to drink. I've never overdone it but I can't go without. I realized that something wasn't going right, due to my drinking. I remember it as if it were now: I was here with a friend of mine, his name was Hagen, we had found who knows where a bottle of aquavit and we were drinking. It was the evening after the rabbit: the aquavit was a good brand, but I didn't like it, that was that. Instead Hagen thought it was excellent; so we argued, each tried to convince the other, and with each glass we got more heated. The more I drank the less I liked it; he insisted, we ended up quarrelling, I told him that he was obstinate and stupid, and Hagen broke the bottle on my head; you see here? I still have the scar. Well, that blow didn't hurt me, on the contrary it gave me a strange, very pleasant sensation such as I had never experienced. I've tried several times to find the words to describe it, and I've never found them: it was somewhat like when you wake up and stretch, while still in bed, but much stronger, more pungent, as though concentrated all in one point.

'I no longer know how the evening ended; the next day the wound didn't bleed anymore, I put a Band-Aid on it, but when I touched it I again felt that sensation, like a tickle, but believe me, so pleasant that I spent the day touching the Band-Aid every time I could, without letting anyone see. Then, little by little, everything went back to normal, I began to like alcohol again, my wound healed, I made up with Hagen and no longer thought about it. But I began to think about it again a few months later.'

'What was this B/41?' Dessauer interrupted.

'It was a benzoyl derivative, I already told you. But it contained a spiranico nucleus.'

Dessauer looked up, surprised. 'A spiranico nucleus? How do you know these things?'

Dybowski smiled a weary smile.

'Forty years,' he replied patiently. 'It's forty years that I've been working in here, and you think that I shouldn't have learned anything at all? To work without learning is no satisfaction. Besides, with all the talk there was about it afterward . . . it was even written up in the newspapers, didn't you read them?'

'Not those of that period,' Dessauer said.

'It's not as though they explained things properly, you know what journalists are like; but at any rate for quite some time the whole town talked of nothing but spirani, as when there is a trial about poisoning. You heard of nothing else, on the trains too, in the air-raid shelters, and even schoolchildren knew about condensed and noncomplanate benzoyl nuclei, about asymmetric carbon speranics, about benzoyl in para- and versaminic activity. Because by now you've understood, haven't you? It was Kleber himself who called them *versamines*: those substances that convert pain into pleasure. Benzoyl had nothing to do with it, or very little: what mattered was precisely the nucleus made in that particular way, almost like the tail flaps of an airplane. If you go up to the second floor, to poor Kleber's study, you will see the spatial models he used to make himself, with his own hands.'

'Did they have a permanent effect?'

'No: it lasted only a few days.'

'That's a pity,' Dessauer let slip. He was listening attentively, but at the same time he was unable to turn his gaze away from the mist and rain outside the windowpanes, or to interrupt a certain line of thought: how he had found his town again, its buildings almost intact, but inwardly ravaged, consumed from below like an island of floating ice, full of a false joie de vivre, sensual without passion, loud without gaiety, skeptical, inert, lost. The capital of neurosis: new only in this; for the rest decrepit, indeed timeless, petrified like Gommorah. The most appropriate setting for the contorted story that the old man was unwinding.

'Pity? Wait for the end. Don't you understand that it was something big? You must know that that B/41 was but a first attempt, a preparation with weak and inconstant effects. Kleber immediately realized that with certain substitute groups, not even that far afield, it was possible to do much more: somewhat like the business of the Hiroshima bomb and the others that came later. It is not by chance, you see, not by chance: some believe they can free humanity from pain, others that they can give it energy gratis, and they do not know that nothing is gratis, ever: everything must be paid for. In any case, he had found the lode. I worked with him, he entrusted me with all the work on the animals; but he continued with the syntheses, developing three or four at the same time. In April he prepared the compound that was much more active than all the others, number 160, the one that became the versamina DN, and turned it over to me for the tests. The dose was small, not more than half a gram. All the animals responded, but not in equal measure: some showed only behavioral anomalies of the type I mentioned before, and returned to normal within a few days; but others seemed – how shall I say? – turned upside down, and they did not recover, as though for them pleasure and pain had definitively changed places. All of these died.

'Looking at them was both horrible and fascinating. I remember a German shepherd, for instance, that we wanted to keep alive at all costs, despite himself, because it seemed he had no other desire than to destroy himself. He sank his fangs into his paws and tail with wild ferocity, and when I put a muzzle on him he bit his tongue. I was forced to put a rubber tampon in his mouth, and I fed him by injection: he then learned to run around the cage and throw himself against the bars with all his strength. At first he hit them at random with his head or with his shoulders, but then he saw that it was better to hit with his nose, and every time he moaned with pleasure. I was forced to tie up his legs too, but he did not complain; on the contrary he quietly wagged his tail all day and all night, because he no longer slept. He had received only a tenth of a gram of versamina in a single dose, but he never recovered: Kleber tried a dozen presumed antidotes on him (he had a theory, he said that they were supposed to act through some sort of protective synthesis) but none of them had any effect, and the thirteenth killed him.

'Then I was given a mongrel, he must have been a year old, a tiny beast to whom I immediately became attached. He seemed mild-tempered, so we let him run free in the garden for several hours every day. We had administered a tenth of a gram to him too, but in small doses, over the course of a month: he survived for a longer time, poor little thing, but he was no longer a dog. There was no longer anything canine about him – he no longer liked meat, he would scratch up dirt and pebbles with his claws and swallow them. He ate salad greens, straw, hay, newspaper. He was afraid of little bitches and courted hens and female cats; actually, one cat took it badly and jumped at his eyes and began to scratch him, and he let her do it, and wagged his tail, lying on his back. If I hadn't arrived in time she would have gouged out his eyes. The hotter the weather, the more trouble I had getting him to drink: when I stood there he pretended to drink, but you could see very well that water repelled him; one time, however, he slipped into the laboratory on the sly, found a basin of isotonic solution and drank it all. Yet when he was eager for water (I fed it to him through a tube), then he would have gone on drinking until he burst.

He howled at the sun, yapped at the moon, wagged his tail for hours on end before the sterilizer and the hammer mill, and when I took him for a walk he snarled at every corner and every tree. In short, he was a counterdog: I assure you that his behavior was sinister enough to alarm anyone who had held on to only a quarter of his brain. Keep in mind: he had not degenerated like the other dog, the shepherd. In my opinion he had understood like a human being, he knew that when you're thirsty you must drink, and that a dog must eat meat and not hay; but error, perversion were stronger than he. In my presence he pretended, made an effort to do the right things, not only to please me and so that I should not get angry, but also, I believe, because he knew, continued to know, what was right. But he died all the same. He was attracted by the racket made by the streetcars and that is how he died: all of a sudden he pulled the leash out of my hand and with his head lowered ran straight into a streetcar. A few days before I had caught him licking the stove: yes, it was lit, almost incandescent. When he saw me, he squatted down, his ears flattened and his tail between his legs, as though he expected to be punished.

'More or less the same thing happened with the guinea pigs and mice. Actually, I don't know if you read about those mice in America the newspapers have talked about: an electric stimulus was connected to one of their pleasure centers in the brain and they learned to excite themselves and persisted until it killed them. Believe me, versamines were involved there; it's an effect that can be obtained with laughable facility, and with little expense. Because, perhaps I didn't yet say this, they are inexpensive substances – not more than a few pennies for a gram, and a gram is enough to wreck a man.

'By now it seemed to me that there was enough to be cautious about: I told him, Kleber too; after all, I was the older man and could take the liberty, even though I was less educated than he, and though I had seen the entire story only from the dogs' side. He answered yes, naturally; but then he wasn't able to resist and talked about it indiscreetly. Indeed, he did worse: he signed a contract with OPG and began to take drugs.

'As you can imagine, I was the first to notice. He made every effort to keep it hidden, but I saw immediately what was up. Do you know how I noticed it? From two things: he stopped smoking and he scratched – excuse my language, but things must be called by their names. To tell the truth, in my presence he continued to smoke but I could see very well that he no longer inhaled the smoke, and did not watch it when he blew it out; and besides, the butts he left in his study kept getting longer, you could tell that he lit up, took a puff out of habit, and threw them away immediately. As for the scratching, he did it only when he thought nobody saw him, or when he was absentminded; but at those moments he would scratch himself ferociously, like a dog, precisely, as though he wanted to dig a hole in himself. He attacked the spots that were already irritated and soon his hands and face were covered with scars. I wouldn't be able to tell you about the rest of his life because he lived alone and spoke to no one. But I don't believe it is by chance that at exactly that time a girl who often phoned asking for him and sometimes waited for him outside the Institute was no longer to be seen.

'As for the arrangement with OPG, it became immediately clear that the matter had begun badly. I don't believe that they paid him much; they organized a low-key, rather clumsy commercial promotion, introducing DN versamine as a new analgesic without mentioning its other aspect. But something must have leaked out –

leaked out from in here, and since I did not talk about it, I would say that it's clear to everyone who did talk. The fact is that the new analgesic was bought up in an instant, and shortly after, the police found a student club here in town where they apparently staged orgies of a kind never seen before. The news appeared in the *Kurier* but without the details; I know them, the details, but I'll spare you them, because it's stuff out of the Middle Ages. Suffice it to say that hundreds of packages of needles were seized, and also tongs and braziers to make them blazing hot. At that time the war had just ended, the Allied Occupation had begun, and the whole thing was quashed: also because it seemed that the daughter of Minister T. was involved in the mess.'

'But what became of Kleber?' Dessauer asked.

'Wait, I'm getting there. I just wanted to tell you one more thing that I found out from none other than Hagen, the fellow with the aquavit, who at the time was office manager at the Ministry of Foreign Affairs. OPG resold the versamine license to the American Navy, making a profit of I don't know how many millions (because that's how things go in this world), and the Navy experimented with a military application. In Korea one of the landing outfits was versaminized. It was thought that they would show unusual courage and contempt for danger; instead, it was frightful – they had plenty of contempt for danger but it seems that in the face of the enemy they behaved in a debased and absurd manner, and what's more, let themselves be killed, all of them.

'You were asking about Kleber. I think I've told you enough for you to guess that the years that followed were not very cheerful for him. I followed him day by day, and I always tried to save him, but I never succeeded in speaking to him man to man: he avoided me, he was ashamed. He lost weight, pined away like someone afflicted by cancer. You could see that he tried to resist, to keep for himself only the good, that avalanche of agreeable, perhaps even delicious sensations that the versamine procured so easily and gratuitously. It only seemed gratuitous, of course, but the illusion must be irresistible. So he forced himself to eat, although he had lost all liking for food; he could no longer sleep, but he had preserved the habits of a methodical man. Every morning he arrived punctually, exactly at eight, and he set to work, but on his face you could read the signs of the struggle he was undergoing, trying not to be betrayed by the bombardment of false messages that came to him from all his senses.

'I can't say whether he continued to take versamine out of weakness, or stubbornness, or whether instead he had stopped and the effects had become chronic; the fact remains that in the winter of '52, which was very cold, I caught him here, right in this room: he was fanning himself with a newspaper and was taking off his undershirt as I entered. He also made mistakes in speaking – sometimes he said "bitter" instead of "sweet," "cold" instead of "hot"; generally he corrected himself quickly, but his hesitation before certain choices didn't escape me, and also a certain at once irritated and guilty glance when he saw that I had noticed. A glance that hurt me: it brought back to mind that other one, his predecessor, the mongrel dog who cowered with flattened ears when I caught him doing things the wrong way round.

'How did he end up? Look, if we go by the newspaper reports, he died because of a traffic accident here in town, in his car, on a summer night. He didn't stop at a traffic light: that's what the police report said. I could have helped them understand, explained to them that for a man in his condition, it mustn't be all that easy to distinguish red from green. But it seemed more charitable to me to keep silent: I've told these things to you because you were friends. I must add that, among so many wrong things, Kleber did one thing right: shortly before dying he destroyed the entire versamine dossier, and all the preparations he was able to get his hands on.'

Here old Dybowski fell silent, and Dessauer also did not say a word. He thought about many things all confused together, and promised himself to sort them out later calmly, perhaps that very evening; he had an appointment, but he would postpone it. He thought about one thing that he hadn't thought of for a long time, because he had suffered much: that pain cannot be taken away, must not, because it is our guardian. Often it is a foolish guardian, because it is inflexible, it is faithful to its order with maniacal obstinacy, and never grows tired, whereas all other sensations grow tired, wear out, especially the pleasant ones. But one must not suppress it, silence it, because it is one with life, it is its custodian.

He also thought, contradictorily, that if he had held the drug in his hand he would have tried it because, if pain is life's guardian, pleasure is its purpose and reward. He thought that to prepare a bit of 4, 4-diaminospirano wouldn't really be all that difficult; he thought that if versamines could convert into joy also the most burdensome and longest of pains, the pain of an absence, of a void around you, the pain of an irreparable failure, the pain of feeling you are finished – well, in that case why not?

But by one of those associations with which memory is so generous, he also thought about a heath in Scotland, never seen but better than seen, a heath filled with rain, lightning bolts and wind, and about the gay-malicious chant of three bearded witches, experts in pains and pleasure and in corrupting the human will:

> '*Fair is foul, and foul is fair:*
> *Hover through the fog and filthy air.*'

The Sleeping Beauty in the Fridge

A Winter's Tale

Characters

LOTTE THÖRL
PETER THÖRL
MARIA LUTZER
ROBERT LUTZER
ILSE
BALDUR
PATRICIA
MARGARETA

Berlin, the year 2115.

Lotte Thörl, alone.

LOTTE. So this year has passed too, it is December nineteenth again, and we're expecting guests for the usual small party. (*Noise of crockery and furniture being moved.*) I personally don't particularly like guests. My husband actually used to call me the 'Big Bear.' Not anymore: over the past few years he's changed so much, has become a serious, boring person. The Little Bear would be our daughter Margareta: poor little thing! she's only four. (*Footsteps; noises as above.*) It's not that I am a shy and skittish woman: it's just that it bothers me to attend parties of more than five or six people. One always ends up by making a great deal of noise, conversations that go around in circles, and I have the painful impression that no one notices my presence – except when I pass around the platters.

On the other hand, we Thörls do not entertain often: twice, three times a year, and we rarely accept invitations. It's natural; no one can offer their guests what we can offer. Some have beautiful antique paintings, Renoir, Picasso, Caravaggio; some have a domesticated orangutan or a pet dog or cat; some have a movable bar with the most up-to-date drugs, but we have Patricia . . . (*sighs*) Patricia!

(*Bell rings.*) Here come the first ones. (*She knocks on a door.*) Come in, Peter: I'm here.

(*Lotte and Peter Thörl; Maria and Robert Lutzer. All exchange greetings and small talk.*)

ROBERT. Good evening, Lotte; good evening, Peter. Awful weather, isn't it? How many months is it that we haven't seen the sun?

PETER. And how many months that we haven't seen you?

LOTTE. Maria! you look younger than ever, and what a marvelous fur! A gift from your husband and master?

ROBERT. They no longer are a rarity. It's a silver marten: it seems the Russians have imported a large quantity of them; you can find them in the eastern sector at very reasonable prices. On the black market, naturally; it is rationed merchandise.

PETER. Robert, I admire and envy you. I know few Berliners who don't complain about the situation, but I don't know anyone who wallows in it as nonchalantly as you. I'm becoming increasingly convinced that true, passionate love of money is a virtue that one doesn't learn but inherits with one's blood.

MARIA. Look at all the flowers! Lotte, I smell a marvelous birthday perfume. All the best, Lotte!

LOTTE (*to the two husbands*). Maria is incorrigible. But take heart, Robert, it isn't marriage that has made her so delightfully scatter-brained. She was like that already in school: we used to call her 'the Cologne amnesiac,' and we used to invite friends from other classes, boys and girls, to attend her exams. (*With jocular severity*) Mrs Lutzer, I must call you to order. Is that how you prepare your history lessons? It is not my birthday today: today is the nineteenth of December, it is Patricia's birthday.

MARIA. Oh, forgive me dear, forgive me. I really have the memory of a chicken. So tonight there will be a defrosting? That will be fantastic!

PETER. Certainly, like every year. We are only waiting for Ilse and Baldur to get here. (*Doorbell*) Here they are: late, as usual.

LOTTE. Be more understanding, Peter! Did you ever see an engaged couple arrive on time?

(*Enter Ilse and Baldur. Greetings and small talk as above. Lotte and Peter; Maria and Robert; Ilse and Baldur.*)

PETER. Good evening, Ilse, good evening, Baldur. Haven't seen you in ages: you're so besotted with each other that old friends no longer exist for you.

BALDUR. You must forgive us. We are drowning in bureaucracy: my doctorate, and the documents for City Hall, and the safe-conduct for Ilse, and the go-ahead from the Party; the visa from the burgomaster has already arrived, but we're still waiting for the visa from Washington and the one from Moscow and above all the one from Peking, which is the most difficult to obtain. It's enough to make your head spin. We haven't seen a soul in ages: we've become savages, we're ashamed to show our faces to the world.

ILSE. We're late, aren't we? We really are two oafs. But why didn't you start without us?

PETER. We wouldn't have dared. The moment of awakening is the most interesting: she's so pretty when she opens her eyes!

ROBERT. Come, Peter, we better get started, otherwise we'll be up till all hours of the night. Go get the manual, so it won't happen like that time – the first time, I think (how many years have passed?) – when you made the wrong move and there was almost an accident.

PETER (*irked*). I've got the manual, here in my pocket; but by now I know it by heart. Shall we go? (*Noise of chairs being moved and footsteps, comments, impatient mutterings.*) . . . One: cut off the nitrogen and the circuit for inert gas. (*He does so: a squeak, a brief puff of gas, twice.*) Two: start the pump, the Wroblewski sterilizer and the microfilter. (*Noise of pump, like a distant motorcycle; a few seconds go by.*) Three: open the oxygen circuit (*an increasingly shrill whistle starts*) and slowly turn the valve until the indicator reaches the twenty-one percent mark . . .

ROBERT (*interrupts*). No, Peter, not twenty-one, twenty-four percent, the manual says twenty-four percent, if I were you I'd wear glasses. Don't take offense, we are the same age, but I wear glasses, at least on certain occasions.

PETER (*annoyed*). Yes, you're right, twenty-four percent. But it doesn't matter whether it's twenty-one or twenty-four: I'd already noticed at other times. Four: gradually change the thermostat, raising the temperature at a speed of approximately two degrees a minute. (*The sound of a metronome ticking.*) Quiet, now, please, or at least, don't speak in a loud voice.

ILSE (*whispers*). Does she suffer during defrosting?

PETER (*as above*). No, not as a rule. But that's just why we must do things properly, follow the instructions to the letter. Also, while she's in the freezer it is indispensable that the temperature be kept constant within very narrow limits.

ROBERT. Certainly: just a couple degrees lower, and good-bye, I read that something or other coagulates in the nerve centers, and they don't wake up again, or they'll wake up stupid and without memory; a couple of degrees higher and they recover consciousness, and then they suffer dreadfully. Just think how horrible, Ilse: to feel all frozen, hands, feet, blood, heart, brain; and not be able to move a finger, bat an eyelid, unable to emit a sound, to ask for help!

ILSE. Terrible. You need a lot of courage and great faith. Faith in the thermostats, I mean. As for me, I'm crazy about winter sports, but to tell the truth, I wouldn't change places with Patricia for all the gold in the world. I've been told that she too would be dead already, if at the time when this business began, they hadn't given her injections of . . . what is it? . . . an-ti-freeze. Yes, yes, exactly what they put in car radiators during the winter. Anyway it makes sense: if not, the blood would freeze. Isn't that so, Mr Thörl?

PETER (*evasive*). You hear all kinds of things . . .

ILSE (*pensive*). I'm not surprised that so few people have gone along with this. I swear, I'm not surprised. She's absolutely beautiful, I've been told: is it true?

ROBERT. Magnificent. I saw her close up last year: a complexion like you don't see anymore. Obviously, despite everything, the twentieth-century diet, still natural to a great extent, must have contained some vital principle that still eludes us. It's not that I distrust chemists; on the contrary, I respect them and hold them in great esteem. But really I believe they're a bit . . . I should say . . . presumptuous, yes, presumptuous. In my opinion there must still be something to discover, even if only of secondary importance.

LOTTE (*grudgingly*). Yes, she is pretty, actually. After all, it's the beauty of her age. She has the skin of a newborn: in my opinion though, it's the result of the deep-freezing. She doesn't have a natural complexion, she is too pink and too white, she seems . . . yes, she looks, she looks like ice cream, if you'll forgive the comparison. Also, her hair is too blond. If I must tell the truth my impression is that she's a bit overripe, *faisandée*, . . . but she is beautiful, nobody can deny that. She's also very cultivated, very educated, very intelligent, very bold, she's altogether superlative, and she frightens me, makes me uneasy, and gives me an inferiority complex. (*She has let herself be carried away; she falls silent, embarrassed, then resumes with effort.*) . . . But I love her anyway, especially when she's frozen.

(*Silence. The metronome continues to beat.*)

ILSE (*whispering*). Can I look through the peephole into the freezer?

PETER (*as above*). Certainly, but don't make any noise. We have already reached minus ten and any sudden emotion might be harmful.

ILSE (*as above*). Ah! she's enchanting! She looks artificial . . . and is she . . . I mean, is she really of the period?

BALDUR (*as above, aside*). Don't ask silly questions!

ILSE (*as above, aside*). It's not a silly question at all. I wanted to know how old she is: she seems so young, and yet they say she is . . . antique.

PETER (*who has heard*). That's soon explained. Patricia is one hundred sixty-three years old, twenty-three of which are normal life and one hundred and forty hibernation. But forgive me, Ilse and Baldur, I thought you already knew this story; you too must forgive me, Maria and Robert, if I repeat things you already know: I'll try briefly to bring these dear children up to date.

As you should know, hibernation technique was perfected around the middle of the twentieth century, essentially for clinical and surgical purposes. But only in

1970 did one attain cryogenics that were truly innocuous and painless and thus suited to the long-term preservation of superior organisms. So a dream became a reality: it seemed possible to 'dispatch' a man into the future. But to how great a distance into the future? And did limits exist? And at what price?

So precisely in order to establish a method of control for the use of posterity, which would be us, in 1975, here in Berlin, a competition for volunteers was initiated.

BALDUR. And Patricia is one of them?

PETER. Precisely. As stated in her personal dossier, which is in the freezer with her, she was in fact the winner of the competition. She had all the requisite qualities: heart, lungs, kidneys, etc., in perfect condition; the nervous system of an astronaut; an imperturbable and resolute personality; limited emotivity and, lastly, a good education and intelligence. Not that education and intelligence are indispensable to endure hibernation, but, all else being equal, preference was given to subjects of a high intellectual level, for obvious reasons of prestige as regards ourselves and our successors.

BALDUR. And so Patricia has slept from 1975 till today?

PETER. Yes, with brief interruptions. The program was agreed upon with her by the commission, whose president was Hugo Thörl, my celebrated ancestor . . .

ILSE. He's the famous one, right, the one we study about in school.

PETER. Precisely, he's the one, my young lady, the discoverer of the fourth principle of thermodynamics . . . . The program, as I was saying, provided for an awakening of a few hours every year, on the nineteenth of December, her birthday.

ILSE. How thoughtful!

PETER. Further awakenings on occasions of particular interest, such as important planetary expeditions, famous crimes and trials, weddings of royalty or film stars, international baseball games, telluric cataclysms and the like: in short, everything that deserves to be seen and handed down to the distant future. And, of course, whenever there is a failure in the current . . . and twice every year for medical checkups. As one can see from the dossier, the total of wakeful intervals, from 1975 till today, has been approximately three hundred days.

BALDUR. . . . And, if I may ask, how is it that Patricia is a guest in your house? Has she been one for a long time?

PETER (*embarrassed*). Patricia is . . . Patricia is, so to speak, part of our family estate. This is a long story and in part obscure. You know, these are matters of other times, a century and a half has passed: it can be considered a miracle that with all the upheavals, blockades, occupations, repressions and plunderings that have been inflicted on Berlin, Patricia was handed down from father to son, undisturbed, without ever leaving our house. In a certain way she represents the family's continuity: she is . . . she is a symbol, there you have it.

BALDUR. . . . But how . . .

PETER. . . . How did Patricia become part of our family? Well, strange though it may seem to you, on this point nothing in writing has been found, and only a verbal tradition survives that Patricia refuses to confirm or deny. It would seem that at the beginning of the experiment, Patricia had lodgings in the university, and in fact in the freezer cell of the Institute of Anatomy, and that around the year 2000 she had a violent quarrel with the faculty: It is said that, actually, this situation did not please her, because she had no privacy and because she was annoyed at having to stay cheek by jowl with corpses set aside for dissection. It appears that during one of her awakenings she formally declared that unless they placed her in a private refrigerator she would have recourse to the law; and that my ancestor, whom I mentioned before, dean of the faculty at that time, in order to resolve the dispute, generously offered to take her in.

ILSE. What a strange woman! Really, if you'll forgive me, hasn't she had enough yet? Who's forcing her? It can't really be all that amusing to be in lethargy all year long, and wake up for only a day or two, and not when you want to, but when someone else wants you to. I'd be bored to death.

PETER. You are mistaken, Ilse. On the contrary, there's never been an existence more intense than Patricia's, her life is concentrated: it contains only the essential, it contains nothing that does not deserve to be lived. As for the time spent in the freezer, it passes for us, not for her. In her it does not leave a trace, neither in her memory nor in her tissues. She does not age; she ages only during the waking hours, from her first birthday in the freezer, which was her twenty-fourth, until today – in a hundred and forty years she has aged scarcely a year. Since last year until today for her about thirty hours have passed.

BALDUR. Three or four for her birthday, and then?

PETER. And then, let's see . . . (*he calculates mentally*), another six or seven for the dentist, for the fitting of a dress, to go out with Lotte to buy a pair of shoes . . .

ILSE. That's understandable; she should keep up with the fashions.

PETER. . . . and that makes ten. Six hours for the first night of *Tristan* at the Opera, and that makes sixteen. Another six for two medical checkups . . .

ILSE. Why, has she been ill? Well, of course, sudden changes in temperature aren't good for anyone. Don't tell me you can get used to them!

PETER. No, no, she is in perfect health. It's those physiologists at the Study Center: punctual as tax collectors, they descend on us twice a year with all their equipment, they defrost her, they turn her over on all sides, X rays, psychological tests, electrocardiograms, blood analysis. . . . Then they leave, and that's the last we hear of them until next time. Professional secrecy: not a word leaks out.

BALDUR. But it's not out of scientific interest that you keep her in your house?

PETER (*embarrassed*). No . . . not only. You know, I am involved in completely different things . . . I'm cut off from the academic world. The fact is that we've become attached to Patricia. And she's become attached to us, like a daughter. She wouldn't leave us for anything in the world.

BALDUR. But in that case why are her waking intervals so rare and short?

PETER. This much is clear: Patricia intends to arrive in the full bloom of youth as far as possible into the century; therefore, she must economize. But you will have the opportunity to hear these things and many others from her herself: there, we've reached thirty-five degrees, she's opening her eyes. Hurry dear, open the hatch and cut the sheath; she's begun to breathe.

(*Click and squeak of hatch; sound of scissors or paper knife.*)

BALDUR. What sort of sheath?

PETER. A hermetic, very closely fitted polyethylene sheath. It reduces losses through evaporation.

(*The metronome, which has been heard in all the pauses as a background noise, throbs louder and louder, then suddenly stops. A beeper rings three times, very distinctly. Complete silence for a few seconds.*)

MARGARETA (*from adjoining room*). Mama! Has Aunt Patricia awakened already? What did she bring me this year?

LOTTE. What do you expect her to bring you? The usual ice cube! In any case it's her birthday, not yours. Keep quiet now. Go to sleep, it's late.

(*Once more silence. A sigh, a rather uncouth yawn, a sneeze. Then, without transition, Patricia starts to speak.*)

PATRICIA (*a mannered, drawling, nasal voice*). Good evening. Good morning. What time is it? So many people! What day is it today? What year?

PETER. It's December nineteenth, 2115. Don't you remember? It's your birthday. Happy birthday, Patricia!

ALL. Happy birthday, Patricia.

(*Voices of everyone confused. One can hear snatches of sentences:*
– Isn't she pretty!
– Miss Patricia, excuse me, I'd like to ask you a few questions.
– Later, later! She must be awfully tired!
– Does she dream when she's in the freezer? What sort of dreams does she have?
– I would like to ask your opinion on . . .)

ILSE. Wonder if she knew Napoleon and Hitler?

BALDUR. Of course not, what are you talking about, they lived two centuries earlier.

LOTTE (*interrupts decisively*). Excuse me, please. Let me through, after all somebody has to take care of practical matters. Patricia may need something. (*To Patricia*) A cup of hot tea? or would you like something more nutritious? A small steak? Do you want to change, to freshen up a bit?

PATRICIA. Tea, thanks. How kind you are, Lotte! No, I don't need anything else for now; you know very well that the defrosting always leaves me with an upset stomach, we'll see about the steak later. But a small one, please. . . . Oh, Peter! how are you? How's your sciatica? What's new? Is the summit meeting over? Is it already cold outside? Oh, I detest winter, I'm so susceptible to colds. . . . And what about you, Lotte?

You seem to be in excellent health, you've even put on a bit of weight, perhaps . . .

MARIA. . . . Ah, well, the years go by for all of us. . . .

BALDUR. They go by for *almost* all of us. If you don't mind, Peter, I heard so much about Patricia, I have waited so anxiously for this meeting, that now I would like . . . (*to Patricia*) Miss Patricia, forgive my boldness, but I know that your time is limited, I would like you to describe our world as seen through your eyes, to speak to me about your past, about your century to which we owe so much, about your plans for the future, what . . .

PATRICIA (*smugly*). It's not at all extraordinary, you know, one becomes accustomed to it right away. For instance, do you see Mr Thörl here, in his fifties (*maliciously*), his hair leaving him, a bit of a paunch, a few aches and pains now and then? Well, for me he was twenty years old two months ago, he wrote poetry and was about to leave as a volunteer with the Uhlans. Three months ago he was ten and called me Aunt Patricia, and he cried when they froze me and wanted to get into the freezer with me. Isn't that true, dear? Oh, a thousand pardons.

And five months ago, not only wasn't he born yet, but he wasn't even distantly scheduled; there was his father, the colonel, but I'm talking about when he was just a lieutenant, he was in the Fourth Mercenary Legion, and at every defrosting he had one more campaign ribbon and a few less hairs. He courted me in the funny way they had in those days: he courted me through eight defrostings . . . you'd say it runs in the Thörls' blood; when it comes to this, I can assure you, they all resemble each other. They do not have – how shall I put it? – a very serious concept of the guardian relationship . . . (*Patricia's voice continues in a fade-out.*) Just think that even the founder, the patriarch . . .

(*Lotte's voice, distinct and close, intervenes, addressing the audience.*)

LOTTE. Did you hear? There, that's what that girl is like. She has no . . . no restraint. It's true that I've put on weight: I don't get to stay in the freezer. But she, she does not put on weight, she's eternal, incorruptible, like asbestos, like a diamond, like gold. But she does like men, and especially other folks' husbands. She's an eternal wheedler, an incorrigible flirt. I appeal to you, ladies and gentlemen: don't I have a good reason not to like her? (*Sighs*) . . . And she appeals to men, at her venerable age: that's the worst of it. You know quite well what men are like, Thörl or no Thörl, and intellectuals more than others: a couple of sighs, a couple of glances in that particular way, a couple of childhood memories, and the trap is sprung. In the long run she is the one who gets into trouble, obviously, since after a month or two she is pestered by some elderly gallants. . . . No, don't think that I'm all blind or all that foolish: I too have noticed that, this time, her tone has changed with my husband, she has become biting, sharp. Obviously, there's another man on the horizon. But you didn't attend those other awakenings. It was enough to flay her! And besides, I've never been able to get proof, to catch them in the act, but are you really certain that between the 'guardian' and the girl everything has always taken place in broad daylight? In other words (*forcefully*), that all defrostings have been properly registered in the personal booklet? I'm not. I'm not sure of it. (*Pause. Confused conversations against the background sounds.*) But this time there's something new, you too must have noticed. It's simple: there's another man on the horizon, a younger man. The little darling likes fresh flesh! Just listen to her: isn't she someone who knows what she wants? (*Voices*) Oh, I didn't think that we had already reached that stage.

(*From the voices in the background emerge those of Baldur and Patricia.*)

BALDUR. . . . an impression such as I've never experienced. I would never have thought it possible to find joined in one person alone the fascination of both youth and eternity. Before you I feel as if I were in the presence of the pyramids, and yet you are so young and so beautiful!

PATRICIA. Yes, Mr . . . Baldur, that's your name, isn't it? Yes, Baldur. But my gifts are three, not two. Eternity, youth and solitude. And the latter is the price paid by those who dare as I have dared.

BALDUR. But what a miraculous experience! Pass in flight where others creep, be able personally to compare customs, events and heroes, at a distance of decades, of centuries! What historian would not be envious? And to think that I proclaim myself a lover of history! (*With sudden élan*) Let me read your diary.

PATRICIA. How do you know . . . I mean, what makes you think that I keep a diary?

BALDUR. So you do keep one! I guessed correctly!

PATRICIA. Yes, I do. It's part of the program, but no one knows about it, not even Thörl. And no one can read it: it's in code, this too is part of the program.

BALDUR. If no one can read it, what's the use of it?

PATRICIA. It's useful for me. I'll use it afterward.

BALDUR. After what?

PATRICIA. Afterward, when I've arrived. I'm counting on publishing it then: I think I won't have any trouble finding a publisher, because it is an intimate diary, the sort that's always successful. (*In a dreamy voice*) You know, I'm planning to devote myself to journalism. And to publish the intimate diaries of all the powerful people of my epoch, Churchill, Stalin, etc. You can make a pile of money.

BALDUR. But how is it that these diaries are in your possession?

PATRICIA. They're not in my possession at all. I'll write them myself. Based on authentic episodes, naturally.

(*Pause*)

BALDUR. Patricia! (*Another pause*) Take me with you.

PATRICIA (*thinks about it, then very coldly*). It wouldn't be a bad idea, in the abstract. But you mustn't believe that it's enough to get into the freezer: you must get injections, go through a training course . . . it's not all that simple. Besides, not everybody's physique is suitable. . . . Certainly, it would be rather nice to have a traveling companion like you, so lively, so passionate, so full of temperament . . . but you're engaged, aren't you?

BALDUR. Engaged? I was.

PATRICIA. Till when?

BALDUR. Till half an hour ago; but now I've met you and everything has changed.

PATRICIA. You're a flatterer, a dangerous man. (*Patricia's voice changes abruptly; it is no longer plangent and languid, but sharp, energetic, cutting.*) In any case, if matters stand as you tell me, an interesting arrangement could develop from it.

BALDUR. Patricia! Why hesitate? Let us leave: come away with me. Not into the future: into the present.

PATRICIA. (*coldly*). Precisely, I was thinking about that too. But when?

BALDUR. Now, immediately. We cross the room and are off.

PATRICIA. Nonsense. We'd immediately have them all at our heels, with him in the lead. Look at him: he's already suspicious . . .

BALDUR. Well, when?

PATRICIA. Tonight. Listen carefully. At midnight everybody leaves, and they refreeze and mothball me. It's much quicker than awakening, it's a bit like with scuba divers, you know quite well, you must go up slowly, but the immersion can be quick. They stuff me into the freezer and connect the compressor without a by-your-leave, but during the first hours I remain quite soft and can easily get back to active life.

BALDUR. And so?

PATRICIA. And so, it's simple. You leave with the others, accompany your . . . I mean that girl home; then you come back here; you slip into the garden, enter through the kitchen window . . .

BALDUR. . . . And it's done! Two more hours and the world is ours! But tell me, Patricia, won't you have regrets? Won't you be sorry at having cut short your race toward future centuries for my sake?

PATRICIA. Look, young man, we'll have plenty of time to discuss these interesting subjects if the caper succeeds. But it must first succeed. Look, they're leaving; go back to your place, take your leave politely and try not to make mistakes. You know, it's not because I want to make a fuss, but I'd hate to waste the opportunity.

(*Voices of the departing guests, the sound of chairs being moved, snatches of sentences:*
– Till next year!
– Good night, if that's what one should say . . .
– Let's go, Robert, I didn't think it was so late.
– Baldur, let's go, you have the honor of escorting me.
Silence. Then Lotte's voice, addressing the audience.)

LOTTE. . . . So, they all left. Peter and I remained alone with Patricia, a thing that's never pleasant for any of us. I don't say this because of the dislike I described a moment ago, a bit impulsively perhaps; no: it is an objectively unpleasant situation, cold, false, filled with embarrassment for all of us. We talked about this or that for a while, then we said good-bye, and Peter put Patricia back into the freezer.

(*The same sounds as during the defrosting, but reversed and accelerated. Sigh, yawn. Zippering of the sheath. The metronome starts up, then the pump, whistles, etc. The metronome continues, the rhythm gradually merging with the slower rhythm of a grandfather clock. One o'clock strikes, half past one, two o'clock. We hear the sound of a car approaching, stopping, the slam of the door. A dog barks in the distance, footsteps on the gravel. A window opens. Footsteps on the wooden floor, which creaks, sounding closer and closer. The freezer door opens.*)

BALDUR (*whispers*). Patricia, it's me!

PATRICIA (*in a confused, muffled voice*). Cu . . . th . . . plstic covr.

BALDUR. Whaaat?

PATRICIA (*a bit more distinctly*). Cut the cover!

(*Sound of cutting.*)

BALDUR. There. And now what? What are we supposed to do? You must forgive me, but I have no experience in this, you know, it's the first time this has happened to me. . . .

PATRICIA. Oh, it's almost all done, I can take care of everything by myself now. Just give me a hand to get out of here.

(*Footsteps. 'Quiet,' 'Shhh,' 'This way.' Window. Footsteps on the gravel, car door, Baldur starts the motor.*)

BALDUR. We're away, Patricia, away from the ice, away from the nightmare. I think I'm dreaming: for two hours I've been living in a dream. I'm afraid of waking up.

PATRICIA (*coldly*). Did you accompany your fiancée home?

BALDUR. Who, Ilse? Yes, I drove her home. I said good-bye to her.

PATRICIA. What do you mean, good-bye? For good?

BALDUR. Yes, it wasn't as difficult as I feared, just a little scene. She didn't even cry.

(*Pause, motor is running.*)

PATRICIA. Young man, don't think badly of me. I believe that the moment has come for an explanation. You must understand: I had to get out of there somehow.

BALDUR. . . . And that's all there was to it? To get out of there?

PATRICIA. That's all. To get out of the freezer and out of Thörl's house. Baldur, I feel that I owe you a confession.

BALDUR. A confession is not enough.

PATRICIA. I can give you nothing else; and it isn't even a handsome confession. I'm really tired: freeze and defrost, freeze and defrost becomes wearying in the long run. And then there's more.

BALDUR. More?

PATRICIA. Yes, more. His visits, at night. At thirty-three degrees Celsius, barely tepid, when I couldn't defend myself in any way. And since I kept quiet, how could I! He probably imagined . . .

BALDUR. My poor dear, how much you must have suffered!

PATRICIA. A real nuisance, you have no idea. I can't tell you how annoying.

(*Sound of the car moving away.*)

LOTTE. . . . And so ends this story. I had suspected something, and that night I had also heard strange noises, but I kept quiet: why should I have sounded the alarm?

I'd say that it's best for everyone this way. Baldur, poor fellow, has told me everything: it seems that on top of everything else, Patricia also asked him for money in order to go I don't know where, to look for a contemporary of hers, who is in America; he too in a freezer, naturally. Nobody cares very much whether Baldur will patch it up with Ilse or not, not even Ilse herself. We sold the freezer. As for Peter, we shall see.

The Measure of Beauty

The beach umbrella next to ours was unoccupied. I went to the torrid shack that bore the inscription MANAGEMENT, to ask whether it was possible to rent it for the entire month; the attendant consulted the list of reservations, then he said, 'No, I'm sorry. It's reserved since June by a gentleman from Milan.' I have good eyesight: next to number 75 was written the name Simpson.

There can't be many Simpsons in Milan; I hoped it wasn't he, *the* Simpson, representative of NATCA. It's not that I dislike him, just the opposite; but my wife and I care a lot for our privacy and vacations are vacations, and any *revenant* from the business world spoils them for me. Furthermore, a certain intolerance of his, a certain puritanical rigidity that had come to light particularly during the episode of the duplicators, had somewhat cooled our relationship, and made him appear to me a not very desirable beach neighbor. But the world is small: three days later Mr Simpson in person showed up under beach umbrella number 75. He carried a very voluminous beach bag, and I had never seen him so embarrassed.

I've known Simpson for many years and I know that he is both astute and naive, like all thoroughbred representatives and middlemen; and besides that he is sociable, loquacious, jovial, a connoisseur of good cooking. Instead, the Simpson that fate had dropped alongside me was reticent and nervous: rather than on a deck chair facing the Adriatic, he seemed to be seated on a fakir's bed. In the few sentences we exchanged he fell into contradiction: he told me that he loved life on the beach, and that he had been coming to Rimini for many years; immediately afterward, that he didn't know how to swim, and that roasting under the sun was for him a great nuisance and waste of time. The next day he disappeared. I made a beeline for the attendant: Simpson had canceled the umbrella. His behavior was beginning to interest me. I made the rounds of the bathing establishments, distributing tips and cigarettes, and in less than two hours I found out (and wasn't astonished by this) that he had looked for and found a beach umbrella at the Sirio baths at the opposite end of the beach.

I'd formed the conviction that puritanical Mr Simpson, abundantly wedded and with a daughter of marrying age, was in Rimini with a girl: this suspicion so excited my curiosity that I decided to spy on his movements from the top of the rotunda. Seeing without being seen, especially from above – this is an occupation that has always enthralled me. 'Peeping Tom,' who chose to die rather than stop peeking at Lady Godiva through the cracks in the shutters, is my hero; spying on my fellow men, independently of what they are doing or are about to do, and of any ultimate discovery, affords me a feeling of power and profound fulfillment: perhaps this is an atavistic memory of the exhausting waits of my hunting ancestors, and reproduces the vital emotions of pursuit and ambush.

But in Simpson's case the discovery seemed to be certain. The hypothesis of a girl immediately fell by the wayside, there wasn't a girl in sight: nevertheless, my man's behavior was peculiar. He lay there and read (or pretended to read) the newspaper, but everything led me to believe that he was intent on an exploratory activity not very dissimilar to mine. At intervals he roused himself from his inertia, poked about in his bag and pulled out a device similar to a movie camera or a small telecamera, pointed it obliquely at the sky, pressed a button, then wrote something in a small notebook. Was he photographing something or someone? I watched more attentively: yes, it was at least probable; cameras provided with a prismatic lens for wide-angle shots, so as not to arouse the suspicion of the person you wish to photograph, are nothing new, especially on beaches.

By the afternoon I no longer had any doubts: Simpson was photographing the bathers who passed in front of him. At times he even moved along the water's edge, and if he found an interesting subject he pointed at the sky and snapped. He did not seem to show any preferences for the prettier bathers and not even for the women bathers *tout court*: he snapped at random adolescents, old matrons, gentlemen all bones and gray fleece, the husky local boys and girls. After every photograph, methodically, he removed his dark glasses and wrote something in a small notebook. One detail seemed inexplicable to me: the photographic devices were two, identical to each other; one for the males, the other for the females.

By now I was certain: this wasn't an innocuous, senile mania (for that matter, I'd give a whole lot to reach the age of sixty as senile as Simpson), but it was something big; at least as big as Simpson's embarrassment at the sight of me and his haste to change umbrellas.

From that moment on my idle voyeurism also became concentrated attention. Simpson's maneuvers had become a challenge to my ingenuity, like a chess problem, indeed, like a mystery of nature; I was determined to get to the bottom of it.

I bought a good pair of binoculars, but it wasn't of much help. Indeed, it further confused my thinking. Simpson was taking notes in English, in a very sloppy handwriting and with many abbreviations; in any event, I was able to discern the fact that every page of the notebook was divided into three columns, and that these were headed: 'Vis. Eval.,' 'Meter' and 'Obos.' Evidently some experimental work on behalf of NATCA; but what?

In the evening I returned to the pensione in a terrible mood. I told my wife the whole business: women often have a surprising intuition for this sort of thing. But my wife too, for different and indefinable reasons, was in a bad mood; she told me that in her opinion Simpson was a filthy old man, and that the whole story did not interest her in the least. I forgot to say that between my wife and Simpson there has been bad blood since last year, when Simpson was selling duplicators and my wife was afraid I would buy one and duplicate her, and she was getting ready to be jealous of herself. But then she thought it over and gave me a striking piece of advice: 'Blackmail him. Threaten to report him to the beach patrol.'

Simpson capitulated precipitously. I was beginning to tell him that I had been unpleasantly surprised by his flight and his lack of trust, and that, in my opinion, our by now long friendship should have reassured him of my capacity for discretion, but I immediately saw that this was a useless approach. Simpson was the usual Simpson: he was dying to tell me everything, from A to Z; evidently, the secrecy had been imposed on him by his company, and all he had been waiting for was a moment of force majeure to violate it. My first hint at reporting him, though vague and maladroit, was for him a sufficient instance of force majeure.

He was satisfied with a sketchy declaration of confidentiality on my part, after which his eyes lit up and he told me that the two apparatuses he carried were not cameras but rather two Kalometers, two beauty measurers. One male and one female.

'This is a new product of ours, a small experimental series. The first specimens have been entrusted to the most senior and trustworthy functionaries,' he told me without false modesty. 'We've been charged to test them under various environmental conditions and on diverse subjects. They have not explained to us the technical details of the mechanism (you know, it's because of the usual patent hassle); and instead they have attached great importance to what they call the *philosophy* of the device.'

'A beauty meter! That seems a bit audacious. What is beauty? Do you know? Did they explain it to you, those people there, at headquarters, at Fort . . . what's it's name?'

'Fort Kiddiwanee. Yes, they did pose the question; but you know, Americans – I should say 'we Americans,' right? but it's so many years now! – Americans are simpler than we. There might have been some uncertainty or doubts until yesterday, but now it's clear: beauty is that which the Kalometer measures. Tell me: what electrician goes to the trouble of finding out about the intimate essence of the difference in potential? The difference of potential is what a voltameter measures; the rest is only a futile complication.'

'Precisely. A voltameter is used by electricians, it is an instrument of their trade. Who can use the Kalometer? NATCA up until now has acquired a good reputation for its office machines, solid, square stuff to be used to calculate, duplicate, compose, translate. I don't understand why they should now devote themselves to the construction of such . . . frivolous devices. Frivolous or philosophical; there's no middle road, it's either/or. I would never buy a Kalometer: what the devil is it good for?'

Mr Simpson became radiant: he placed his left index finger against his nose, strongly deviating it to the right, then he said, 'Do you know how many advance orders we have already? Not less than forty thousand in the States alone, and the publicity campaign hasn't even started. I'll be able to tell you in much greater detail in a few days, when a number of legal aspects relative to the possible uses of the device will have been clarified; you certainly don't think that NATCA can afford to plan and launch a model without serious market research! In fact, the idea has tempted also our, shall I say, colleagues behind the Iron Curtain. Didn't you know? It's high-level gossip that even made the newspapers (but they spoke in general terms about 'a new discovery of strategic importance'), it made the rounds of all our branch offices, and even aroused some apprehension. The Soviets maintain the contrary, as usual; but we have reliable proof that one of our researchers three years ago sent to Moscow to the Ministry of Education the fundamental idea of the Kalometer, and one of the first complete drawings. Of course it's no secret to anyone that NATCA is a den of crypto-communists, intellectuals and malcontents.

'Luckily for us, the whole business ended up in the hands of the bureaucrats and the theoreticians of Marxist esthetics; thanks to the former, a few years have been wasted; thanks to the latter, the sort of device that they'll come up with down there will in no way be able to compete with ours. It is destined to other uses: it apparently is a Kalogoniometer that measures beauty in relation to the angle of social approach, and that doesn't concern us in the least. Our point of view is very different, more concrete. Beauty, I was about to say, is a pure number: it is a relationship, or rather an ensemble of relationships. I don't want to parade with another's feathers: you will find all I'm saying and expressed in loftier terms in the publicity booklet of the Kalometer which is already prepared in America and is now being translated; you know I'm just a small engineer, and what's more, atrophied by twenty years of commercial activity (prosperous, however). Beauty, according to our philosophy, is relative to a model, variable at will, at the judgment of fashion, or even any observer whatsoever, and privileged observers do not exist. The judgment of an artist, of a hidden persuader, or even quite simply of a single customer. Therefore each Kalometer must be tuned before being used, and the fine-tuning is a delicate and fundamental operation: for example, the device you see here was tuned on the basis of Sebastiano del Piombo's *Fantesca*.'

'So, if I've understood correctly, we have here a differential apparatus.'

'Certainly. Of course, one can't expect every user to have evolved and differentiated tastes: not all men possess a well-defined female ideal. So, during this initial phase of perfecting and commercial introduction NATCA is concentrating on three models: a *blank* model, which is tuned, free of charge, on a specimen sample chosen by the customer; and two models with standard tuning, for the measuring of female and male beauty respectively. For experimental purposes, all through the current year the female model, called Paris, will be tuned on the features of Elizabeth Taylor, and the male model (which for the time being is not in great demand) on the features of Burt Lancaster. Apropos, just this morning I received a confidential letter from Fort Kiddiwanee, Oklahoma: they inform me that till now no satisfactory name has been found for this model, and that a competition has been opened among us senior functionaries. The prize, naturally, is a Kalometer, any one of the three models. You are a cultivated person, would you like to compete? I'd be glad to let you compete under my name. . . .'

I won't claim that Semiramis is a very original or even very pertinent name: obviously the other competitors' imagination and culture were even more sluggish than mine. I won the competition, or more precisely I got Simpson to win it, who received and turned over to me a *blank* Kalometer, making me happy for a month.

I also tried the device just as it had been sent to me, but without achieving anything: it scored off 100 no matter what object was presented to it. I sent it back to the branch office, and got them to tune it on a good color reproduction of the *Portrait of Madame Lunia Czechowska*; it was returned to me with laudable promptness and I tried it out in various situations.

To express a final judgment would perhaps be premature and presumptuous; yet it seems to me I can affirm that the Kalometer is a sensitive and ingenious device. If its purpose is that of reproducing human judgment, that purpose is amply achieved: but it reproduces the judgment of an observer whose tastes are extremely limited and narrow, or rather that of a maniac. My apparatus, for instance, assigns low scores to all roundish female faces and absolves elongated faces; to such a point that it has assigned a score of K32 to our milk vendor, who is considered one of the beauties of the quarter but is rather plump, and it has attributed K28 to the *Gioconda*, which I submitted to it in a reproduction. On the other hand, the device is extraordinarily partial to long, slender necks.

Its most surprising quality (actually, after closer examination, the only quality that distinguishes it from a banal system of photometers) is its indifference to the position of the subject and to its distance. I've asked my wife, who turned out to be a good K75, with a high score of K79 when she's rested and serene and under good light conditions, to submit herself to measurements in different positions, full face, right and left profile, lying down, with hat or without, with eyes open or closed, and I've always obtained readings fluctuating within five K units.

The readings are decisively altered only when the face forms an angle of more than ninety degrees; if the subject is completely turned away, that is, presents the nape of the neck to the device, the readings are very low.

I must mention here that my wife has an oval, very elongated face, a slender neck and a slightly upturned nose; in my opinion she would deserve an even higher score if it weren't for her hair, which is black, while that of the tuning model is dark blond.

If one points the Paris at male faces, one usually obtains responses below K20, and below K10 if the subject wears a mustache or beard. It is remarkable that the Kalometer rarely gives rigorously zero readings: similarly to what happens with children, it recognizes the human face also in its coarsest or most casual imitations. I've amused myself by slowly gliding the lens over an irregularly variegated surface (to be precise, wallpaper): every jerk of the needle responded to an area in which it was possible to recognize a vaguely anthropomorphic semblance. I've obtained zero readings only on decisively asymmetric or shapeless subjects, and naturally against solid-color backgrounds.

My wife detests the Kalometer but, as is her habit, she won't or cannot give me a reason. Whenever she sees me holding the device or hears me mention it, she turns frosty and her mood plummets. This is an injustice on her part because, as I said, she has not been judged badly; K79 is an excellent score. In the beginning I thought that she had extended to the Kalometer her general distrust for the apparatuses that Simpson sells me or lets me have on trial, and for Simpson himself; in any event her silence and her unease weighed on me so much that the other evening I deliberately provoked her indignation by fiddling around for a good hour and all over the house with the Kalometer: and actually, I must say that her opinions, though expressed in an emotional manner, are well founded and reasonable.

In short, my wife is scandalized by the device's extreme docility. According to her, rather than measuring beauty, it measures conformity and is therefore an exquisitely conformist instrument. I tried to defend the Kalometer (which, according to my wife, should more appropriately be called the 'homeometer') by pointing out to her that anyone who passes a judgment is a conformist, inasmuch as, consciously or not, he refers back to a model: I reminded her of the tempestuous debut of the Impressionists; the hatred of public opinion for single innovators (in all fields), which is transformed into quiet love when the innovators are innovators no longer; finally I tried to demonstate to her that the establishing of a fashion, of a style, the collective 'getting used to' a new mode of expression, is the exact analogue of a Kalometer's tuning. I insisted on what I consider the most alarming phenomenon of today's civilization, which is that the average man can be tuned in the most incredible ways: he can be made to believe that Swedish furniture and plastic flowers, and they alone, are beautiful; that only a particular toothpaste is good, only a particular surgeon skillful, only a particular party the depository of truth; in short, I declared that it is not very sporting to despise a machine only because it reproduces a human mental process. But my wife is a hopeless case of a Crocean education: she answered 'maybe' and I don't think I convinced her.

On the other hand, during recent times I too have lost some of my enthusiasm, but for different reasons. I again met Simpson, at a Rotary dinner: he was in an excellent mood, and announced two 'great victories' of his.

'Now I can relinquish all my reservations about the sales campaign,' he told me. 'You won't believe me, but in all of our entire catalogue there isn't a machine easier to place. Tomorrow I'm sending off my monthly report to Fort Kiddiwanee; you can bet there'll be a promotion! I always say, for a salesman there are two great virtues: knowledge of your fellow beings and imagination.' He waxed confidential and lowered his voice: '. . . Call girl centers! Nobody had yet thought about it, not even in America. It is a true spontaneous census: I didn't think there were so many. All the managers have immediately understood the commercial importance of a new index, completed by an objective Kalometric score: Magda, age twenty-two, K eighty-seven; Wilma, age twenty-six, K seventy-seven . . . do you understand?

'Then I had another brainstorm: . . . well, to tell the truth, this isn't entirely to my credit, it was suggested to me by circumstances. I sold a Paris to my friend Gilberto: do you know what he did? As soon as he got it, he interfered with it, untuned it and then retuned it on himself.'

'And so?'

'But don't you see? It's an idea that you can make arise so to speak spontaneously in the mind of most customers. I've already prepared a draft of the publicity leaflet that I would like to distribute for the next holidays: in fact, if you'd be so kind as to take a look at it . . . you know, I'm not all that sure about my Italian. Once the fashion is launched, who won't make his wife (or her husband) the present of a Kalometer tuned on his or her photograph? You'll see, very few will resist the flattery of a K one hundred: remember the witch in *Snow White*. Everybody likes to be praised and agreed with, even if only by a mirror or a printed circuit.'

I hadn't known this cynical side of Simpson's character. We separated coldly and I fear that our friendship is seriously compromised.

Full Employment

'Exactly the same as in 1929,' Mr Simpson said. 'You're young and cannot remember, but it's exactly the same as then: disheartenment, inertia, lack of initiative. And do you think that over there in the States, where after all things aren't going that badly, they would give me a hand? Just the opposite: precisely this year, when we needed something new, something revolutionary, do you know what the NATCA planning office, with its four hundred technicians and fifty scientists, has come up with? Here, look: this is all.' He pulled a metal box from his pocket and plunked it on the table scornfully.

'You tell me, how can a person be a representative with love? It's a pretty little machine, I won't deny it, but, believe me, it requires quite a bit of courage to run from customer to customer all year long with nothing else in hand, and try to convince them that this is the great 1966 NATCA innovation.'

'What can it do?' I asked.

'There, that's exactly the point: it can do everything and nothing. As a rule, machines are specialized: a tractor pulls, a saw saws, a versifier makes verses, a photometer measures light. This one here instead can do everything, or almost. It's called the Minibrain; not even the name is a success, in my opinion. It's presumptuous and vague, and cannot be translated. In short it has no commercial appeal whatsoever. It's a four-track selector, that's what it is: do you want to know how many women named Eleonora were operated on for appendicitis in Sicily in 1940? Or how many of the suicides in the entire world from 1900 to date were left-handed and at the same time blonds? You only have to push this key and you'll have your answer in an instant: but only if you have first introduced the protocols here; I'm sorry, forgive me if it's not much. In short, as far as I'm concerned it's a huge mistake, and they will pay dearly for it. According to them, the innovation consists in the fact that it is pocket-size and also in its price. Do you want it? Twenty-four thousand lire and it's yours: you'd think it was made in Japan. But do you know what? If within the year they don't give me something more original, with all my sixty years and thirty-five working for them, I'll leave them flat. No, no, I'm not joking. Luckily I have other cards in hand; I don't want to sound conceited, but I feel up to doing something better than placing selectors at a moment of crisis.'

All through this outburst, which was taking place at the end of one of those prodigal banquets that despite everything NATCA continues to organize every year for its best customers, I had followed Simpson's mood with curiosity. In contrast to his words, he did not seem at all discouraged; on the contrary, he was unusually animated and gay. Behind his thick glasses, his gray eyes gleamed vivaciously: or was it perhaps only the effect of the wine that both of us had drunk in abundance? I decided to smooth the path to confidentiality for him.

'I too am convinced that, with your experience, you can do something better than going around selling office machines. Selling is difficult, often disagreeable; and yet it is an occupation that fosters human contacts, that teaches something new every day. . . . And, in the end, NATCA isn't the whole world.'

Simpson promptly accepted my gambit. 'That's precisely the crux of the matter: at NATCA they're either wrong or they exaggerate. This is an old idea of mine: machines are important, we can no longer do without them, they shape our world, but they are not always the best solution for our problems.'

The gist of all this was not very clear; I attempted a new probe. 'Certainly, the human brain is irreplacable. This is a truth that those who design electronic brains tend to forget.'

'No, no,' Simpson answered impatiently, 'don't talk to me about the human brain. First of all it is too complicated; besides, it is not at all proven that it can manage to understand itself; and finally there are too many people working on it. Good people, disinterested, I'll agree to that, but too many; there are mountains of books and thousands of organizations, other NATCAS, neither better nor worse than mine, where the human brain is being cooked in all the sauces. Freud, Pavlov, Turing, the cyberneticists, the sociologists, all of them manipulating it, denaturing it, and all our machines try to copy it. No, my idea is something else.' He paused, as though he were hesitating, then he leaned over the table and said in a low voice, 'It's not only an idea. Would you like to come and see me on Sunday?'

It was an old villa in the hills that Simpson had bought cheaply at the end of the war. The Simpsons welcomed my wife and me with cordiality and courtesy; I was very happy to finally meet Mrs Simpson, a slim, gray-haired woman, mild and reserved, and yet full of human warmth. They asked us to sit down in the garden at the edge of a pond; the conversation limped on, distracted and vague, chiefly on account of Simpson. He looked into the air, shifted in his chair, continually lit his pipe and let it go out: it was clear that he was in an almost comical hurry to get through the preambles and come down to cases.

I must admit he managed this quite elegantly. While Mrs Simpson was serving tea, he asked my wife, 'Would you like some blueberries? There are a great many and they're excellent, on the other side of the valley.' 'Please don't go to any trouble . . .,' my wife began; Simpson answered, 'Not at all!' Then he pulled a small instrument from his pocket that seemed similar to a panpipe and blew three notes. We heard a light, sharp flutter of wings, the water of the pond rippled, and a swarm of dragonflies passed over our heads. 'Two minutes!' Simpson exclaimed triumphantly, and clicked his wrist chronometer; with a proud and at the same time shamefaced smile, Mrs Simpson went into the house, reappeared with a crystal bowl, and placed it empty on the small table. At the end of the second minute the dragonflies returned, like a minuscule wave of bombers; there must have been several hundred. They hovered above us in stationary flight, amid a metallic, almost musical rustle; then one by one, abruptly, they descended over the bowl, slowed their flight, dropped a blueberry and flew off in a flash. In a few instants, the bowl was full: not one blueberry had missed it, and they were still freshly gleaming with dew.

'It never fails,' Simpson said. 'It is a spectacular demonstration, but it's not very rigorous. In any event, since you've seen it, there's no need for me to try and convince you with words. Now you tell me: if it is possible to do this, what would be the point of developing a machine that one could order to gather blueberries in two acres of woods? And do you believe that it would be possible to design a machine able to execute the order in two minutes without the slightest noise, without consuming fuel, without being damaged and without damaging the woods? And what about the cost, just think of it. What is the price of a swarm of dragonflies? Which, besides all else, actually are very pretty.'

'Are they . . . conditioned dragonflies?' I asked foolishly. I had not been able to restrain myself from throwing a furtive glance of alarm at my wife, and I was afraid that Simpson might have noticed it and might have understood its meaning. My wife's face was impassive, but I distinctly sensed her disquiet.

'They're not conditioned, they are at my service. Indeed, more precisely, we have come to an agreement.' Simpson leaned back against the backrest of his chair and smiled benevolently, gloating over the effect of his pronouncement; then he resumed: 'Of course, it might be better to take things from the beginning. You have read, I imagine, about Von Frisch's brilliant work on the language of the bees: the dance in eights, its modalities and its meaning in relation to distance, direction and amount of food. The subject fascinated me twelve years ago, and since then I've devoted all my free weekend hours to the bees. In the beginning I only wanted to try to speak to the bees in their language. It seems absurd that no one thought of it before – you can do so with extraordinary ease. Come and see.'

He showed me a beehive on which he had replaced the front panel with a frosted pane of glass. With a finger he traced several oblique eights on the external face of the glass, and soon a small swarm issued buzzing from the little door.

'I'm sorry I deceived them, this time. Southeast, at a distance of two hundred meters, there is nothing, poor dears: I only wanted to show you how I broke the ice, the wall of incomprehension that separates us from the insects. I had made things hard for myself at the beginning: just think that, for several months, I danced in figure eights myself, all of me, I mean, not only with my finger – yes, right in front here, on the meadow. They understood all the same, but with difficulty, and besides it was fatiguing and ridiculous. Eventually I realized that much less is enough: any signal whatsoever, as you saw, even with a twig, with a finger, provided it conforms with their code.'

'And also with the dragonflies . . . .?'

'With the dragonflies I have only indirect relations for the time being. There was a second step: I realized quite soon that the language of the bees goes far beyond the figure-eight dance signaling food. Today I can prove that they have other dances, I mean other figures; I haven't yet understood them all, but I've already been able to compile a small glossary containing a few hundred entries. Here it is: There are the equivalents of a good number of nouns such as 'sun,' 'wind,' 'rain,' 'cold,' 'heat,' etc. There is a vast assortment of plant names: in this connection I've noticed that they have at least twelve distinct figures to indicate, for example, an apple tree, depending on whether the tree is large, small, old, healthy, grown wild, and so on – something like what we do with horses. They know how to say 'gather,' 'sting,' 'fall,' 'fly'; here too they have a surprising number of synonyms for flight: their own 'to fly' is different from that of mosquitoes, butterflies and sparrows. However, they do not make any distinction between walking, running, swimming, and traveling on wheels: for them, all movements on ground level or over water are a 'sliding.' In regard to other insects, and above all flying insects, their lexical patrimony is just barely inferior to ours; however, they are satisfied with an extremely generic nomenclature for the larger animals. Their signs for quadrupeds, respectively from the mouse to the dog and the sheep on up, are only two, and they could approximately be rendered by 'small four' and 'big four.' They don't even distinguish between man and woman; I had to explain the difference to them.'

'And you speak this language?'

'Badly, for now; but I understand it well enough, and I've used it to get them to explain to me some of the greater mysteries of the beehive; how they decide on what day to slaughter the males, when and why they authorize the queens to lock in combat until death, how they establish the numerical relationship between drones and workers. They haven't told me everything, however: they keep certain secrets. They are a race with great dignity.'

'Do they also speak to the dragonflies by dancing?'

'No, bees only use dancing to communicate among themselves and (forgive my lack of modesty) with me. As for other species, I must tell you first of all that the bees have regular relationships only with those most evolved, especially with other social insects, and with those that have gregarious habits. For instance, they have rather close – though not always friendly – contacts with ants, wasps, and, precisely, dragonflies; with locusts, on the other hand, and the orthoptera in general they confine themselves to commands and threats. In any case, with all the other insects the bees communicate by means of their antennae. Theirs is a rudimentary code, but on the other hand it is so swift that I've absolutely been unable to follow it, and I feel that it is irremediably beyond human capabilities. If you must know, not only don't I have any hope, but I don't even have any desire to make contact with other insects, aside from the bees: it would seem rather indelicate toward them; and anyway, they act as mediators with great enthusiasm, almost as though they enjoyed it. To return to the code – the, let us call it, interinsectic code – I have the impression that it is not a true and proper language: rather than rigidly conventional, it seems to me to rely on the intuition and imagination of the moment. It must be vaguely similar to the complicated and at the same time succinct method whereby we men communicate with dogs (I'm sure you've noticed, haven't you? that there does not exist a man-dog language, and yet the understanding in both directions is considerable): but it is certainly richer, as you yourself will be able to see from the results.'

He led us to the garden and the arbor and pointed out to us that there wasn't a single ant in the area, and not because of insecticides: his wife didn't like ants (Mrs Simpson, who was following us, blushed deeply), so he had offered them a deal: he would provide for the support of all their colonies, all the way to the perimeter wall (an expense of two or three thousand lire a year, he explained to me), and they would agree to demobilize all the anthills within a radius of fifty meters from the villa, not to open new ones, and each day for two hours, from five to seven, to perform all operations of microcleaning and destruction of noxious larvae in the garden and villa. The ants had agreed; however, shortly afterward, through the bees' mediation, they had complained about a certain colony of ant lions that infested a sandy strip at the edge of the wood. Simpson confessed to me that at the time he didn't even know that ant lions were the larvae of dragonflies: he had gone to the site, and with extreme horror he had seen their bloodthirsty habits. The sand was studded with small conical holes: just then an ant ventured to the rim and had immediately plunged into the depths together with the loose sand. From the depths there emerged a pair of ferocious curved mandibles, and Simpson had been forced to admit that the ants' protest was justified. He told me that he had felt both proud and confused at the arbitration that had been asked of him: the good name of all of mankind would depend on his decision.

He had summoned a small meeting. 'It was last September, a memorable assembly. Bees, ants and dragonflies participated – adult dragonflies, who rigorously and urbanely defended the rights of their larvae. They pointed out to me that the latter could in no way be held responsible for their feeding habits; they had very poor locomotion, and all they could do was lay traps for the ants or starve to death. At that I proposed to allot to them an adequate daily ration of balanced feed, the same as we give to our chickens. The dragonflies requested a trial feeding: the larvae showed they liked it, and at that the dragonflies declared themselves ready to interpose their good offices so that all threats to the ants would be discontinued. It was on that occasion that I offered them a bonus for every expedition into the blueberry woods: but that is a service I rarely ask of them. They are among the most intelligent and hardy insects, and I expect a lot from them.'

He explained to me that it had seemed improper to him to propose any type of contract to the bees, who were already too busy; on the other hand, he was involved in advanced negotiations with flies and mosquitoes. Flies, he said, were stupid, and you couldn't get much out of them: just that they shouldn't be a nuisance in autumn and should not frequent the stable and dung heap. In exchange for four milligrams of milk per day per head, they had agreed: Simpson was planning to assign them simple urgent messages, at least until he could have a phone installed in the villa. With the mosquitoes the negotiations promised to be difficult for other reasons: not only were they good for nothing, but they had made it clear that they did not want to, indeed could not, give up human blood, or at least that of mammals. Due to the proximity of the pond the mosquitoes constituted a considerable nuisance; so Simpson considered an agreement desirable: he had consulted with the town veterinarian, and he proposed to draw every two months half a liter of blood from a cow in the stable. With a bit of citrate, it would not coagulate, and according to the census, it should be enough for all the local mosquitoes. He pointed out that in itself it wasn't a great bargain, but it was still less costly than spraying DDT, and furthermore it would not disturb the biological balance in the area. This detail was not without importance because the method could be patented and utilized in all regions affected by malaria: he thought that the mosquitoes would understand rather quickly that it was to their obvious interest to avoid becoming infested with plasmodium, and as for the plasmodia themselves, even if they became extinct it would be no great loss. I asked him whether it wouldn't be possible to make analogous nonaggression pacts with other parasites that infest people and dwellings: Simpson assured me that so far contacts with nongregarious insects had proved to be difficult; that, on the other hand, he had not devoted himself to this with particular diligence in view of the scant profit one could hope for even in the best of cases; that furthermore he believed they were not gregarious precisely because of their inability to communicate. Nevertheless, on the subject of harmful insects, he had already prepared a draft agreement, approved by the Food and Agriculture Organization, and he planned to discuss it with a delegation of locusts immediately after the season of metamorphosis, thanks to the mediation of a friend of his, the NATCA representative for UAR and Lebanon.

The sun had set by now, and we went into the living room. My wife and I were filled with admiration and dismay. We couldn't tell Simpson what we thought; then my wife made up her mind, and with great difficulty she said that he had gotten his hands on . . . on 'something' new and big, pregnant with scientific and even poetic possibilities. Simpson stopped her. 'My dear lady, I never forget that I'm a businessman: actually, I haven't yet told you about the biggest deal. I must beg you not to speak about it in public yet, but I want you to know that this work of mine is of the greatest interest to the NATCA top brass, especially to the Fort Kiddiwanee think tank. I've informed them, after of course having clarified the patent situation, and it would seem that an interesting arrangement is in the offing. Now look what I have in here.'

He handed me a tiny cardboard box, no bigger than a thimble. I opened it.

'There's nothing in here!'

'Almost nothing,' Simpson retorted.

He gave me a magnifying glass: against the white background of the box I saw a filament, thinner than a hair, perhaps a centimeter long; around the middle one could distinguish a slight thickening.

'It's a resistor,' Simpson said. 'The thread is two thousandths of a micron thick, the connection is five thousandths micron, and the whole thing costs four thousand lire; but soon it will cost only two hundred. The specimen is the first that was assembled by my ants, by the pine-tree workers, the strongest and most skillful. In one summer I taught a team of ten, and they have trained all the others. You should see them, it is a unique spectacle: two of them seize the two electrodes with their mandibles, another gives them three twists and fastens them with a tiny drop of resin, then all three of them place the piece on the conveyor.

It takes three of them forty seconds to assemble a resistor, including dead time, and they work twenty hours out of twenty-four. This has given rise to a union problem, inevitably, but these things can always be settled; they are satisfied, no doubt about it. They receive payment in kind, divided into two lots: one so to speak personal, which the ants consume during their work breaks, and the other collective, meant for the ant heap's stockpiles, which they store in their abdominal pockets; all told, fifteen grams per day for the entire working squad, which is made up of five hundred workers. It is three times as much as what they were able to scrape together during a day's foraging in the wood. But this is just the beginning: I'm training other squads for other 'impossible' jobs. One squad to trace the diffraction reticule of a spectrometer. One thousand lines within eight millimeters; another squad to repair miniaturized printed circuits, which until now were thrown away when broken; another yet to retouch photographic negatives; four teams to perform auxiliary work during brain surgery, and I can tell you already at this point that they have proven to be irreplaceable in stopping hemorrhages of the capillaries. You only have to think about it for a moment, and immediately dozens of jobs come to mind that require a minimum output of energy but cannot be performed economically because our fingers are too thick and slow, because a micromanipulator is too costly, or because they entail too many operations over too vast an area. I have already made contact with an agricultural station for extremely exciting experiments: I would like to train an anthill to distribute fertilizers by 'home delivery.' I mean, one grain per seed; train another anthill to reclaim rice paddies by removing infesting weeds before they germinate; another to clean the silos; another yet, to perform cellular micrographs. . . . Life is short, believe me: I curse myself for having started so late. There is so little one can do on one's own!'

'Why don't you get a partner?'

'You think I haven't tried? I almost ended up in jail. I've been convinced that . . . what does that proverb of yours say? Better alone.'

'In jail?'

'Yes, because of O'Toole. Only six months ago. Young, optimistic, intelligent, indefatigable, and also full of imagination, a mine of ideas. But one day I found a peculiar small object on his desk, a small hollow plastic ball, no larger than a grape with some powder inside. I was holding it in my hand, you understand, when there was a knock at the door. It was Interpol, eight agents. I had to hire a battery of lawyers to get out of it, to convince them that I was in the dark about everything.'

'In the dark about what?'

'About the business with the eels. You know of course that they're not insects, but they too migrate in shoals, thousands and thousands every year. That wretch had made a deal with them: as if I weren't paying him enough. He had corrupted them with a couple of dead flies, and they would come to shore one by one before starting on their journey to the Sargasso sea; two grams of heroin each, in those little balls tied to their backs. Down there of course there was Rick Papaleos' yacht waiting for them. Now, as I was saying, all suspicions against me have been disproven; but the whole thing has come out into the open, and the tax collectors are hounding me. They imagine that I'm making enormous sums of money; they're investigating. The same old story, right? You invent fire and make a gift of it to mankind, then a vulture gnaws at your liver for eternity.'

The Sixth Day

Characters

ARIMANE
ORMUZ
SECRETARY
ANATOMY ADVISER
COMPTROLLER
MINISTER OF WATERWAYS
PSYCHOLOGICAL ADVISER
THERMODYNAMICS ADVISER
MESSENGER
CHEMICAL ADVISER
MECHANICAL ADVISER

The scene, as open and deep as possible. A very massive, crude table, chairs carved from blocks of stone. An enormous clock with a very slow and noisy beat, whose face instead of hours displays hieroglyphs, algebraic symbols, signs of the zodiac. A door at the back.

ARIMANE (*holds in his hand, open, a letter with many seals; he seems to be continuing an already started speech*). Most venerable gentlemen, we must therefore conclude, I should say crown, our by now long work. As I've had the honor of explaining to you, though with a few minor reservations, and with the intention of making some inessential changes in our operation, the management is basically satisfied both with the organization established by us and its present functioning. The elegant and practical solution of the problem of oxygen regeneration has been particularly praised (*he nods toward the thermodynamics adviser, who bows in thanks*); the successful procedure submitted and realized by the adviser for chemistry (*nod and bow as above*) for the closure of the nitrogen cycle; and in another, no less important field, the perfecting of the wing-flapping-frequency movement for which I'm glad to convey to the adviser on mechanics (*nod and bow as above*) the high praise of management, together with the request to pass it on to the bird foreman and the insect foreman who have assisted him. Lastly, I must praise the diligence and skill of the workers, thanks to whom, even though our production experience cannot be considered lengthy, the waste, the specimens that did not pass the test, and production discards can be considered reduced to more than satisfactory margins. In today's communication, management (*holds up the letter*) reiterates, in a more explicit form, its recommendations that the planning work relative to the Man model be speedily completed. In order to better follow the superior instructions from above it will therefore be advisable to enter resolutely into the project's details.

ORMUZ (*a sad and unassuming character. All through Arimane's speech he has given signs of restlessness and disapproval; several times he has been about to speak up, then, as though he did not dare, he has sat down again. He speaks in a timid voice, with hesitations and pauses, as though he were at a loss for words*). I would like to beg my most venerable colleague and brother to give a public reading of the motion that some time ago was approved by the executive board, relative to the problem Man. Quite some time has passed since then, and I feel that some of the interested parties no longer recall it.

ARIMANE (*visibly annoyed: he looks at his wristwatch ostentatiously, then at the big clock*). Colleague secretary, I would beg you to seek out the motion Man among the papers. The final draft. I don't exactly remember the date, but you should be able to find it approximately during the period of the first test reports concerning placentiferous beings. Please hurry: the fourth glacial age is about to begin, and I would not want us to postpone everything once again.

SECRETARY (*in the meantime has looked for and found the motion in a voluminous dossier; he reads in an official tone*). 'The executive board of directors, convinced that (*incomprehensible muttering*) . . .; considering . . . (*as above*) . . .; with the purpose of . . . (*as above*); in conformity with the superior interest of . . . (*as above*); considers appropriate the planning and creation of an animal species distinct from those until now realized and characterized by the following requisites:

(a) a particular aptitude for the creation and utilization of tools;

(b) capability to express themselves articulately, for instance by means of signs, sounds, or any other means that the competent technical gentlemen will consider apt to the purpose;

(c) fitness for life under conditions of extreme labor;

(d) a certain degree of preference for social life, whose optimum value is to be determined experimentally.

The board of directors *urges* the technicians and all the officers concerned to evince the greatest interest in the above-mentioned problem, which is a matter of the utmost urgency, and looks forward to a rapid and brilliant solution thereof.'

ORMUZ (*jumps to his feet and speaks with the precipitousness typical of the timid*). I never disguised my opposition in principle to the creation of so-called Man. Already at the time when the board of directors quite irresponsibly (*murmurs: Ormuz takes a deep breath, hesitates, then continues*) formulated the first draft of the motion that was just read, I had indicated the dangers connected with the insertion of so called Man into the present planetary balance. Naturally, being aware of the importance that for all too obvious reasons management attaches to the problem in question, and the proverbial obstinacy (*murmurs, comments*) of management itself, I realized that it is by now too late to obtain the motion's withdrawal. I shall therefore confine myself to suggesting, one at a time and in a purely consultative manner, the modifications and attenuations to the board's ambitious program which in my opinion allow for its implementation without excessive long or shorter shocks.

ARIMANE. All right, all right, my venerable colleague. Your reservations are known, your personal skepticism and pessimism are known, and finally, known is your interesting report on the questionable outcome of similar experiments performed by yourself in various epochs and on other planets, at a time when all of us had greater freedom. Let it be said among us – those attempts of yours to produce Superbeasts, all brain and balance, filled *ab ovum* with geometry, music and wisdom, would make a cat laugh. They smacked of antiseptic and inorganic chemistry. For anyone with a certain experience of the things of this world, or for that matter of any other world, their incompatibility with the environment surrounding them would have been easily intuited, an environment that is of necessity both florid and putrid, pullulating, confused, changeable.

I will take the liberty of repeating to you that precisely because of these failures, management now insists and urges that at last this old problem be confronted squarely, with seriousness and competence (*repeats meaningfully*), I said both seriousness and competence, so that the awaited guest may make his appearance, (*lyrically*) the dominator, the knower of good and evil; in short, the one whom the executive board of directors has elegantly defined as the being built in the image and semblance of his creator. (*Dignified and official applause.*) And so to work, gentlemen; and once again allow me to remind you that time is of the essence.

ANATOMY ADVISER. I ask for the floor.

ARIMANE. The anatomy adviser has the floor.

ANATOMY ADVISER. I shall say in brief what my specific competence suggests to me as to how the problem should be approached. In the first place, it would be illogical to start from zero, neglecting all the good work that has until now been done on earth. We already possess an approximately balanced animal and vegetable world; I would therefore recommend to our planning colleagues to abstain from too reckless deviations from and too audacious innovations to the already realized models. The field is in itself already too vast. If I were allowed any indiscretions that verge on the limits of professional reserve, I would speak to you at length about the many projects that are accumulating on my desk (not to mention those fit for the wastepaper basket). Please take note, this is often very interesting and at any rate original material: organisms designed for temperatures varying between minus two hundred seventy and plus three hundred degrees Celsius, studies on colloidal systems in liquid carbonic anhydride, metabolisms without nitrogen and without carbon, and so on. One fine fellow even proposed to me a line of exclusively metallic living models; another proposed a most ingenious, almost completely self-contained vesicular organism, lighter than air because filled with hydrogen, which it draws from water by means of a theoretically irreproachable enzymatic system, and meant to navigate with the wind over the entire terrestrial surface, without a noticeable expenditure of energy.

I mention these curiosities essentially in order to give you an idea of the, shall I say, negative aspect of my mandate. We have here, in several instances, potentially fruitful themes: but it would in my opinion be a mistake to allow oneself to be distracted by their indisputable appeal. It seems to me, if only for the sake of time and simplicity, that undoubtedly in the project under examination the point of departure must be sought in one of the fields in which our experience has been tested best and at the greatest length. This time we cannot afford attempts, second efforts, rectifications: let us be warned by the disastrous failure of the great saurians, which in fact held such great promise on paper and, at bottom, were not far removed from traditional patterns. Discarding for obvious reasons the vegetal realm, I bring to the planners' attention the mammals and Arthropoda (*a long, muttering buzz, comments*); nor will I conceal from you that my personal preference inclines to the latter.

COMPTROLLER. As it is both my habit and duty, I must intervene even though not asked. My dear anatomy colleague, tell me: what, in your opinion, should the dimensions of Man be?

ANATOMY ADVISER (*taken by surprise*). Well . . . actually . . . (*He makes calculations under his breath, scribbling figures and sketches on a sheet of paper in front of him.*) Let's see . . . let's see . . . there, approximately sixty centimeters to fifteen or twenty linear meters. In accordance with the unit price and locomotion requirements, I should opt for the larger dimensions: it seems to me they guarantee a more probable success in the inevitable competition with other species.

COMPTROLLER. In view of your preference for Arthropoda, are you therefore envisaging a Man approximately twenty meters long and with an external skeleton?

ANATOMY ADVISER. Certainly: I will take the liberty of reminding you, in all modesty, of the elegance of this innovation of mine. With the external-carrying skeleton we satisfy by means of a single structure all the requirements of support, locomotion, and defense; the difficulties of growth, as is well known, can be easily circumvented by the molting artifice, recently perfected by me. The introduction of chitin as a building material . . .

COMPTROLLER (*frostily*) . . . . Are you aware of the cost of chitin?

ANATOMY ADVISER. No, but in any case . . .

COMPTROLLER. That's enough. I have sufficient elements to decisively oppose your proposal for a twenty-meter-long arthropod Man. And, come to think of it, not even five, not even one meter will do. If you must make him arthropod that's your business; but if he's going to be bigger than a stag beetle, I won't be responsible for anything, and you'll have to see about the budget.

ARIMANE. My dear anatomy colleague, the comptroller's opinion (besides being in my view perfectly justified) unfortunately cannot be appealed. It furthermore appears to me that, besides the mammal you mentioned just before, the order of the vertebrates still offers interesting possibilities among reptiles, birds, and fishes . . .

MINISTER OF WATERWAYS (*a perky little old man, with a blue beard and a small trident in his hand*). There, there, that's the right word. It is inconceivable to my mind that in this room no mention had yet been made of an aquatic solution. But of course, it is a desperately dry room: stone, cement, wood, not a puddle, what am I saying? not even a faucet. Enough to make you feel you're coagulating!

And yet everyone knows that water covers three quarters of the terrestrial surface; and besides, emerged earth is a surface, it has but two dimensions, two coordinates, four cardinal points; whereas the ocean, gentlemen, the ocean . . .

ARIMANE. I would have no basic objections in principle to an entirely or partly aquatic Man; but subparagraph (a) of the motion Man speaks of tools, and I ask myself from what material a floating or subaqueous Man could forge them for himself.

MINISTER OF WATERWAYS. I don't see the difficulty. An aquatic Man, especially if he has coastal habits, would have at his disposal the shells of mollusks, bones and teeth of all kinds, various minerals, many of them easily worked, algae with strong fibers; indeed, in this regard, a simple word of mine to my friend in charge of vegetals, would suffice, and in the course of a few thousand generations we would be able to abundantly avail ourselves of any similar material, for example to wood, hemp or cord, whose properties we might propose to him; of course within the limits of good sense and existing technology.

PSYCHOLOGICAL ADVISER (*decked out like a Martian, with helmet, enormous spectacles, antennae, filaments, etc.*). Gentlemen, we have in fact gone astray. I have this very moment, and with the greatest unconcern, heard talk about a coastal Man without anyone standing up to call attention to the extreme precariousness of life to which creatures living between earth and water are subject, exposed as they are to the dangers of both elements. Just think of the troubles of seals! But there is much more: it seems clear to me, from at least three or four subsections of the motion, that Man is implicitly understood to be reasonable.

MINISTER OF WATERWAYS. Obviously! And what of it? Are you perhaps trying to insinuate that one can't reason while under water? In that case, what am I here for, since I spend almost all my working hours under water?

PSYCHOLOGICAL ADVISER. I beg you, my venerable colleague, calm down and let me talk. There's nothing easier than to prepare a nice roll of drawings, in plain view and cross section, with all the structural details, of a lovely large beast or a tiny beastie with wings or without, with nails or horns, with two eyes or eight eyes, or one hundred and eight eyes, or even one thousand feet, like that time you made me sweat blood to repair the nervous system of the millipede.

Then you make a tiny empty circle inside the head with next to it, written with stencils: 'Cranial cavity for installation of encephalon,' and the chief psychologist must make do. And up until now I have made do, no one can deny that, but – and listen carefully – haven't you realized that if anyone should have a say on the subject of aquatic or terrestrial or flying man, that's me? Tools, articulated language, and social life all at one blow and right away, and (I bet) probably someone will still find something to criticize because the sense of direction isn't all that it might be, or someone else (*he stares at the comptroller meaningfully*) will protest because per pound he costs more than a mole or cayman! (*Murmurs of approval, a few dissents. The psychological adviser takes off his Martian helmet to scratch his head and wipe off his sweat, then he puts it back on and continues.*) In short, listen carefully, and if someone will go to the trouble of reporting this to the higher-ups, all the better. You have one of three choices: either from now on I'll be taken seriously and will no longer be presented with already completed and signed projects; or I will be given a reasonable period of time to straighten out the mess; or I hand in my resignation and in that case, instead of having the small empty circle my anatomy colleague will be free to put into the head of his most ingenious creation a pack of connective tissue or an emergency stomach or, best of all, a nice big dumpling of reserve fat. And that's it.

(*Silence full of compunction and guilt from which at last arises Arimane's persuasive voice.*)

ARIMANE. My venerable psychological colleague, I can give you formal assurance that no one in this assemblage ever thought even for an instant of underestimating the difficulties and responsibilities of your work; what's more, you have taught us that compromise solutions are the rule rather than the exception, and it is our common task to try to resolve each problem in the spirit of the utmost possible cooperation. In fact, in the case under discussion, the preeminent importance of your opinion is clear to all, and your specific competence is well known. So the floor is yours.

PSYCHOLOGICAL ADVISER (*instantly mollified, takes a deep breath*). Gentlemen, it is my opinion, which for the rest can be amply documented, that in order to put together a Man answering to the prescribed characteristics, and at the same time vital, enonomical and reasonably durable, we should go back to the beginning and set up this animal along definitely new lines.

ARIMANE (*interrupts*). No, no, not all . . .

PSYCHOLOGICAL ADVISER. Very well then, venerable colleagues, the objection of urgency was foreseen and discounted. May I, however, be permitted to regret that once again extrinsic motives come to trouble what could have been (and this is rare!) an interesting little job; for the rest, this seems to be the fate of us technicians.

So then, to return to the basic question, I have no doubt, Man must be terrestrial and not aquatic. I will briefly outline the reasons for this. It seems clear to me that this Man will possess rather well developed mental faculties, and this, given the present state of our knowledge, cannot be realized without a corresponding development of the sensory organs. Now, for a submerged or floating animal, the development of the senses encounters serious difficulties. In the first place, taste and the olfactory sense will evidently be combined for use in a single sense; which would still be the lesser evil. But think of the conditions of homogeneity, I might say monotony, of the aqueous environment: I do not wish to mortgage the future, but the best eyes fabricated up until now cannot explore more than about ten meters of limpid water, and a few centimeters of turbid water; therefore we shall either give Man rudimentary eyes or they will become so due to nonuse in a few thousand centuries. The same, more or less, can be said of the ears . . .

MINISTER OF WATERWAYS (*interrupts*). Water carries sounds exceptionally well, my dear sir! and twenty-seven times faster than the air!

MANY VOICES. Calm down, stop exaggerating!

PSYCHOLOGICAL ADVISER (*continuing*) . . . can be said of the ears: it is indeed very easy to construct a subaqueous ear, but it is equally difficult to generate sounds in the water. I confess that I wouldn't know how to explain the physical reason, which in any case is not my job; but let the minister of waters and my venerable anatomy colleague explain the singular circumstance of the fish's proverbial mutism. This may perhaps be a sign of wisdom, but it seems to me that, during my inspection trips, I have been compelled to travel to the remotest corner of the sea of the Antilles to find a fish that emits sounds; and these were neither very articulated nor at all pleasant sounds which as far as I've been able to determine the above-mentioned fish, whose name escapes me . . .

VOICES. The cow fish! the cow fish!

PSYCHOLOGICAL ADVISER. . . . emits in a completely haphazard manner, at the moment when he empties his swim bladder. And, a curious detail, before emitting these sounds he emerges. In conclusion, I ask myself and I ask you what the perfected ear of the Man-fish is supposed to hear, if not thunder when he approaches the surface, the crash of the surf when he approaches the shore, and the occasional bellows of his colleagues of the Antilles. The decision is up to you: but I must remind you that, given our present construction possibilities, this creature would be half blind and if not deaf, mute; and whether this represents an advantage for . . . (*seizes the motion about Man lying on the table and reads aloud*) '. . . ability to express himself articulately, etc., etc.,' and further on: '. . . prosperity to social life . . .,' I let each of you be the judge.

ARIMANE. I will now bring an end to this first fruitful exchange of views, summing them up as follows: Man will therefore be neither arthropode nor fish; it remains to decide whether he will be a Man mammal, Man reptile or Man bird. If I may be permitted on this occasion to express an opinion of mine dictated, more than by reason, by emotion and sympathy, I would like to recommend the reptiles to your attention.

I will not conceal from you that among the many shapes

and figures created by your art and your ingenuity, none has aroused my admiration more than that of the serpent.

It is strong and astute: 'It is the most astute among terrestrial creatures,' as was said by a much loftier Judge (*all rise to their feet and bow*). Its structure is of exceptional simplicity and elegance, and it would be a pity not to subject it to further improvements. It is a skillful and sure poisoner; it should not be difficult for it to become, in keeping with your hopes, the master of the earth, even perhaps by creating a void all around itself.

ANATOMY ADVISER. That is all true: and I might add that serpents are extraordinarily economical, that they lend themselves to numerous and highly interesting modifications, that for example it would not be difficult to enlarge their skull by a good forty percent, and so on. But I must remind you that not one of the reptiles constructed up until now would be able to survive in a cold climate; thus subsection C of the motion would not be fulfilled. I would be grateful to my thermo-dynamics colleague if he were to confirm this assertion of mine with some numerical data.

THERMODYNAMICS ADVISER (*sharp and dry*). Median average annual temperature above ten degrees Celsius; never temperatures under fifteen degrees below zero. That's it in a nutshell.

ARIMANE (*laughs, green in the face*). I must confess that the circumstance, though obvious, had escaped me; nor shall I conceal from you a certain disappointment, for during recent times I've often thought of the suggestive appearance the earth's surface would present if furrowed in every direction by powerful, varicolored pythons, and of their cities, which I liked to imagine excavated among the roots of gigantic trees and provided with vast rooms for rest and meditation for the individual pythons returning from an abundant meal. But since I'm being assured that all this cannot be, let us abandon the thought of it, and since our choice is now restricted to one between mammals and birds, we shall devote all our energy to a speedy solution. I see that our venerable psychological colleague is asking for the floor: and since no one would deny that on him weighs a good part of the responsibility for the project, I beg all of you to listen to him attentively.

PSYCHOLOGICAL ADVISER (*erupts into speech before the other has finished*). As far as I'm concerned, as I've already indicated, the solution should be sought elsewhere. Ever since I published my famous cycle of research on termites and ants . . . (*interruptions from all sides*) . . . I have had in my drawer a little project . . . (*the interruptions increase in violence*) . . . several most original automatisms that ensure an incredible saving of nervous tissue . . .

(*Pandemonium erupts, which Arimane has trouble subduing*).

ARIMANE. I told you once already that these innovations of yours do not interest us. We absolutely lack the time to study, launch, develop and test a new animal model, and you ought to be the first to teach us that: and precisely with regard to the Hymenoptera so dear to you, tell me, isn't it true, that between their prototype and their stabilization in today's morphology there passed a number of years that can be expressed in eight or ten figures? I therefore call you to order, and let this be the last time; otherwise we might find ourselves compelled to renounce your precious assistance, considering that before you were hired your colleagues without too much ado for example perfected the splendid Coelenterata, which function perfectly well to this day, never break down, reproduce in great quantities without fuss and cost a pittance. Those were the days, let that be said without offense to anyone! Many working and few criticizing, many deeds and few words, and everything that left the factory worked fine without the complications thought up by you modernists. Now, before a work project is approved, we need the signature of the psychologist and the neurologist and the histologist and the test certificate and the OK of the esthetic committee in three copies, and who knows what else. And I'm told that's not enough, and that we'll soon be actually hiring a superintendent in charge of spiritual matters, who will put us all at attention . . . (*He realizes that he has gone too far, abruptly falls silent and looks around with a certain embarrassment. Then he again addresses the psychological adviser.*) Anyway, think about it, and then explain to us clearly whether in your opinion we ought to study a bird Man or a mammal Man, and the reasons on which your opinion is founded.

PSYCHOLOGICAL ADVISER (*gulps several times, sucks on his pencil, etc.; then speaks*). If the choice comes down to these two possibilities, it is my opinion that Man must be a bird. (*Uproar, comments. All exchange signs of satisfaction, nod approval; two or three are about to get up, as though everything were over.*) Just a moment, damn it! I didn't mean to say that it is enough to fish out of the files the Sparrow project or the Barn Owl project, change the registration number and three or four paragraphs, and send it on to the Test Center for the realization of the prototype!

Now please listen to me carefully; I will try to present to you briefly (because I see you're in a hurry) the main considerations on the subject. Everything is fine as regards points b and d of the motion. There already exists today such an assortment of songbirds that the problem of articulated language, at least from its anatomical aspect, can be considered solved; whereas nothing of the kind has until now been done among the mammals. Am I correct, my anatomy colleague?

ANATOMY ADVISER. Absolutely, absolutely.

PSYCHOLOGICAL ADVISER. Of course, there remains to be studied a brain suited to create and use language, but this problem, which concerns me exclusively, would remain more or less the same no matter what form it is decided to assign to Man. As for point c, 'fitness to live under extreme working conditions,' it does not seem to me that from this one can deduce a criterion of choice between mammals and birds: in both classes there exist genera that have easily adapted to the most disparate climates and environments. It is, however, evident that the faculty of moving rapidly in flight constitutes an important element in favor of the bird Man, inasmuch as it would allow for exchange of information and transportation of provisions from continent to continent, it would facilitate the immediate establishment of a single language and a single civilization for the entire human genus, it would nullify existing geographical obstacles, and render futile the creation of artificial territorial demarcations between one tribe and another. There is no need for me to insist on the other, more immediate advantages offered by rapid flight, as regards defense and offense against all earthbound and aquatic species, and as regards the prompt discovery of ever new territories suited for hunting, cultivation and exploitation: so that it seems legitimate to me to formulate the axiom: 'The animal that flies does not go hungry.'

ORMUZ. Forgive the interruption, my venerable colleague: how will your bird Man reproduce himself?

PSYCHOLOGICAL ADVISER (*surprised and irritated*). What a strange question! He will reproduce like other birds: the male will attract the female, or vice versa; the female will be fertilized, the nest will be built, the eggs laid and hatched, and the young will be raised and educated by both parents, until they have reached a minimum of independence. The fittest will survive. I see no reason to change.

ORMUZ (*at first uncertain, then increasingly excited and impassioned*). No, gentlemen, the matter does not seem that simple to me. Many of you know . . . and in any case I never made a secret of it with anyone . . . in short, sexual differentiation has always rubbed me the wrong way. It may have its advantages for the species; it may also have advantages for the individual (although, according to what I'm told, these advantages have a very brief duration); but any objective observer must admit that sex has in the first place been a frightful complication and, secondly, a permanent source of dangers and troubles.

Nothing is so valuable as experience: since we're dealing with social life, keep in mind that the only example of social life successfully realized and lasting from the Tertiary to this day without the slightest inconvenience is and remains that of the Hymenoptera; in which, due to a great extent to my intercession, the sexual drama has been eluded and relegated to the extreme margins of the productive society.

Gentlemen, it is a heartfelt prayer I address to you: weigh your words before you utter them. Whether Man be bird or mammal, it is our duty to make every effort to smooth his path, because the burden he will have to carry will be heavy. Having created it, we know the brain, and we know of what portentous activities it is at least potentially capable, but we also know its measure and its limits; we also know, having had a hand in it, the energies that lie dormant and awaken in the play of the sexes. I do not deny that the experiment of combining these two mechanisms is interesting, but I confess my hesitation, I confess my fears.

What will become of this creature? Will it be twofold, will it be a centaur, a man to his innermost entrails and hence a wild beast; or will it be linked to a cycle of sexual heats, and in that case how will it maintain sufficiently uniform behavior? It will not follow (do not laugh!) the Good and the True, but two goods and two trues. And when two men will desire the same woman, or two women the same man, what will become of their social institutions and the laws that were designed to protect them?

And apropos of Man, what shall we say about those famous 'elegant and economical solutions,' which are the boast of the here-present anatomy adviser and enthusiastically subscribed to by the here-present comptroller, so that orifices and channels meant for excretion have been utilized for sexual purposes with the greatest nonchalance? This circumstance, which we know to be due to a pure calculation to reduce encumbrances and costs, cannot appear to this thinking animal as anything but a mocking symbol, an abject and disturbing confusion, the sacred-foul mark of a two-headed unreason, of chaos, fixed in his body like a jewel, unrenounceable, eternal.

Here is my conclusion, gentlemen: Let Man be made, if Man must be made; and let him be a bird if you so wish. But may I already, beginning with this moment, be allowed to attack the problem, expunge at the start all the conflicts that will inevitably explode tomorrow, so that in the foreseeable future we shall not be compelled to watch the execrable spectacle of a male Man who leads his people into a war in order to conquer a female, or a female Man who distracts a male's mind from noble enterprises and thoughts so as to subjugate him. Remember: the one who is about to be born will be our judge. Not only our errors but all his or her errors through centuries to come will fall on our heads.

ARIMANE. You may even be right, but I don't see the urgency of bandaging heads before they are broken. That is, I do not see the possibility nor the opportuneness of refrigerating Man in the planning stage – and doing this with the obvious intent of expediting the work. If at a later date your anguished predictions should take on substance, well, we shall see; we shall lack neither the occasion nor the time to correct the model with the modifications that will seem most advisable. However, since Man, it would appear, will be a bird, I don't see any reason for dramatizing matters. The difficulties and risks that worry you will be easily contained: the sexual interest can be reduced to extremely brief periods, perhaps to not more than a few minutes a year; no pregnancy, no suckling, a precise and powerful tendency to monogamy, a short hatching period, the young issuing from the egg ready or almost ready for autonomous life. We should be able to achieve this without overhauling the anatomical patterns presently in force, which, besides all else, would involve frightful obstacles of a bureaucratic and administrative nature.

No, gentlemen, the decision is made, and Man will be a bird: a bird in every respect, neither penguin nor ostrich, but a flying bird, with beak, feathers, claws, eggs and nest. There remain to be defined only a few important construction details, that is:

(1) What will be the optimal dimensions?

(2) Will it be preferable to envisage him as sedentary or migratory . . . (*At Arimane's last words, the door at the end of the room has been cautiously opened. The head and shoulder of the messenger have appeared, who, not daring to interrupt, gestures excitedly and glances about to attract the attention of those present. As a result, there is a growing murmur and bustle that Arimane finally notices.*) What is it? What's happening?

MESSENGER (*winks at Arimane with the air of officious familiarity typical of school custodians and beadles*). Come outside for a moment, your venerability. Important news from . . . (*he signals by nodding backward.*)

ARIMANE (*follows him out through the door; we hear a heated discussion through the buzz and comments of the others. Suddenly the slightly opened door is violently closed from the outside, and reopened shortly afterward. Arimane reenters, slowly, his head lowered. He is silent for a long time, then speaks*). . . . Let us go home now, gentlemen, it is all over and everything is solved. Home, let's go home. What are we staying here for?

They didn't wait for us: wasn't I right to be in a hurry? Once again they've decided to prove to us that we are not necessary, that they can manage by themselves, they do not need anatomists, nor psychologists, nor comptrollers. They can do whatever they want to do.

. . . No, gentlemen, I don't have many details. I don't know whether they've consulted with someone, or have followed a line of reasoning, or a long-meditated plan, or a moment's intuition. I know that they have taken seven measures of clay and have kneaded it with river and seawater; I know that they have molded the mud in the shape that appeared best to them. Apparently, what is involved is a vertical beast, almost without hairs, helpless, which to the messenger here present looked like something between a monkey and a bear: an animal without wings or feathers, and hence to be considered basically mammal. It furthermore appears the Man's female was created from one of his ribs . . . (*cries, questions*) . . . from one of his ribs, yes, by a process that is not clear to me, that I would not hesitate to call heterodox, and I don't know if they intend to preserve it for generations to come.

Into this creature they have infused I don't know what sort of breath, and it moved. And so Man is born, gentlemen, far from our assembly: quite simple, isn't it? Whether and to what extent he corresponds to the requirements that were imposed on us, or whether, on the other hand, it is Man purely by definition and convention, I do not have the elements to ascertain.

There is nothing left for us but to wish this anomalous creature a long and prosperous career. Our colleague secretary will be kind enough to undertake the drafting of the inaugural message, the ratification chart, registration in the rolls, cost estimates, etc.; everyone else is relieved of any and all commitments. Take heart, gentlemen; the meeting is adjourned.

Retirement Fund

I had gone to the Fair without having to and without any particular curiosity, impelled by that irrational sense of duty which all Milanese know, and without whose existence the Fair would not be the Fair, that is, it would be deserted most of the time, and comfortable and easy to visit.

I was very surprised to find Simpson at the NATCA booth. He welcomed me with a sunny smile. 'You didn't expect to see me, eh, behind this counter instead of the usual pretty girl or the rookie representative. In fact it's not my job, standing here to answer the foolish questions of casual visitors (ahem . . . present company excluded of course), and instead trying to guess who the incognito competitors are – which after all is not at all difficult, because their questions are less foolish. But I've come here of my own will, I couldn't say why myself. Actually, why not say so? There's nothing to be ashamed of: I've come here out of gratitude.'

'Gratitude to whom?'

'To NATCA, obviously. Yesterday was a great day for me.'

'Did you get a promotion?'

'What do you mean, a promotion? There's no way I could have gone any higher . . . no, no . . . : I'm retiring. Come, let's go to the bar: I'll buy you a whiskey.'

He told me that normally he should have retired two years later, but had asked for early retirement, and just the day before had received a telex informing him of the management's consent.

'It isn't that I no longer feel like working,' he told me. 'Just the opposite, as you know, but I have other interests now, and I feel the need to have the whole day to myself. They've understood this very well at Fort Kiddiwanee, and in any case, it's also in their interest, because of the assembly-ants, you know.'

'Congratulations: I didn't know that the deal had gone through.'

'Yes, yes, I've gotten an exclusive agreement with them: one pound of trained ants per month at three dollars per ant. So they decided not to be sticklers: complete severance pay, an eight-thousand-dollar bonus, a first-degree pension, and in addition a present that I really must show you. A present that is unique in the world, at least for now.'

Meanwhile we had returned to the booth and we sat down on the two armchairs in the back. 'It's nothing new for you,' Simpson continued. 'Also, apart from the business of social insects, by now I've become a bit fed up with the "new frontier" of those fine people. Last year, for instance, with the scarcity of executives that exists in America they threw on the market a whole series of measuring apparatuses that are supposed to replace aptitude tests and personnel interviews, and they insisted that I should sell them also in Italy. They're supposed to be set up like a cascade: the candidate enters, goes through a tunnel the same as in a car wash, and when he comes out on the other side of his chart there are already printed his qualifications, his score, his mental profile, his IQ. . . .'

'What's that you say?'

'Oh yes, I'm sorry: his intelligence quotient, the tasks to be set him and the salary to be offered. In the past I used to love these little games; now, however, I don't enjoy them in the least, and they even give me a vague feeling of uneasiness. And wait till you see this!'

Mr Simpson took out of the showcase a small black container that looked to me like a geodetic instrument.

'This is a VIP-SCAN; yes sir, that's what they call it. A probe for VIPs, Very Important Persons: this too should be used to select management personnel. It's supposed to be used (on the sly, of course) during the preliminary "cordial conversation." Excuse me for a moment: you don't mind, do you?'

He pointed the lens at me and held the shutter release down for a minute or so. 'Speak, please; it doesn't matter, say anything you want. Take a few steps back and forth. Enough, that's it. Let's see: twenty-eight hundredths. Don't take this badly, but you're not a VIP. You see, these are precisely the things that annoy me: twenty-eight to someone like you! But you mustn't be upset; in fact I wanted to show you that this little gismo is a judge not worth a cent, and besides it's adjusted to American standards. No, I don't know exactly how it works, and it doesn't interest me much either, I swear; I only know that the points are based on factors such as the cut and design of one's clothes, the size of one's cigar (and you don't smoke), the condition of one's teeth, the pace and rhythm of one's speech. Forgive me, perhaps I shouldn't have done it; but if this can serve as reassurance, look, I barely get as high as twenty-five, when I'm freshly shaved, otherwise I don't get more than twenty points. In sum, it's rubbish. Either they don't sell, and in that case things will look bad for Italian NATCA; or they do sell, and in that case it's enough to make you shudder thinking of a managerial class completely made up of perfect hundreds. Do you understand? – this is another good reason to quit.'

He lowered his voice and confidentially placed his hand on my knee: '. . . But if you come to see me one of these days, after the Fair, I will show you my first and principal reason. It's the present I mentioned: A Torec, a Total Recorder. With that in the house, a small assortment of tapes, a decent pension, and my bees, why should I continue to make myself sick over customers?'

Simpson apologized for receiving me at the office and not at home.

'Here perhaps we'll be a little less comfortable, but

quieter: there's nothing more annoying than a phone call during a fruition, and here nobody ever calls outside office hours. Besides, I must confess to you, this little device doesn't meet with my wife's approval and she doesn't even want to see it around her.'

He described the Torec to me quite skillfully and with that incapacity for amazement which is typical of him and which in my opinion springs from his long past as a salesman of marvels. The Torec, he explained, is a total recorder. It is not one of your usual office machines; it is a revolutionary mechanism. It is based on the Andrac, the device created and described by R. Vacca, and put to work by him on his own person – that is to say, on the basis of direct communication between nervous circuits and electronic circuits. With the Andrac, by submitting to a small surgical intervention, one can for instance activate a Telex or drive a car simply by means of nervous impulses, without the use of the muscles: in other words, it is enough to 'wish it.' The Torec, by contrast, exploits the corresponding receptive mechanism inasmuch as it arouses sensations in the brain without the mediation of the senses: unlike the Andrac, however, the Torec does not require any invasive intervention. The transmission of the sensations recorded on the tape takes place through cutaneous electrodes, without the need of any preliminary operation.

The listener, or more accurately the fruitioner, only has to put on a helmet, and all during the time the tape rolls he receives the entire orderly sequence of sensations that the tape itself contains: visual, aural, tactile, olfactory, gustatory, anesthetic and painful sensations, besides the so to speak inner sensations which all of us in the waking state receive from our memory. In short, all the afferent messages that the brain, or more precisely (to use Aristotle's words) the patient intellect, is capable of receiving. The transmission does not take place through the fruitioner's sensory organs, which remain cut off, but directly on the nervous level, by means of a code that NATCA keeps secret; the result is a total experience. The spectator integrally relives the sequence of events that the tape suggests to him, and feels he's participating in it or even that he is the chief actor: this sensation has nothing in common with hallucinations or with dreams, because, while the tape lasts, it is indistinguishable from reality. When the tape is finished, you keep a normal memory of it, but during each fruition, the natural memory is supplanted by the artificial memory recorded on the tape; therefore one does not remember prior fruitions, and neither wariness nor boredom sets in. Every fruition of a particular tape can be repeated an infinite number of times, and every time it is as vivid and rich in surprises as the first time.

'With the Torec,' Simpson concluded, 'you need nothing else. You understand: whatever sensation one might wish to obtain, one only has to pick a tape. Do you want to go on a cruise to the Antilles? Or climb Mount Cervino? Or circle the earth for an hour, in the absence of gravity? Or be Sergeant Able F. Cooper, and wipe out a band of Vietcong? Well, you lock yourself up in your room, slip on the helmet, relax and leave it to him, to the Torec.'

I remained silent for a few moments while Simpson watched me through his glasses with benevolent curiosity. 'You seem perplexed,' he said then.

'I would say,' I replied, 'that this Torec is a definitive instrument. A subversive instrument, I mean to say: no other NATCA machine, indeed, no machine that was ever invented contains so great a threat to our habits and our social order. It will discourage all initiative, indeed, all human activity: it will be the last great step, after mass entertainment and mass communications. For example, in our house since we bought a TV set my son spends hours in front of it without ever playing, dazzled like a rabbit by the headlights of a car. I'm not; I leave, but it costs me an effort. But who will have the willpower to escape a Torec spectacle? It seems to me much more dangerous than any drug: who would ever work again? Who would still take care of his family?'

'I didn't tell you that the Torec is for sale,' Simpson said. 'Indeed, I've told you that I've received it as a present, that it is a present unlike any other, and that they sent it to me on the occasion of my retirement. If we're splitting hairs, I should add that it isn't even a true gift; legally, the apparatus continues to belong to NATCA, and it has been entrusted to me for an indefinite period of time not only as a reward but also so I can study its long-term effects.'

'In any case,' I said, 'if they researched it and built it, it's because they plan to put it on the market.'

'The matter is simple. In everything they do, the people who own NATCA have only two purposes, which in fact come down to one: making money and acquiring prestige, which actually means making more money. Obviously they would like to have a standard production of Torec and sell millions of copies of them, but they are still reasonable enough to understand that Congress would not stay on the sidelines when faced by the unchecked spread of such an instrument. Therefore, during these last months, after realization of the prototype, they are first of all busy encasing it in an armor of patents, so that not even one nut remains uncovered; secondly, they are busy extorting from the legislature permission to distribute it in all rest homes, and to issue it free of charge to all invalids and incurable patients. Finally, and this is their most ambitious program, they would like the right to a Torec for the entire active population to mature by law alongside the right to a pension.'

'And so you would be, in some sense, the prototype of tomorrow's pensioner?'

'Yes, and I assure you that the experience does not displease me in the least. I received the Torec only two weeks ago, but it has already given me enchanting evenings: of course, you're right, will and common sense are needed so as not to be overwhelmed, not to devote whole days to it, and I would never put it in the hands of a youth, but at my age it is precious. Would you like to try it? I have given my word never to lend it or sell it, but you are a discreet person and I believe that I can make an exception for you. You know, they've also asked me to study its possibilities as a teaching aid, for example, for the study of geography and the natural sciences, and I would set great store by your opinion.'

'Make yourself comfortable,' he said to me. 'Perhaps it would be best to close the shutters. Yes, like this, with your back to the lamp will be fine. At this time I only possess about thirty tapes, but another seventy are going through customs in Genoa and I hope to receive them soon: that way I'll have the entire series of tapes in existence to date.'

'Who manufactures the tapes? How do you get them? How are they made?'

'There is talk of producing artificial tapes, but for the time being they are all made by recordings. The process is known only in its general outlines: over there at Fort Kiddiwanee at the Torec division they propose a cycle of recordings to any person who normally or occasionally has some experience that lends itself to commercial exploitation – to aviators, explorers, scuba divers, seducers or seductresses, and to other numerous categories of individuals that you yourself can imagine if you think about for a moment. Let us say the subject accepts, and an agreement is reached concerning rights: as for this, I heard that rather large sums are involved, between two and five thousand dollars a tape, but that often in order to obtain a usable tape the recording must be repeated ten or twenty times. So: if an agreement is reached, they slip over his head a helmet more or less like this one, and all he has to do is wear it the whole time the recording is being made; and that's it. All his sensations are transmitted via radio to the recording switchboard, and then from the first tape as many copies as they wish are printed with the usual techniques.'

'But then . . . if the subject *knows* that every one of his sensations is recorded, in that case also this awareness of his must be recorded on the tape. You will not relive the lift-off of just any astronaut but that of an astronaut who knows he has a Torec helmet on his head and is the object of a recording.'

'Precisely,' Simpson said. 'In fact, in the majority of tapes that I have enjoyed this background awareness can be distinctly perceived, but with training some of the subjects learn how to repress it during the recording, and to relegate it to the subconscious, where the Torec does not reach. In any case, it's not too much of a bother. As for the helmet, it's no trouble at all: the sensation "helmet-on-head" which is recorded on all of our tapes coincides with the sensation provoked directly by the reception helmet.'

I was about to present him with a number of other difficulties of a philosophical nature that I had thought of, but Simpson interrupted me. 'Would you like to begin with this? It's one of my favorites. You know, soccer isn't very popular in the United States, but ever since I've been living in Italy I've become a devoted fan of the Milan team; actually I'm the one who put through the deal between Rasmussen and NATCA, and I myself directed the recording. He made three million lire and NATCA made a terrific tape. What a center forward, unbelievable, awesome! There, sit down, put on the helmet, and then tell me what you think.'

'But I don't understand the first thing about soccer. Not only did I never play it, not even as a kid, but I never even saw a game, not even on television!'

'It doesn't matter,' Simpson said, still vibrant with enthusiasm, and he turned on the current.

The sun was low and hot, the air dusty: I perceived an intense odor of churned-up dirt. I was sweating and one of my ankles hurt me a bit: I ran with extremely light strides after the soccer ball, I looked to my left out the corner of my eye and felt agile and ready like a coiled-up spring. Another black and red player entered my field of vision; I passed the ball to him, skimming it along the ground, surprising an opponent, then flung myself forward as the goalie was coming out to the right. I heard the burgeoning roar of the spectators, I saw the ball pushed back over to me and slightly ahead to take advantage of my forward movement: I was on top of it in a flash and my left foot kicked it into the goal with precision, effortlessly, neatly, right past the outstretched hands of the goalie. I felt a wave of delight surge in my blood, and shortly after the bitter taste of the adrenaline discharge in my mouth; then everything ended and I was sitting in the armchair.

'Did you see? It's very brief, but it is a little gem. Were you aware of the recording? No, isn't that so? When you're near the goal, you've got other things on your mind.'

'Exactly. I must admit it, it's a strange sensation, it's exalting to feel one's body so young and docile: a sensation lost for decades. Yes, scoring is beautiful too: one thinks of nothing else, one is as if concentrated on a single point, like a projectile. And the roar of the crowd! Yet, I don't know if you noticed, in that instant in which I expected . . . in which *he* expected the pass, an extraneous thought comes through: a tall, dark-haired girl, whose name is Claudia and with whom he has an appointment at nine in Saint Babila. It lasts barely a second, but it is very clear: time, place, precedents, everything. Did you experience it?'

'Yes, certainly, but these things are unimportant; actually they heighten the sense of reality. Obviously one cannot turn oneself into a tabula rasa, and show up for the recording as though one had been born an instant before: I've heard that many refuse to sign a contract precisely for reasons of this kind, because they have some memory they want to keep secret. So, what do you think about it? Would you like to try again?'

I asked Simpson to let me see the titles of the other tapes he had. They were very concise and scarcely suggestive; some were even incomprehensible, perhaps because of the translation.

'I think you'd better advise me,' I said. 'I wouldn't know how to choose.'

'You're right. You can't trust the titles, just as with books and films. And keep in mind that, as I told you, for the time being there are only about one hundred available tapes: but not long ago I saw the draft of the most recent catalogue and it's stuff to make your head spin. But let me show it to you: it seems to me instructive from the point of view of the "American way of life," and more in general as an attempt at a systematization of thinkable experiences.'

The catalogue contained more than nine hundred titles, each of which was followed by a Dewey decimal classification number, and was divided into seven sections. The first was headed 'Art and Nature'; the corresponding tapes were marked by a white band and had titles such as 'Sunset in Venice,' 'Paestum and Metaponte Seen by Quasimodo,' 'The Hurricane Magdalen,' 'A Day with the Cod Fishermen,' 'The Polar Route,' 'Chicago as Seen by Allen Ginsburg,' 'We Scuba Divers,' 'Meditations on the Sphinx by Emily S. Stoddard.' Simpson pointed out to me that these were not ordinary sensations, like those of a crude, uneducated man visiting Venice or casually witnessing a spectacle of nature; each subject had been recorded by hiring good writers and poets who had agreed to put their culture and sensibility at thc fruitioners' disposal.

The second section was composed of tapes with a red band and the heading 'Power.' This section was further subdivided into the subsections 'Violence,' 'War,' 'Authority,' 'Wealth,' 'Miscellaneous.'

'This is an arbitrary categorization,' Simpson said. 'I, for example, would certainly have put a white instead of a red band on the tape you just had on, 'A Goal by Rasmussen.' In general, I'm not very interested in the red tapes; but I've been told that in America a black market in these tapes is already being born: they slip out of NATCA's studios in a mysterious way and are bought up by youths who own clandestine Torecs put together any old way by unscrupulous radio technicians. Well, the red tapes are in the greatest demand. Perhaps it's not a bad thing: a young man who buys a brawl in a bar is not likely to take part in one for fear of getting his skull cracked.'

'Why? If he acquires a taste for it . . . Don't you think it might be the same as for the leopards, who once they've tasted man's blood can no longer go without it?'

Simpson looked at me with a curious expression. 'Of course, you're an Italian intellectual: I know you people quite well. A good middle-class family, plenty of money, a devout and possessive mother, a parish school, no military service, no competitive sports, except for a bit of tennis. One or more women courted without passion, one married, a lifelong quiet job. That's how it is, isn't that so?'

'Well, not exactly, at least where I'm concerned . . .'

'Of course, I may have been wrong about some of the details, but that's the substance, don't deny it. The struggle for life is avoided, you've never had a fistfight and you're left with a yearning for it into old age. At bottom, that's why you accepted Mussolini: you wanted a tough guy, a fighter, and he, who wasn't a fighter but wasn't stupid either, played the part as long as he could. But let's not get off the subject: do you want to see what fun it is to have a fistfight? Here, put on the helmet, and then you can tell me.'

I was seated, the others around me were standing. There were three of them, they wore striped T-shirts and looked at me with a smirk. One of them, Bernie, spoke to me in a language which, when I thought about it later, I understood to be very slangy American, but at that time I understood it perfectly, and I spoke it too; actually I even remember a few expressions – he called me 'bright boy' and 'goddamn rat' and he mocked me for quite a while, with patience and cruelty. He derided me because I was a Wop, and more precisely a Dago; I didn't answer, and continued to drink with studied indifference. In truth I felt both anger and fear; I was conscious of the theatrical fiction but the insults had struck and stung me, and then the fiction reproduced a situation that wasn't new, even though I'd never been able to get used to it. I was nineteen years old, heavyset and muscular, and I really was a Wop, a son of Italian immigrants; I was deeply ashamed of it, and at the same time proud. My persecutors were authentic persecutors, neighbors of the same part of town and enemies since childhood: blond, Anglo-Saxon and Protestant. I detested them and yet I admired them a little. They had never dared to attack me openly: the contract with NATCA had offered them a splendid opportunity and impunity. I knew that they and I had all been hired for a recording, but this did not diminish our mutual hatred; indeed, the very fact of having accepted money to have a fight with them doubled my hostility and rage.

When, imitating my way of speaking, Bernie said, 'Wassa matta, Momma's boy!,' and threw me a clownish kiss with the tips of his fingers. I grabbed my beer mug and flung it into his face: I saw his blood spurt and was filled by a ferocious exhilaration. Immediately after that I knocked over the table, and holding it in front of me like a shield I started for the exit. I felt a fist hit me in the ribs: I dropped the table and lunged at Andrew. I hit him on the jaw: he flew back and crashed stunned into the bar, but meanwhile Bernie had come to, and he and Tom pushed me into a corner raining blows on my stomach and liver. I was gasping for breath and saw them only as blurred shadows; but when they said to me, 'Come on, bimbo, ask for mercy,' I took two steps forward, then I pretended to fall and instead threw myself headfirst at Tom like a charging bull. I floored him, tripped over his body and fell on top of him; while I was trying to get up I was hit by a furious uppercut to the chin that literally lifted me off the ground and seemed about to tear my head off my shoulders. I lost consciousness; I regained it together with the impression of an ice-cold shower splashing down on my head, then everything was over.

'That's enough, thank you,' I told Simpson, massaging my chin which, who knows why, still hurt me a little.

'You're right: I don't have the least desire to start over again, neither for real nor by proxy.'

'Neither do I,' Simpson said. 'I did it only once and that was enough. But I believe that for an authentic Wop it might offer some satisfaction, if only for the fact of fighting one against three. In my opinion, NATCA has recorded this tape precisely for them; you know very well, they never do anything without market research.'

'But I believe that they recorded it for those others, for the blond Anglo-Saxon Protestants, and for the racists of all races. Just think what a refined pleasure, to feel oneself suffer in the shoes of the one who wishes to inflict suffering! Well, let's forget it. What are those tapes with the green band? What does "Encounters" mean?'

Mr Simpson smiled. 'It's a euphemism if ever there was one. You know that in our country also, censorship is a serious business. These are supposed to be "encounters" with famous personalities, for customers who wish to have a brief conversation with the great of the earth. As a matter of fact, here are a few of them: look. "DeGaulle," "Francisco Franco Bahamonde," "Conrad Adenauer," "Mao Ze Dong," (yes, he too was there: these Chinese are hard to understand), "Fidel Castro." But they only function as a cover: for the most part they are about something completely different, they are porn tapes. There is an encounter, but in a different sense: you see, these are different names that rarely make the first pages in the newspapers . . . Sina Rasinko, Ingebaum, Corrada Colli . . .'

At this point I began to blush. This is an annoying defect that I've had since adolescence: I only have to think 'I'm sure you'll blush now' (and no one can stop from thinking this) and sure enough the mechanism trips: I feel myself getting red, I'm ashamed of getting red, and so I get even redder, until I begin to stream with sweat, my throat goes dry, and I can no longer speak. This time, the almost casual stimulus had originated with the name Corrada Colli, the model made famous by the well-known scandal, for whom, I had suddenly realized,

I felt a salacious attraction, never confessed to anyone, not even to myself.

Simpson was watching me, hesitating between laughter and alarm: in fact, my congested condition was so evident that he could not have decently pretended not to notice it. 'Don't you feel well?' he finally asked. 'Would you like a breath of fresh air?'

'No, no,' I said gasping, while my blood tumultuously flowed back to its deeper source. 'It's nothing, it happens to me often.'

'Are you telling me,' Simpson foolishly said, 'that the name of the Colli woman has put you in such a state?' He lowered his voice: '. . . Or perhaps you too are part of that bunch?'

'Of course not, what are you talking about!' I protested while the phenomenon was repeated with double intensity, blatantly giving me the lie.

Simpson, perplexed, kept silent; he pretended that he was looking out the window, but every so often he shot me a quick glance. Then he made up his mind. 'Listen, this is man to man, and we've known each other for twenty years. You are here to try out the Torec, right? Well, I've got that tape: don't stand on ceremony, if you want to have this pleasure you only have to tell me: it will stay between us, obviously; besides, look, the tape is still in its original case, sealed, and I don't even know exactly what it contains. It might be the most innocent thing in the world; but in any case there's nothing to be ashamed of. I think that no theologian would find anything wrong with it – after all, you're not the one who's sinning. Come on, put on the helmet.'

I was in a theater dressing room, sitting on a stool, with my back to the mirror and the dressing table, and I experienced a vivid impression of lightness: I immediately realized that this was due to my very scant attire. I knew I was waiting for someone; indeed, someone knocked at the door and I said, 'You may come in.' It wasn't 'my' voice and that was natural; but it was a female voice and that was less natural. As the man come in,

I turned toward the mirror to arrange my hair and the image was hers, her image, Corrada's, seen a thousand times in the popular magazines: her pale cat's eyes, her triangular face, her black plait wrapped around her head with perverse innocence, her snow-white skin – but I was there inside that skin.

Meanwhile the man had come in: he was of average height, with an olive complexion, jovial; he wore a sporty sweater and had a mustache. I experienced toward him an extremely violent and distinctly ambivalent sensation. The tape imposed on me a sequence of passionate memories, some filled with furious desire, others with rebellion and hostility, and he appeared in all of them: his name was Rinaldo, he had been my lover for two years, he betrayed me, I was wildly in love with him, then he had finally returned; and at the same time my true identity repelled the topsy-turvy suggestion, rebelled against the impossible, monstrous thing that was about to happen, now, immediately, there on the couch. I suffered acutely, and I had the vague perception of fumbling around the helmet, of desperately trying to detach it from my head.

As from a stellar distance, Simpson's quiet voice reached me: 'What the hell are you doing? What is happening to you? Wait, let me take care of it, or you'll rip out the cable.'

Then everything became dark and silent; Simpson had cut off the current.

I was furious. 'What sort of joke is this? Why me, of all people! A friend, fifty years old, married and with two children, a guaranteed heterosexual! Enough, give me my hat and keep your deviltries!'

Simpson looked at me without understanding; then he rushed to check the title of the tape and turned pale as wax. 'You must believe me, I would never have taken such a liberty. I really didn't know. It was a mistake – unpardonable, but a mistake. Look here: I was convinced the label read "Corrada Colli, an evening with," and instead it reads "Corrada Colli, an evening of." It's a tape for the ladies. I never tried it, I told you so before.'

We looked at each other with mutual embarrassment. Even though I still was very perturbed, at that instant I remembered Simpson's hint at the Torec's possible didactic applications, and I was barely able to contain a burst of bitter laughter. Then Simpson said, 'And yet not by surprise like this but knowing about it in advance, this might be an interesting experience too. Unique: nobody ever went through it, even if the Greeks attributed it to Tiresias. Of course they had studied all sorts of things; just think, recently I read that they had already thought of domesticating ants as I've done, and of speaking with dolphins like Lilly.'

I answered quite curtly, 'I don't want to try, certainly not. You go ahead and try, if you think it's important, then you can tell me all about it.' But his mortification and good faith were so evident that I felt sorry for him; as soon as he had recovered a little I made up to him and asked:

'What are these tapes with the gray band?'

'You have forgiven me, haven't you? I thank you and I promise you that I'll be more careful. This is the "Epic" series, a fascinating experiment.'

'Epic? Are they war, wild westerns or Marines in battle, the sort of thing that you Americans are so fond of?'

Simpson, like a good Christian, ignored the provocation.

'No, epic has nothing at all to do with it. These are recordings of the so-called Epicurean effect: they are based on the fact that the cessation of a state of suffering or need . . . But, look, why don't you give me a chance to redeem myself? All right? You are a sensible man: you'll see that you won't have reason to regret it. Besides, I know this "thirst" tape very well, and I can assure you that there won't be any surprises. That is, there will be surprises, but permissible, decent ones.'

The heat was intense: I found myself in a desolate landscape of dark boulders and sand. I had an atrocious thirst, but I was not tired and did not feel anxious; I knew it was a Torec recording, I knew that behind me stood the

NATCA jeep, that I had signed a contract, and that by contract I hadn't had anything to drink for three days, that I was a chronically unemployed person from Salt Lake City, and that shortly I would drink. They had told me to proceed in a certain direction, and I was walking: my thirst was already at the stage in which not only the throat and mouth but also the eyes dry out, and I saw huge yellow stars flash on and off. I walked for five minutes tripping over the rocks, then I saw a sandy clearing surrounded by the ruins of a dry stone wall; at the center stood a well, with a rope and a wooden bucket. I let down the bucket and pulled it up full of clear, fresh water; I knew very well that it wasn't springwater, that the well had been dug the day before, and that the tank truck that had filled it was nearby, parked in the shadow of a cliff. But the thirst was there, it was real, ferocious and urgent, and I drank like a calf, immersing my entire face in the water: I drank at length through the mouth and the nose, stopping every now and then to breathe, totally pervaded by the most intense and simple of the pleasures granted to the living, that of restoring one's osmotic tension. But it did not last long: I hadn't drunk even a liter when the water no longer gave me any pleasure. Here the desert scene vanished and was replaced by another one, quite similar: I was in a canoe, in the midst of a torrid, blue and empty sea. Here too there were the thirst and awareness of the artifice, and the certainty that water would come; but this time I was asking myself from where, because all around I saw nothing but sea and sky. Then, about a hundred meters from me emerged a small submarine with the writing NATCA II, and the scene came to its conclusion with a delicious draft of water. Then I successively found myself in a prison, in a sealed wagon, before a glassmaker's furnace, tied to a pole, in a hospital bed, and each time my brief but tormenting thirst was more than rewarded by the arrival of ice-cold water or other beverages, in always different, generally artificial or puerile circumstances.

'The plot is a bit monotonous and the staging is weak,

but the purpose is no doubt achieved,' I told Simpson. 'You're right, it's a unique, acute, almost intolerable pleasure.'

'Everybody knows it,' Simpson said, 'but without the Torec it would not have been possible to condense seven satisfactions into a twenty-minute spectacle, entirely eliminating danger, and almost entirely the negative part of the experience, that is the long torment of thirst which is inevitable in reality. It is for this reason that all Epic tapes are anthological, that is made up of segments: in fact they exploit a disagreeable sensation, which is suitably brief, and a sensation of relief, which is intense but brief by its very nature. Besides thirst, several tapes concerning the cessation of hunger and at least a dozen kinds of physical and spiritual pain are being programmed.'

'These Epic tapes,' I said, 'leave me perplexed. Perhaps something good might even come from the others: by and large the substantially positive gain one draws from a victory in sports, or a natural spectacle, or a real live love. But here, what is one to squeeze from these frigid little games at the expense of pain if not a canned pleasure, an end in itself, solipsistic, solitary? In short, they seem an evasion to me; I don't think they're moral.'

'Perhaps you're right,' Simpson said after a brief silence, 'but will you still think like this when you're seventy years old, or eighty? And can a paralyzed man, a man tied to a bed, a man who lives only to die, think the same as you do?'

Simpson briefly described to me the so-called superego tapes, with a blue band (rescues, sacrifices, the recorded experiences of painters, musicians and poets at the peak of their creative effort), and the yellow-band tapes which reproduce the mystical and religious experiences of various denominations; with regard to these, he mentioned that a number of missionaries had already requested them in order to furnish their catechumens with a sample of their future lives as converts.

As for the tapes of the seventh series, with a black band, they are difficult to catalogue. The company puts them together at random under the heading 'Special Effects': most of them are experimental recordings at the edge of what is possible today, in order to establish what will be possible tomorrow. Some, as Simpson had mentioned to me earlier, are synthetic tapes, that is, not live recordings but built through special techniques image by image, wave by wave, in the way synthetic music and animated drawings are fabricated. In this fashion sensations that never existed and never were conceived of before have been obtained: Simpson also told me that in one of the NATCA studios a group of technicians is busy composing on tape an episode of Socrates' life as seen by Phaedon.

'Not all the black tapes,' Simpson said, 'contain agreeable experiences; some are meant exclusively for scientific purposes. There are for instance recordings made on just-born babies, neurotics, psychotics, geniuses, idiots, even animals.'

'On animals?' I repeated flabbergasted.

'Yes, on superior animals whose nervous systems are akin to ours. There are tapes on dogs – "grow a tail!" the catalogue suggests enthusiastically; tapes of cats, monkeys, horses, elephants. For the time being, I have only one of those black tapes, but I recommend it to you as a conclusion to the evening.'

The sun was dazzlingly reflected by the glaciers; there was not a cloud to be seen. I was gliding, supported by my wings (or my arms?), and beneath me an Alpine valley slowly unwound. Its bottom was at least two thousand meters below me, but I could make out every stone, every blade of grass, every ripple on the water of the stream, because my eyes were endowed with extraordinary acuity. Also, my field of vision was greater than usual: it embraced a good two thirds of the horizon and included the point perpendicularly beneath me, yet in an upward direction it was limited by a black shadow; what's more, I could not see my nose, indeed, any nose.

I saw, I heard the rustle of the wind and the distant crash of the stream, I felt the changing pressure of the air against my wings and tail, but behind this mosaic of sensations my mind was in a state of torpor, paralysis. I perceived a tension, similar to what one ordinarily experiences behind the sternum when one remembers that 'one must do something' and one has forgotten what it is. I had to 'do a certain thing,' perform an action, I didn't know what, but I knew that I must perform it in a certain direction, complete it in a certain place that was imprinted on my memory with perfect clarity: a jagged ridge on my right, at the base of the first peak a brown spot where the snowfield ended, a bush that now was hidden in the shadow – a place like a million others, but there were my nest, my female and my young baby.

I tacked windward, glided over a huge long crest and followed it, skimming the ground from south to north: now my huge shadow preceded me, cutting at full speed across the terraces of grass and dirt, shards and snow patches. A sentinel marmot whistled two, three, four times before I was able to see it; at the same instant I saw several stalks of wild oats shiver beneath me: a hare still in its winter coat went downhill toward its burrow with desperate leaps. I gathered my wings to my body and fell upon it like a stone; it was less than a meter from its shelter when I was upon it. I spread my wings to break the fall and unsheathed my claws. I snatched it up in full flight, and regained height by just exploiting the impetus without beating my wings. When the impetus was exhausted, I killed the hare with two blows of my beak: now I knew what it was that 'had to be done'; the sense of tension had ceased and I aimed my flight to the nest.

Since it had gotten quite late, I said good-bye to Simpson and thanked him for the demonstration, above all for the last tape, which had satisfied me deeply. Simpson apologized again for the mishap. 'Of course one must be very careful; an error can have unexpected consequences. I still wanted to tell you what happened to Chris Webster, one of the men on the Torec project, with the first industrial tape they had been able to record – it was a parachute jump. When he tried to check the recording, Webster found himself on the ground, a bit bruised, and the deflated parachute beside him. All of a sudden the cloth panel rose from the ground, swelled as though a strong wind were blowing from below, and Webster felt himself torn from the ground and slowly pulled upward while the pain from his bruises instantly disappeared. He quietly rose for a couple of minutes, then the traction ropes gave a jerk and the climb accelerated vertiginously, taking away his breath; at the same instant, the parachute closed like an umbrella, folded over several times lengthwise, and rolled up with a snap and adhered to his shoulders. As he was climbing like a rocket he saw the airplane come over him, flying backward with the hatch open: Webster was sucked into it headfirst and found himself in the cabin filled with fear over the impending jump. You know what happened, don't you? He had put the tape into the Torec backward.'

Simpson affectionately extorted a promise from me to come and see him again in November when his tape collection would be complete, and we separated late at night.

Poor Simpson! I'm afraid it's all over for him. After so many years of faithful service with NATCA, NATCA's last machine has defeated him, and precisely the machine that was supposed to ensure for him a varied and serene old age. He struggled with the Torec like Jacob with the angel, but the battle was lost before it began. He sacrificed everything to it: his peace, his work, his sleep, wife and books. The Torec palls on you, unfortunately; every tape can be used an infinite number of times, and every time genuine memory is extinguished and the picked-up memory recorded on the tape itself flares up. Therefore Simpson experiences no boredom during fruition, but he is oppressed by a boredom vast as the sea, as heavy as the world, when the tape ends: then nothing is left to him but to start another one. He has gone from the two hours per day that he had set himself to five, then to ten, now to eighteen or twenty: without the Torec he would be lost, with the Torec he is equally lost. He has aged twenty years in six months, he is a shadow of his former self.

Between one tape and the next, he rereads *Ecclesiastes*: it is the only book that still says something to him. In *Ecclesiastes* he has told me he finds himself and his condition: '. . . All the rivers run into the sea; yet the sea is not full; . . . the eye is not satisfied with seeing, nor the ear filled with hearing. The thing that hath been, it is that which shall be; and that which is done is that which shall be done; and there is no new thing under the sun.' And also: '. . . For in much wisdom there is much grief; and he that increaseth knowledge increaseth sorrow.' In the few days when he is at peace with himself, Simpson feels close to the old and just king, satiated with wisdom and days, who had seven hundred wives and infinite riches and the friendship of the black queen, who had worshipped the true God and the false gods Astarte and Milcom, and had clothed his wisdom in song.

But Solomon's wisdom had been acquired in pain over a long life filled with works and sins; Simpson's is the fruit of a complicated electronic circuit and eight-track tapes and he knows it and is ashamed of it, and to escape his shame he plunges back into the Torec. He's headed for death; he knows this and is not afraid of it: he has already experienced it six times, in six different versions, recorded on six tapes with a black band.

Westward

'Forget about the movie camera: look, look with your own eyes, and try to count them!'

Anna put down the apparatus and looked down into the valley: it was a rocky, narrow valley that communicated with the interior only through a square notch and ended at the sea in a vast, muddy beach. At last, after weeks of lying in wait and pursuit, they were successful: the army of lemmings, wave after wave, came to the pass and descended precipitously along the slope, raising a brown cloud of dust; where the incline was less steep, the gray-blue waves again merged into a compact torrent which moved in an orderly fashion toward the sea.

Within a few minutes the beach was invaded: in the warm light of the sunset you could distinguish the individual rodents that advanced in the mud, sinking into it up to their bellies; they went forward with difficulty but without hesitation, entered the water and continued on by swimming. You saw the heads emerge about one hundred meters from the water's edge; some isolated heads could still be seen at two hundred meters' distance, where the waves of the fjord broke; farther out, nothing. In the sky, another army flashed restlessly: a flotilla of predators, many falcons, a few buzzards, and then sparrow hawks, kites and others that the two naturalists were unable to identify. They swirled and wheeled, screeching and fighting among themselves; now and then one of them dropped down like a stone, came to a halt with an abrupt milling of its wings, and landed attracted by an invisible target, and then around it the flood of lemmings split open as around a small island.

'There,' Walter said, 'now we've also seen it. Now it is different; we no longer have any alibis. It is something that exists, that exists in nature, that has existed always, and therefore must have a cause, and so that cause must be found.'

'It's a challenge, isn't it?' Anna said in an almost maternal tone; but Walter already felt up to his neck in this and did not answer. 'Let's go,' he said; he picked up the mesh bag and flew down the slope all the way to where the more hurried lemmings passed between his legs without showing fear. He caught four of them, then it occurred to him that perhaps the ones that were already halfway down the slope did not represent an average sample: they might be the strongest, or the youngest, or the most resolute. He freed three of them, then advanced in the midst of the gray swarm and captured another five at various spots in the valley. He climbed back up to the tent with the six small animals, which twittered feebly but did not bite each other.

'Poor little things!' Anna said. 'But after all they would have died in any case.' Walter was already calling the forest ranger's helicopter over the radio. 'They'll be here tomorrow,' he said. 'We can have dinner now.' Anna looked up questioningly; Walter said, 'No, actually not yet. In fact give them something to eat too; but not much, so as not to alter their condition.'

They spoke about it at length three days later, with Professor Osiasson, but without settling anything. They returned to their hotel.

'What did you expect from him, after all? That he should criticize the theory he himself propounded?'

'No,' Walter said, 'but at least that he would pay attention to my objections. It is easy to repeat the same thing throughout an entire career and with a good conscience; you only have to reject new facts.'

'Are you sure of those new facts?'

'I'm sure today, and I'll be even more so tomorrow. You saw it yourself: the six we captured at the end of the march were very well nourished: twenty-eight percent fat, more than the average of the lemmings captured on the plateaus. But if it's not enough, I'll go back there . . .'

'We will go back.'

'. . . we'll go back, and catch sixty of them, or six hundred, and then we'll see if there'll be an Osiasson who will dare to go on repeating that what moves them is hunger.'

'Or overpopulation . . .'

'It's nonsense. No animal will react to overcrowding with worse overcrowding. Those we have seen came from all the folds of the highlands; the fact is, they did not avoid each other, on the contrary they sought each other out, tribe with tribe, individual with individual. They have marched for two months, always westward, and every day they became denser.'

'And so?'

'So . . . you see, I don't know yet, I cannot yet formulate my thought exactly, but I . . . I believe that they really want to die.'

'Why would a living being want to die?'

'And why should it want to live?' Why should it *always* want to live?'

'Because . . . well, I don't know, but we all want to live. We are alive because we want to live. It is characteristic property of living substance; I want to live, I have no doubt. Life is better than death: that seems an axiom to me.'

'You never had any doubts? Be honest!'

'No, never.'

Anna meditated, then she added: 'Almost never.'

'You said *almost*.'

'Yes, you know very well. After Mary was born. It lasted only a short time, a few months, but it was pretty awful: I had the impression that I would never get out of it, that I would remain like that forever.'

'And what did you think about during those months? How did you see the world?'

'I no longer remember. I've done everything to forget.'

'Forget what?'

'That hole. That void. That feeling . . . useless, with all around me useless, drowned in a sea of uselessness. Alone also in the midst of a crowd: buried alive amidst everybody else buried alive. But let's stop this, please let me be. Keep to more general topics.'

'Let's see . . . listen, let's try this. This is the rule, that each of us human beings but also the animals, and . . . yes, also the plants, everything that is alive struggles to live and does not know why. The why is inscribed in every cell, but in a language that we cannot read with our minds; but we do read it with all of our being, and we obey the message with all our behaviour. But the message can be more or less imperative: the species in which the messages are incised deeply and clearly survive, the others become extinct, are extinct. But also those in whom the message is clear can have gaps. Individuals without love for life can be born; others may lose it for a short or long time, perhaps for all the life they have left; and finally . . . here, perhaps I've got it: also groups of individuals may lose it, epochs, nations, families. Such things have happened; human history is full of them.'

'Fine. There's a semblance of order now; you're getting close. But now you must explain to me, indeed, explain to yourself, how that love can disappear in a group.'

'I'll think about it later. Now I also wanted to tell you that between a person who possesses the love of life and a person who has lost it there exists no common language. The same event is described by both in two ways that have nothing in common: one person draws joy from it, the other torment, each draws from it the confirmation of his own vision of the world.'

'They can't both be right.'

'No. In general, you know, and one must have the courage to say so, it's the others who are right.'

'The lemmings?'

'Why not: let's call them lemmings.'

'And what about us?'

'We are wrong, and we know it, but we find it more agreeable to keep our eyes shut. Life does *not* have a purpose; pain always prevails over joy; we are all sentenced to death, and the day of one's execution has not been revealed; we are condemned to watch the end of those dearest to us; there are compensations, but they are few. We know all this and yet something protects us and supports us and keeps us away from the shipwreck. And what is this protection? Perhaps only habit: the habit of living that we contract at birth by being born.'

'In my opinion, the protection is not the same for all. Some find a defense in religion, some in altruism, some in obtuseness, some in vice; some are able to distract themselves uninterruptedly.'

'All true,' Walter said. 'I might add that the most common and also the least ignoble defense is the one that exploits our essential ignorance of tomorrow. And, you see, here too there is symmetry. This uncertainty is the same uncertainty that makes life bearable for the . . . the lemmings. For everyone else, the will to live is something profound and confused, something within us and at the same time beside us, separate from consciousness, almost an organ that as a rule functions in silence, quite obediently, and so is ignored; but it can become diseased or atrophied, be wounded or amputated. In that case one goes on living, but with effort, with pain, like someone who has lost his stomach or a lung.'

'Yes,' said Anna, 'this is the principal defense, the natural defense that is given to us together with life so that life can be endured. But there are others, I believe: the ones I mentioned before.'

'Indeed, all defenses must have something in common. If we can answer the question we've left hanging, that is, what acts within a group, we will also know what the various defenses share. Two suppositions can be made: the first is that one "lemming" contaminates all its neighbors; the other is that this is a matter of an intoxication or a deficiency.'

Nothing is more vivifying than a hypothesis. The Forest Rangers' Laboratory was mobilized within a few days, and the results were soon evident, but for a long time they were negative. The blood of migrating lemmings was identical to that of stationary lemmings: the same for the urine, the amount of fat, everything. Walter thought and spoke of nothing else. One evening he talked about it with Bruno, their glasses full before them, and they hit on the idea together.

'This, for instance, is useful,' Bruno said. 'It's old knowledge, common knowledge.'

'It's a very rudimentary medicine. Alcohol is not innocuous, it is difficult to dose and its effect is very brief.'

'But one could work on it.'

The following day they were in front of the lemming enclosure on the Institute's grounds. It had been necessary to reinforce the mesh of the wire fence on the side facing in the direction of the sea, and sink it two hefty meters below ground level, because the small beasts found no peace: there were about a hundred of them by now, and all day long, and through half of the night they crowded against the wire fence, trampling over each other, trying to climb up and push each other back; some dug tunnels that inevitably came to a halt against the buried fence, they came out crawling backward, began again; the other three sides of the enclosure were deserted. Walter went inside, caught four of them, tied a marker to their paw and with a probe administered to them one gram of alcohol. The four, put back in the enclosure, paused for a few moments, with bristling hair and dilated nostrils, then they moved away and quietly began to munch on the heather; nevertheless, an hour later, they had one by one resumed their places in the melee of lemmings determined to migrate westward.

Walter and Bruno agreed in concluding that it wasn't much, but it was a clue.

A month later, the pharmacology department was going full blast. The proposed theme was simple and terrifying: to identify or synthesize the hormone that inhibits the existential void. Anna was perplexed and said so openly.

'Say we find it, will it be good or bad?'

'Good for the individual, certainly. Whether it will be good for the human species is doubtful, but it is a boundless doubt—which applies to any drug, not only to this. Any medicine, indeed any medical intervention makes the unfit fit: would you object to all medication and all doctors? The human species has chosen this path for centuries, the path of artificial survival, and it does not seem to me that it's been weakened by it. Humanity has turned its back on nature for quite some time: it is made up of individuals and stakes everything on individual survival, on the prolongation of life and on the victory over death and pain.'

'But there are other ways to vanquish pain, this pain: other struggles that each of us has a duty to wage with his own means, without outside help. Those who win prove they are strong, and in so doing become strong, are enriched and better themselves.'

'And those who do not win? Those who give in, collapsing with a crash or little by little? What will you say, what will I say, if we shall also find ourselves . . . walking westward? Will we be able to rejoice in the name of the species, and of those others who within themselves find the strength to reverse their course?'

Six more months went by and for Anna and Walter they were unusual months. They went up the Amazon river on a passenger service boat, then on a smaller boat up the Cinto river, and finally in a native canoe up a nameless tributary: the guide who accompanied them had promised them a journey of four days, but it was only on the seventh day that they negotiated the

Sacayo rapids and came in sight of the village. From a distance they could distinguish the crumbling buttresses of the Spanish fortress, and they said nothing because there was no need and it was nothing new for them, another element in the landscape: in the sky a dense interweaving of predatory flights which seemed to center directly above the fortress.

The village of Arunde sheltered the last remnants of the Arunde tribe; they had learned of its existence by chance, from an article that appeared in an anthropological review. The Arunde, once spread over a territory as large as Belgium, had withdrawn within ever narrower borders since their number was in continuous decline. This was not the consequence of illnesses, or of wars with bordering tribes, nor even of insufficient food, but only because of the enormous number of suicides: it was exactly because of this that Walter had decided to request financing of the expedition.

They were received by the village's elder, who was only thirty-nine years old and spoke Spanish quite correctly. Walter, who hated preambles, came straight to the point; he expected from the elder reserve, shyness, perhaps suspicion or coldness before a stranger's pitiless curiosity, and instead found before him a serene man, conscious and mature as though he had prepared for that interview for years, perhaps for his entire life.

The elder confirmed that the Arunde had since time immemorial lacked metaphysical convictions: alone among all their neighbors they had neither churches nor priests nor witch doctors, and did not expect succor from the heavens nor the earth nor from the lower depths. They believed neither in rewards nor punishments. Their soil was not poor, they enjoyed just laws, a humane and expeditious administration; they knew neither hunger nor discord, they possessed a rich and original popular culture, and they often made merry in festivities and banquets. Interrogated by Walter about the constant numerical decline of the population, the elder answered that he was aware of the fundamental difference between their belief and those of other people, near or distant, of which he had heard.

The Arunde, he said, attributed little value to individual survival, and none to that of the nation. Each of them was taught from infancy to evaluate life exclusively in terms of pleasure and pain, factoring in, of course, also the pleasures and pains the behavior of each individual caused his fellow men. When, in the judgment of each individual, the balance sheet tended to become permanently negative, when, that is, the citizen felt he suffered and produced more sorrows than joys, he was invited to an open discussion before the council of elders, and if his judgment was confirmed, the conclusion was encouraged and facilitated. After his dismissal, he was led to the area of the ktan fields: ktan is a cereal very widespread in this country, and its seed, sifted and ground, is used to make a kind of flat bread. If it is not sifted, the very minute seeds produce an infesting weed, which has a drugging and toxic effect.

The man is handed over to the ktan cultivators: he lives on bread made from unsifted seed, and in a few days, or a few weeks, as he may choose, he reaches a state of agreeable stupor, which is followed by definitive rest. A very few change their minds and return from the ktan fields to the fortified town: there they are welcomed with joyful affection. Unsifted seeds are smuggled past the walls, but the volume is not preoccupying and the practice is tolerated.

Upon their return, Anna and Walter were met by an important piece of news. The 'missing substance' had been found – more precisely, it had first been created from nothing by synthesis, through an exhausting labor of evaluation of innumerable compounds suspected of having a specific effect on the nervous system; shortly after, it had been identified in normal blood. Strangely, Bruno's intuition had hit the mark: in fact the most efficacious compound was an alcohol, even though its structure was rather complex. The dosage was quite small, so small as to justify the failure of the analyst, who had not identified it as a normal component of the blood of all healthy mammals, including man, and who therefore had not been able to notice its absence in the blood of the migrating lemmings. Walter had his quarter hour of success and notoriety: the blood samples he had collected from the Arunde did not contain even a trace of the active principle.

This, which had been called factor L, was soon produced on a pilot scale. It was active if or when taken orally and proved miraculous in restoring the will for life in subjects that lacked it, or had lost it as the result of illnesses, calamities or traumas; in other people, taken in normal doses it did not produce noteworthy effects or signs of sensitivization or accumulation.

The opportunity for a confirmation was immediately evident to everyone: in fact, for a twofold confirmation, concerning the migratory lemmings and their human analogues. Walter sent the elder of the Arunde a small package which contained a dose of factor L sufficient for one hundred persons and for one year; under separate cover he wrote him a long letter in which he explained in great detail how the medication must be administered, and begged him to extend the experiment also to the people sent to the ktan fields; but he did not have the time to wait for an answer, because the Forest Rangers had informed him that a column of lemmings was rapidly approaching the mouth of Molde river, at the end of Penndal fjord.

It was not an easy job: Walter had to avail himself of the help of four young assistants besides Anna's enthusiastic collaboration. Fortunately, the L factor was water soluble and water was abundantly available on the spot; Walter planned to scatter the solution beyond the gorge, where the heather grew thickly, and one could expect that the lemmings would stop to munch on it. But it became clear that his plan could not be realized: the area was too broad, and the columns of lemmings were already approaching, heralded by high dust swirls visible at a distance of twenty kilometers.

At that Walter decided to spray the solution directly above the columns, along the sole path that ran immediately below the gorge. He would not be able to act upon the entire population, but he believed that the effect would nevertheless be demonstrative.

The first lemmings showed up at the gorge around nine o'clock; by ten the valley was already crowded and the flow promised to increase. Walter descended into the valley with the sprayer attached to his back; he leaned against a boulder and opened the tap of the propellant. There was no wind: from high up on the ridge Anna distinctly saw the whitish cloud spurt out, streaming out in the direction of the valley. She saw the gray tide stop in a swirl, like the water of a river against the pylon of a bridge: the lemmings that had inhaled the solution seemed uncertain whether to continue, to stop or go back up. But then she saw a massive wave of restless bodies wash over the first, and a third over the second, so that the rolling mass reached up to Walter's waist; she saw Walter make rapid gestures with his free hand, confused, convulsed gestures that seemed to her a call for help, then she saw Walter totter, torn away from the boulder's shelter, fall and get carried along, buried and again carried farther, visible for short stretches like a swelling beneath the flood of the innumerable small desperate creatures that were running toward death, their death and his death, toward the swamp and the nearby sea.

That same day the package that Walter had sent across the ocean came back, returned to the sender. Anna gained possession of it only three days later, when Walter's body had already been recovered: it contained a laconic message addressed to Walter 'y a todos los sábios del mundo civil.' It said: 'The Arunde people, soon to be no longer a people, greets you and thanks you. We do not wish to offend, but we return your medicament, so that those among you who wish to may profit from it: we prefer freedom to drugs and death to illusion.'

Seen from Afar

Declaration in good faith: We have been promised that within a very few years, perhaps even within the current year, 1967, human beings will set foot on the moon, irreversibly carrying there our cellular mechanisms, our infections and our civilization.

At the moment when this takes place and when the first report of the first visitors is published, all the illustrious and less illustrious fantasies that the literatures of all times have expressed about the Selenites will be routed and rendered empty and vain. Therefore, I should be pleased if the present essay were read and understood as a last reverent homage to Lucian of Samosata, Voltaire, Swedenborg, Rostand, E. A. Poe, Flammarion and H. G. Wells.

Declaration in bad faith: The deciphering of the present Report, which has reached us in Selenitic linear B characters, has presented serious technical difficulties to the FBI decoders to whom it was entrusted; we therefore beg the reader to be indulgent toward its incongruities and gaps. We must furthermore point out that, for the sake of simplicity, it has seemed advisable to adopt for the transcription, to the extent that this is possible, terrestrial measurements, dates and geographical terms corresponding to the expressions contained in the original.

Therefore, when for example one speaks of cities or ships, one should remember that they are 'cities' (i.e., dense conglomerations of human dwelling) and 'ships' (i.e., voluminous floating objects built and piloted by man) for us, not for the unknown anonymous compiler of the Report, to whom both cities and ships appear under a much less revealing light.

REPORT

1. VALIDITY. In the present Report are described some variations and movements that were observed on the terrestrial surface in recent times. By contrast, not described are variations and movements whose periodicity coincides with the sidereal year or the lunar month, such as the cycles of the polar caps, the variations in color of plains and mountains, the tides, the variations of transparency in the atmosphere, etc.: these phenomena have been known for a long time, have been the object of numerous previous reports, and are certainly connected with astronomical cycles. Hence they seem irrelevant to any discussion concerning the presence of life on earth.

2. CITIES. For the description, nomenclature and location of the main Cities and Ports, we refer the reader back to the preceding Report No. 8, dated January 15, 1876. Thanks to the recent improvement of the resolving power of our optical instruments, it has been observed that the majority of the Cities are in a phase of rapid expansion, and that the atmosphere above them tends to become increasingly opaque, rich in fine dust, carbon dioxide, and sulfurous or sulfuric anhydride.

It has furthermore been possible to establish that they are not simple areas of color different from the surrounding terrain. In many of them we have observed a 'fine structure': some, for example Paris, Tokyo and Milan, have a well-defined center from which irradiate filaments; other filaments surround the center at varying distances, with a circular or polygonal pattern. However, other cities, and among these all or almost all Ports, present a reticular structure, constituted by tendentially rectilinear and orthogonal filaments which subdivide the urban area into rectangles or squares.

2.1. Evening Light. From 1905 to 1910 on, all the above mentioned urban filaments become suddenly luminous after the local setting of the Sun. More precisely: approximately thirty to sixty minutes after the terminator's passage, the filaments of each single City light up in rapid succession; each filament lights up instantaneously and the lightings-up follow each other within five to ten seconds. The luminosity lasts throughout the night, and ceases suddenly approximately thirty minutes before the new passage of the terminator. The phenomenon, quite spectacular and carefully studied by many observers, presents surprising characteristics of regularity. for every single city, interruptions of luminosity have been observed only on one or two nights out of every thousand, mostly coinciding with serious atmospheric disturbances in the vicinity, so that the hypothesis that it is a matter of an electrical phenomenon does not appear inappropriate.

Concerning alterations in the Evening Light during the Anomalous Period, see point 5 below. At the end of said period the phenomenon again manifested itself with the customary regularity; however, spectroscopic examination of urban luminosity has demonstrated that until around 1950 its spectrum was prevalently continuous (due to incadescence) while thereafter, with ever-increasing intensity, banded or linear spectrums of the kind emitted by rarefied gases or fluorescence are superimposed on this luminosity.

During the winter of 1965–66, a total extinguishing was observed in the city of New York, although the sky was clear.

2.2. Expansion. As mentioned, many Cities seem to be in a state of active expansion. Generally, this expansion involves the structure of the preexisting reticulate: the radiating Cities expand along their radia, the reticular Cities expand through new layers in the shape of orthogonal reticulates. The analogy with crystalline growth is evident, and allows us to assume that the Cities are vast areas of the terrestrial surface characterized by pronounced crystallization; for that matter, we have an example of this on the Moon, in the imposing formations of well-crystallized orthoclases, which cover several hectares of ground within the basin of Aristarchus.

The hypothesis as to the crystalline nature of the Cities is reinforced by the recent discovery of structures of a regular shape, apparently to be ascribed to the trimetric system, which rise several hundreds of meters above the city-plan. They can easily be observed at dusk, thanks to their shadow: their cross-section is rectangular or square and in some cases it has been possible to witness their formation, which takes place at a velocity of 10 to 20 meters per month along the vertical axis. It is very rare for these structures to show up beyond the confines of the urban areas. Under favorable geometric conditions, some of them specularly reflect the solar light, which has facilitated the measuring of the crystallographic constants.

Other signs of a bidimensional crystalline arrangement can perhaps be discerned in the rectangular structures of slightly varying colors observed on many terrestrial plains.

2.3. ELLIPTICAL CRATERS. The existence of elliptical (more rarely circular or semicircular) craters within certain Cities or in their immediate vicinity was already pointed out in previous Reports. They formed slowly (in the course of five to fifteen years) even in very ancient times near various Cities of the Mediterranean area; but there is no record of their having been observed before the eighth century BC. The majority of these ancient craters were later more or less completely obliterated, perhaps due to erosion or as a consequence of natural catastrophes. During the last sixty years many other craters have formed with great regularity within or close to all the Cities, with an extension superior to 30 to 50 hectares; the largest Cities often have two or more.

They never appear on inclines, and their shapes and dimensions are very uniform. Rather than being of a precisely elliptical design, they consist of a rectangle measuring approximately 160 by 200 meters, completed on the two short sides by two semicircumferences. Their orientation appears haphazard, both in respect to the urban reticulate, and to the cardinal points. That these are craters has been clearly recognized on the basis of the profile of their shadows at dusk: their rim is 12 to 20 meters high in relation to the ground, it drops sheerly on the outside, and toward the inside has a declivity of approximately 50 percent. Some of them, during the summer season, emit at times a tenuous luminosity during the early hours of the night.

Their volcanic origin is deemed probable, but their relationship to the urban formations is obscure. Just as mysterious is the weekly rhythm to which the craters seem to be typically subject, and which we shall describe here below.

3. NONASTRONOMICAL PERIODICITY. A certain number of phenomena observed on earth follow a seven-day rhythm. Only the optical instruments at our disposal for a few decades have allowed us to highlight this singularity; therefore, we are not in a position to establish whether its origins are recent or remote, or even if this singularity goes back to the solidifying of the terrestrial crust. It is certainly not an astronomic rhythm: as is well known, neither the terrestrial month (synodic or sidereal) nor the year (solar or sidereal) contains a number of days which is a multiple of 7.

The weekly rhythm is extremely rigid. The phenomena which we shall call OTSD (Of The Seventh Day), and which mainly concern the Cities and their immediate surroundings, take place simultaneously on the entire terrestrial surface; allowances being made, of course, for discrepancies in local times. This fact is not explained, nor have truly satisfactory hypotheses been advanced: just as a matter of curiosity we point out that some observers have formulated the supposition of a biological rhythm. Any possible life (vegetal and/or animal) on Earth, that in this hypothesis would have to be accepted as rigorously monogenetic, would be subject to an extremely general cycle, in which activity and rest (or vice versa) follow each other in periods of six days and one day.

3.1. THE OTSD ACTIVITY OF THE CRATERS. As mentioned, the elliptical characters referred to under section 2.3 are subject to a weekly rhythm.

Every seven days their contours, which normally are whitish, become gray or black within a few hours (generally during the early afternoon hours): they maintain this dark coloration for approximately two hours, and then in about fifteen to twenty minutes they resume the original whitish tint. Only exceptionally has the phenomenon been observed on other days than the seventh. The internal area of the crater does not present appreciable variations in color.

3.2. OTHER OTSD ACTIVITIES. During the early diurnal hours of the seven days, the peripheral (radial) urban filaments appear slightly darker. During the successive early evening hours, above all in the summer season, they appear, however, feebly luminous also outside the urban perimeter; under particular conditions of angulation, this luminosity appears divided into two parallel and contiguous filaments, one of white light and the other of red light.

Also certain portions of the marine shoreline are subject to OTSD darkening. This has been observed on shorelines of a peculiar yellowish color, not too distant from Cities and not subject to very high tides: it takes place only during the seasons and in the localities of greatest solar impact, and it lasts from two to four hours after dawn until the local sunset. On some of the beaches in question this obscuring is noticed not only on the seventh day but daily for a period of fifteen to thirty days, which begins approximately one month after the summer solstice.

3.3. OTSD ANOMALIES. During recent months it has been demonstrated that in certain regions of North Africa, Southern Asia and the Malay archipelago, the OTSD phenomenon takes place two days in advance in respect to the rest of the Earth, and only one day in advance on a narrow strip of the isthmus that joins Asia to Africa. In the British Isles, however, they appear distributed between the sixth and the seventh day.

4. PORTS AND PORT ACTIVITIES. For 'Ports,' as is known, we mean Cities situated on the shores of seas, large lakes or rivers. For the definition of these geographical concepts, we refer you to the preceding Reports, but we wish to remind the reader that the liquid nature of seas, lakes and rivers must at this point be considered confirmed by the polarimetric examination of the solar image reflected by it, and that, given the temperature and pressure conditions existing on the terrestrial surface, it is today universally admitted that the liquid in question is water. The relationships between water, snow, polar caps, glaciers, atmospheric humidity and cloudiness were described in Report No. 7, to which we refer you.

Here we will concern ourselves specifically with maritime Ports; we must point out that it already did not escape the most ancient observers that they were always located in more or less deep indentations on the coasts, and often at the mouths of rivers. All the phenomena situated in the land Cities are observed also in the Ports, but in the latter specific activities of great interest are carried out.

4.1 SHIPS. For the sake of simplicity, we shall indicate by the name of 'ships' particular floating objects of an elongated shape that modern optical instruments have allowed us to make out. They move through the water longitudinally at speeds that are greatly varied but rarely superior to 70 km/hr; their maximum length is approximately 300 meters, the minimum is inferior to the resolving power of our instruments (about 50 meters).

Their importance is fundamental: they are the only objects that we see materially move on the terrestrial surface, with the exception of ice fragments that are often seen detaching themselves from the polar banks. But whereas the movements of the latter are slow and appear haphazard, the motions of the ships are subject to interesting peculiarities.

4.1.1. SHIPS' MOVEMENTS. Ships are divided into periodic and aperiodic. The first travel fixed to-and-fro routes between two Ports, often stopping for a few hours at intermediate Ports; a rough proportionality has been noticed between their dimensions and the length of their voyages. They only exceptionally stop in the open sea; they move with a speed that is extremely constant for every ship, both by day and night, and their route is very close to the shortest line between the points of departure and arrival.

At night they emanate a feeble luminosity; occasionally they stop in the Ports for some months.

Also the aperiodic ships move from Port to Port, but without apparent regularity. Their stops are usually longer (up to ten days); some of them roam irregularly on the open sea, or are stationed there for long periods. They are not luminous, and on the average they are less speedy. No ship comes into contact with terra firma save in the Ports.

4.1.2. GENESIS AND DISAPPEARANCE OF SHIPS. All ships are formed in relatively few fixed spots, all of them situated in small or large Ports. The formation process lasts from a few months to one to two years: it seems to take place by transversal growth starting from the main axis, which is formed during a first phase. The life of ships extends over thirty to fifty years; normally, after a more or less prolonged stay in a Port, which is sometimes that of origin, they seem to undergo a rapid process of disintegration or decomposition. In rare instances they have been seen to disappear on the open seas; on this subject, however, see section 5.

4.1.3. Hypotheses on the Nature of Ships. It is by now excluded that they are floating blocks of pumice or ice. Attention should be given to a recent bold theory according to which ships are nothing but aquatic animals, intelligent when periodic, less intelligent (or less endowed with a sense of orientation) when aperiodic. The former supposedly take nourishment at the expense of some material or living species to be found in the Ports; the latter, perhaps, at the expense of smaller ships (invisible to us) on the open sea; however, according to some observations, they are thought to manifest a tropism for hydrocarbons.

In fact many aperiodic ships frequent Ports situated in areas in which the atmosphere reveals traces of methane and ethane. Also in the Ports there is thought to take place the reproductive cycle of both varieties, for the time being obscure to us.

4.2. Terrestrial Ports. In the vicinity of many Cities are seen areas denominated 'terrestrial Ports,' and characterized by a particular network of filaments of a gray color, luminous at night; these are one or more rectangles 50 to 80 meters wide and 3,000 or more meters long. From one terrestrial Port to another there have been observed movements of singular objects constituted by a long white cloud in the shape of an elongated isosceles triangle whose vertex advances at a velocity of 800 to 1,000 km/hr.

5. Anomalous Period. This name is generally used to indicate the 1939–45 period, which was typified by numerous deviations from the terrestrial norm.

As already mentioned, in a great number of cities the phenomenon of the evening light (2.1.) appeared disturbed or interrupted. Also the growth appeared greatly slowed down or nonexistent (2.2.). The OTSD darkening of the craters was less intense and regular (3.1.); and so was the darkening of the shoreline (3.2.); the OTSD luminosity of the urban centers (3.2.), of the craters (2.3.) and of the periodic ships (4.1.) disappeared.

The pendular rhythm of the latter (4.1.1.) appeared seriously disturbed; on the contrary, the number and volume of aperiodic ships increased, as though the latter had overcome the former. The phenomenon (4.1.2.) of the sudden disappearance of ships in the open sea, normally very rare, occurred with great frequency: not less than eight hundred disappearances were noticed, taking place at tempos which varied from four minutes to several hours, but due to the incompleteness of the observations, and the impossibility of controlling at every instant more than half the terrestrial surface, this figure must certainly be multiplied by 2 and probably by a higher factor.

Some disappearances of ships were preceded by intense but instantaneous luminous phenomena; other analogous phenomena have been noticed during the same period in various terrestrial regions, particularly in Europe, the Far East, and along the northern coast of Africa. The end of the anomalous epoch was marked by two very lively explosions, both of which took place in Japan at a distance of two days from one another. Other similar or stronger explosions were observed during the ten subsequent years on various small islands in the Pacific and in a restricted region of central Asia: at the moment of this Report the phenomenon seems extinct or latent.

The Hard-Sellers

The place was pleasant, luminous and gay; the light, which came attenuated from all directions, was blue-white and trembled slightly. The walls were white and opaque, and were lost toward the top in an indistinct shimmer. Also the columns were white: smooth and cylindrical, they joined with the barely visible vaulted ceiling.

S., in a white smock, sat on a high stool before a drafting table. He was very young, almost a boy, and was intent on tracing on a sheet of paper a complicated graph made of long diagonal lines which irradiated from a point situated on the lower left, and converged with orderly elegance toward another point, which by an effect of perspective seemed to be beyond the sheet of paper, at an extreme distance. The sheet was yellowish and the ink was brown; thc drawing was crowded with erasures and words and explanatory sentences scribbled hurriedly, as though pushed by the anxiety of not letting an idea escape. Table and stool were in the middle of the floor, very far from the walls, and the floor was empty. S. worked intently, but without continuity: he alternated bursts of intense activity with pauses in which he seemed to meditate in pursuit of a thought, or perhaps had become distracted.

A bell rang in the distance, but S. did not hear it and continued to work. After about ten seconds the bell rang again: S. lifted his head for a moment and then went back to drawing. At the third ring, which was more insistent, S. sighed, laid down his pencil, got off the stool and headed for the end of the large room; his figure appeared minute in relation to the vast squared-off sections of the floor, and his footsteps resounded at length beneath the silent vault. He went down broad corridors and entered the reception room: this was small, and its ceiling was so low you could touch it with your hand. Here were waiting for him a robust young man, a blond and beautiful middle-aged woman, and a thin man with salt-and-pepper hair; they stood near the table, and the young man held a small suitcase by its handle. S. stopped for an instant on the threshold, as though irked; then he collected himself and said, 'Sit down, please.' He sat down and the three did the same. S. was annoyed at having been forced to interrupt his work. He said, 'What can I do for you?'; then he noticed the suitcase that the young man had placed on the table and he added, with disappointment, 'Oh, I understand.'

The young man did not waste time on preambles. He opened the suitcase and said, 'No, look, we might as well avoid misunderstandings from the start. We are not insurance agents and neither did we come all the way here to sell: or, more precisely, not to sell merchandise. We are functionaries.'

'Then you have come for . . .'

'Exactly, you've guessed correctly.'

'And what are you offering me?'

'The Earth,' the young man answered, winking cordially. 'We are Earth specialists – as you know, the third planet of the Solar System. A beautiful place, for the rest, as we shall try to demonstrate to you, if you will allow us to do so.' He caught a slight hesitation in S.'s glance, and added, 'Are you surprised? You weren't expecting us?'

'Yes, to tell the truth . . . I thought I'd seen a certain movement, recently. There have been rumors, a number of colleagues had disappeared, just like that, silently, without warning. But . . . well, I don't feel I'm ready; I've made no calculations, no preparations. You know very well what happens when there isn't a deadline: one prefers to let the days go by, and stay like that, up in the air, without making decisions.'

The young man intervened with professional

efficiency. 'But of course, don't worry. It's normal, this is what almost always happens; it's very difficult to find a candidate who meets us with a definite yes or no. At any rate, it's easy to understand; it's impossible to form an opinion like this, alone, without witnesses, without testimonials, without serious documentation. But that's precisely what we're here for: if you'll be kind enough to listen to us for a moment . . . No, we will not take up much of your time – even though you people . . . you'll surely agree, have plenty of time. Not like us, who are always in a hurry, but mustn't show it, or else what sort of business deals could we put through?'

As he spoke, the young man rummaged in his case; he took from it several illustrations of the Earth, some of the scholastic type, others taken from great heights or from cosmic distances. He showed them to S. one by one, describing them in a professional, concrete tone.

'Here we are. As I mentioned, we deal with the Earth and in particular with the Human Species. Hard times have been over for quite a while; by now it is a well-equipped planet, indeed comfortable, with temperature variations that do not go beyond one hundred twenty degrees Celsius between the maximum and the absolute minimum, and an atmospheric pressure which is practically constant in time and space. A day has twenty-four hours, the year approximately three hundred and sixty-five days; there is a pretty little satellite that causes moderate tides and gently illuminates the night. It is much smaller than the sun, but it was intelligently positioned in such a way as to have the same apparent diameter as the sun: thus are obtained solar eclipses highly appreciated by connoisseurs there – just look at this one here, with a complete view of the corona. Besides, there is also an ocean of salt water designed without stinting, this is it, you see? Now I'll show it to you in motion.'

Within the square of the photograph, which represented a vast seascape facing a sandy shoreline extending all the way to the horizon, the waves docilely began to move.

'It isn't really that impressive on the photograph, but it is one of the most suggestive terrestrial spectacles. I know of some clients of ours who, also quite old, spend hours contemplating the waves, this eternal rhythm, always the same and always different; they say it is worth the trip. It is a pity that we have so little free time, because otherwise . . . Oh, I forgot to tell you that the terrestrial axis is inclined on the ecliptic of a small angle, here it is.'

He drew from the pile a schematic image of Earth, with meridians and parallels: at his command, the Earth began to turn slowly.

'By this simple device it's been possible to obtain an agreeable variety of climates over a good part of the planet. Finally, we have at our disposal an absolutely exceptional atmosphere, unique in the galaxy, and I won't tell you how much effort and time it has cost us: just think, more than twenty percent of oxygen, an inestimable wealth and a source of energy that will never come to an end. You know, it's easy to say petroleum here, coal there, hydrogen, methane. I know planets that are full of methane – so full that it spills over. But if they're without oxygen, what can they do with it? Well, enough, it isn't right to speak badly of the competition's products. Please, forgive me, I've let myself be carried away and I've forgotten my manners.'

He took a calling card from his pocket and handed it to S.

'Here, that's me, my name is G., and I am in charge of the general organization; these are my assistants, our Mrs B., who will speak to you about problems of human relations, and my colleague R., who will answer your questions of a historical and philosophical nature.'

Mrs B. smiled and bent her head; Mr R. rose to his feet and bowed stiffly. Both handed S. their business cards.

'Delighted,' S. said. 'I'm at your disposal. But without commitment, right? I wouldn't want that . . .'

'You may rest assured,' G. said. 'With this discussion you do not make any commitment whatsoever, and we, for our part, will try to avoid any and all pressure with regard to your choice. We shall present our data in the most objective and thorough manner. However, it is our duty to warn you: there will not be a second visit. I'm sure you understand, the candidates are many, and we, who work at this business of slipping souls into bodies, are very few indeed. It is not an easy profession, you know: it gives great satisfaction, but few people succeed. So, our day is full, and save for rare exceptions we cannot call on the same candidate twice. You'll see, you'll judge, and you'll make a completely free decision; you'll tell us yes or no, and we shall in any case part as good friends. And now we can begin.'

G. pulled another packet of illustrations from his case, handed it to S., and continued. 'These are our samples: our strength is all here. It is absolutely up-to-date material, completely reliable – just think, we renew it every six months.'

S. leafed through the illustrations with curiosity: they were splendid figures, in brilliant, harmonious colors. The majority represented magnificent human specimens – young and very beautiful women, athletic men with a slightly fatuous smile who moved a bit within the square, as though impatient to fly into action.

'Are these the men?'

'Men and women,' G. answered. 'You are aware of the difference, right? It is small but fundamental. . . . A young Polynesian woman . . . a Senegalese hunter . . . a Los Angeles bank clerk . . . an Australian boxer – should we watch him as he fights? There – look at the agility, the power: he's like a panther. . . . A young Indian mother . . .'

The Indian mother must have slipped into that packet of illustrations by mistake; as a matter of fact, her appearance was not very agreeable. She was skeleton-thin from starvation and clutched to her bosom an undernourished little boy with a swollen belly and legs like sticks. G. promptly whisked away the image before S. could ask any questions and replaced it with that of a Danish girl student, blond and admirably shaped. S.

considered the sheet attentively and then he asked, 'Are they born like this? I mean, so well developed?'

Mrs B. intervened with a smile. 'Oh no, there is a certain growth, evidently; they are born much smaller, and in my opinion also much prettier.' She turned to G. 'Would you look for one of the growth sequences, please?'

After searching for a few moments (the contents of the case did not seem to be kept in very good order), G. drew out an image and handed it to the woman, who in turn presented it to S.; it pictured a young man with a musculature so developed that it was almost monstrous: he was standing, naked, his legs set apart, his hands closed in fists held over his shoulders and his biceps prominent, and he smiled the smile of a wild beast. Suddenly, without changing position but only growing smaller, the young man turned into an adolescent, then into a boy, a child, an infant, a newborn, all of them smiling and all splendidly nourished. Mrs B. said to G. quite softly, 'No, in the other direction, if you don't mind, and a bit more slowly.'

In S.'s hands the reverse metamorphosis unfolded without a hitch until it reached the original athlete, who in the end warmly greeted S. by shaking his joined hands over his head.

'There,' Mrs B. said, 'this way it seems quite clear to me. It is the same individual at the age of one month, one year, six, fourteen, eighteen and thirty.'

'That's interesting,' S. admitted. 'The same happens with the women, I should imagine?'

'Certainly,' the woman answered. 'Would you like to see the sequence?'

'No, don't bother; if it's the same, there's no need. Instead, I would like to know what happens before and after. Does one continue to grow?'

'Not exactly to grow; but other changes take place that are difficult to reproduce with images. There is a certain physical decline . . .'

Here another accident took place: while Mrs B. was uttering the words 'physical decline,' the image S. was holding was replaced by that of a mature, bald man, then by that of an elderly obese, pale man, and finally by that of a failing old man. The woman quickly tucked the photograph away in the case and continued blithely:

'. . . which is however compensated by greater prudence and life experience, and often by great serenity. But it is "before" that is extremely interesting.'

She turned to G. and asked, 'Do we have any births?'

'No, Mrs B., you know very well that we can show neither births nor sexual embraces.' Then he continued, addressing S., 'It's not that there's anything illicit behind this, but we are dealing here with a peculiar procedure, a technology unique in its kind, and so bold that in a nonborn such as yourself it might arouse a certain perturbation, even if only at the subconscious level. Forgive me, but these are our instructions.'

'. . . But we can show him the sample cards of couples, isn't that true?' Mrs B. intervened with warmth.

'Certainly,' G. resumed. 'It is absolutely exciting, you'll see. As you know, the male and the female, in our case, the man and the woman, are strictly complementary, not only morphologically; therefore the conjugal condition, or at any rate life in a twosome, is the basic prerequisite for peace of the spirit. In any case just look here: this is a documentation that is self-explanatory. Look at this couple . . . this other one, in a rowboat . . . these other two: those pinkish prisms on the background are the Dolomites, an absolutely beautiful place, I went there on vacation last year; but going there alone is totally blah. This is a Congolese couple engaged to be married . . . aren't they darling? These are two married people . . . of a certain age . . .'

Here Mrs B.'s warm, slightly hoarse voice cut in. 'Believe me, by now we have a lot of experience with such matters, and we can guarantee you that the true great terrestrial adventure is precisely this, to find a partner of a different sex and live together, at least for a few years but if possible throughout one's life. Don't give this up, believe me: if you'll happen to be born female, don't neglect to get yourself fertilized as soon as a reasonable opportunity presents itself to you. And breast-feeding (here it is, look) creates an affective tie so sweet and profound, so . . . how shall I say? pervasive that it is difficult to describe it without having experienced it.'

'And . . . did you experience it?' asked S., who in fact felt slightly perturbed.

'Certainly. We functionaries are given our license only if we can present a complete terrestrial curriculum.'

Mr G. broke in. 'Also being born a man, of course, presents advantages: indeed, advantages and disadvantages compensate each other to such a point that the choices, at all times, have always been distributed between the two sexes with singular equality. Do you see this table, and this graph with the T in abscissa? Fifty-fifty, disregarding decimals.'

G. took a pack of cigarettes from his pocket and offered them around; then he leaned against the backrest of his chair and said, 'What about taking a break?'

But he must have been truly suffering from an irresistible need for activity, for instead of relaxing he went on rummaging through his case, and in no time pulled from it several objects that he arranged on the table before S.

'This is not part of my job: it is a private initiative of mine, a collection that I'm in the habit of carrying around with me. In my opinion, these objects say a lot: they'll help you form an idea on what you are bound to encounter. This, for example, is a ballpoint pen, it costs only fifty lire and with it you can write one hundred thousand words without effort and without making a dirty mess. These are nylon stockings: look how light they are! They are worn for years and can be washed in an instant. This . . . no, this isn't an artifact, it is a skullcap: do you see how thin and strong it is? I do not carry other anatomical specimens with me, because they are rather perishable; but look at this, it is a mitral valve made of plastic – yes, a cardiac valve. A gem, isn't it? and besides, it offers great tranquillity. And this is detergent:

with it you can do a wash in a moment.'

'Excuse me for interrupting,' S. said, 'but would you mind showing me again for a moment one of those last . . . Yes, that one with the Congolese couple, and those others . . . They don't all have the same skin color, am I right? I thought that men were all the same.'

Mr R., who until that moment had remained silent, broke in. 'Basically they are; these are negligible differences without any biological significance. We do not have here with us samples of mixed couples, but they exist in abundance, and they are as fertile as the others, if not more. It is only an . . . an epidermic matter, precisely: a matter of pigmentation. Black skin offers the tissues better protection against the sun's ultraviolet rays and so it is better suited for individuals who live in the tropics. There are also some who are yellow here and there.'

'Oh, I understand. So these are varieties: they are interchangeable, is that right? Like two nuts with the same thread?'

R. and Mrs B. turned to G. hesitantly. G., a bit less jovial than before, said, 'We are not in the habit of depicting everything in rosy tints, nor is that our task. Look, not everything goes smoothly all the time: there have been some problems and there still are. These aren't very serious matters, in most cases everybody lives on his own, or white and blacks crossbreed and the problem ceases to exist. But there are, yes there are, cases of tension, with a few broken windowpanes, perhaps even a few broken bones. After all, not everything on Earth is programmed; a margin of freedom (and thus of unpredictability) does exist; the fabric has a few flaws, we cannot deny it. Taking everything into account, I should say that today it is perhaps better to be born white, but this is a transitory fact; I believe that within a century or two nobody will talk about it any longer.'

'But as you well know it's now that I'm supposed to be born, right?' G. was about to answer, but R. butted in:

'Certainly; if it suits you even tomorrow: the time to prepare the papers. We're no bureaucrats, we don't like things to drag on.'

'No, I'd like to think about it for a while. I'm not all that convinced. I don't like this business of being born different: it can only lead to trouble.'

R. answered in a somewhat resentful tone, 'I know what you're trying to say. But, first of all, the blacks are few, and therefore the probabilities of being born black are scant; furthermore not everybody is born in the zones of friction, so they are a minority within the minority. In short, there is no game without risks, and here the risk is very small.'

S. seemed to be very sensitive on the subject, or perhaps someone had influenced him beforehand: politely, but with decisiveness, he expressed a desire to see something more, the images of some typical situation.

'Gladly,' G. answered, 'everything is here, the beautiful and the less beautiful. We wouldn't be honest if our documentation were not complete, don't you agree? Here, look here: this is a peaceful demonstration . . .; this is an integrated school experiment . . .; this is the crew of a merchant vessel, do you see? they work together . . .'

While G. talked, S. had cautiously approached the case; suddenly, catching the three functionaries by surprise, he seized a photograph that pictured a conflict between blacks and police: there was a close-up of a policeman with his gun drawn. He asked, 'And this? What does this represent?'

Rather irked, G. answered, 'Listen, you shouldn't behave like this, we're doing our job, after all, and you ought to let us work as we see fit. We attach the same importance to objectivity as to success, you must understand us: in that case there are confidential things, documents meant for a completely different purpose. So, you'll forgive me, but the choice is up to us . . . Well, you've already seen it: yes, it is a street confrontation, it happens at times, I told you that we haven't come here to sow illusions. It happens for territorial reasons, or reasons of rank, or pure aggressiveness, as in the entire animal world; it happens less and less, this . . .'

For one instant, the image S. was holding was replaced by another: it showed a gallows platform, a man wearing a hood and a black man hanging.

'. . . This, for instance, hasn't been seen for a while, but it happens, yes it does.'

S. was carefully examining the image: he pointed to a detail and asked, 'And what's this?'

'It's a pistol, that's what it is,' G. answered with a touch of ill temper. 'Look, it's shooting: are you happy now?'

Still between S.'s hands, the image became animated for a moment: the policeman shot and the black escaped stumbling from the frame, then everything stopped again.

'What became of him?' S. asked anxiously.

'Of whom?'

'The one who was here before. The one who was hit, the black.'

'Good heavens! How am I supposed to know? I don't know them all by heart; anyway, you saw it yourself, he left the frame.'

'But is he . . . is he dead?'

Embarrassed and frowning, G. took the image from S.'s hands and put it away without answering him. R. spoke in his place. 'You mustn't be too impressed by a single case, of which furthermore you have gained knowledge in a completely irregular manner. The episode you've seen has a marginal character; such things don't happen every day, or else we'd be in a sorry state. You'll have to admit that, in order to form an opinion, it is much more useful to dwell on general, typical situations: just a moment, please.'

He searched in the case and showed S. three images. In the first, against a serene sky at dusk, one could see a group of young peasant women returning home down a path and singing. In the second, a procession of skiers descending a steep slope lit up by the moon, each of them carrying a burning torch. In the third, one could see the spacious room of a library, in which several young people studied intently; S. paused, to look at it attentively. 'Just a minute, let me see this for a minute. This one is interesting: it's almost like here. They are studying, aren't they?'

'Yes, it would seem so,' G. answered.

'What are they studying?'

'I don't know, but we can find out. Wait.'

One by one the various students were focused on within the picture and successively enlarged, so that it was possible to distinguish the books each had in front of him. Although there was no need to, G. commented. 'This one, for instance, studies architecture. This girl is preparing for an examination on theoretical physics. This other one . . . wait, let us look at him a bit more closely: we can't make it out too well this way . . . you know, when there aren't any illustrations it's more difficult. There: he's studying philosophy, actually the history of philosophy.'

'Oh. And what happens to him afterward?'

'After what?'

'After he's finished studying; or does he study all his life long?'

'I don't know that either. I told you, it's already quite surprising if we manage to remember all the images we carry with us: how can you expect that just like that, at a moment's notice, we should be able to tell the why and wherefore, the before and after, the causes and the effects of our entire catalogue?'

S. was showing himself for what he was: a well-mannered but hardheaded young man. He politely insisted. 'Why don't you get him to move? As you did before?'

'If you really care that much I can try,' G. answered.

Within the square the image became confused or disintegrated into a swarm of tiny spots and colored lines, which shortly after coagulated into a new figure: the ex-student was sitting behind the window of a post office. 'One year later,' said G.; there followed a renewed swarming, G. said, 'Two years later,' and the same image became visible from a slightly different angle. Ten years later the ex-student wore eyeglasses, but the scene was substantially the same. Thirty years later you still saw the post office, and the ex-student's hair was white.

'Obviously he lacks initiative,' G. remarked. 'But let me tell you as a friend, you're a bit too distrustful. We'd be in real trouble if everyone was like you!' But perhaps he was joking, because in his voice one could perceive more admiration than reproach.

'But you must understand me, after all,' S. answered. 'The choice is up to me, and I would like to know what I'm doing. Therefore, don't take offense, but I would like to see the afterward of . . . there, also of this one.'

He had again picked up the photograph of the library, and he was pointing to another reader. 'Let's see,' G. said. 'Here he is two years later.'

The reader sat in a comfortable armchair with a lamp overhead: he was reading. 'Here he is, four years later . . . no, forgive me, five years later.'

The reader, changed very little, sat at a table facing a young woman; between the two, on a small chair, was a child with a spoon in his hand. 'An attractive family, isn't it?' G. remarked with satisfaction. 'This is seven years later,' he then announced.

As though the mechanism had escaped G.'s control, in the frame various scenes appeared in rapid succession:

The reader was in uniform: saying good-bye to his wife, who was crying.

The reader was boarding a military airplane.

A festoon of parachutes detached itself from the airplane.

The reader, with his tommy gun pointed downward, was landing.

The reader had landed on a dark plain: he was behind a boulder, in ambush.

The reader had been hit: a black stain was spreading underneath him.

A rough wooden cross on a mound of earth.

'This . . . this is war, isn't it?' S. asked after a moment's silence. G., very embarrassed, didn't say a word; R. answered:

'Yes, we know, there's a lot of talk about it, but I'd like to warn you about certain platitudes. First of all, keep this in mind, it's not at all proven that war is rooted in the human species, that it is written in the destiny of all countries, of all epochs and all individuals. Precisely during this period, we are experiencing a very well put together peace plan, based on the balance of fears and aggressive potentialities: well, it's been working for twenty-five years in a manner which, when all is said and done, is quite satisfactory; we've had only half a dozen small, peripheral wars. Nothing of this kind has been seen for many centuries; the pictures you've looked at could by now have only . . . ahem, a retrospective value, and the second golden age may already have begun in silence, furtively. Besides, I should like to remind you that war isn't always an evil, or rather an evil for everyone. We've heard about several of our clients who have survived the last conflict not only in good health and without damages, but also making quite a bit of money out of it . . .'

Here G. cleared his throat, as if to interrupt, but R. didn't notice and went on.

'. . . Others have become famous and esteemed, and others yet, actually the greater part of humanity, weren't even aware of it.'

'In short,' G. intervened, 'I don't think there is any reason to dramatize. Think about it for a moment: what are fifty million dead when you have a population of three billion? Life, you must understand, life is a single fabric, even though it has a right and a wrong side; it has bright days and dark days, it is an interweaving of defeats and victories, but it pays for itself, it is an inestimable good. I know very well that you up here have a tendency to pose all questions on a cosmic scale, but once on Earth you will be individuals, you will have one head, which besides is different from all others, and one skin, and you'll become aware of a great difference between what is inside the skin and what is outside. I, you must realize, have no arguments to prove which of the two is right, the nonborn or the born, but one thing I can affirm from personal experience: anyone who has tasted the fruit of life can no longer go without it. The born, all the born, with very few exceptions, cling to life with a tenacity that surprises even us propagandists, and which is the best praise of life itself. They don't let it go as long as they have breath in their body: it is a unique spectacle. Look.'

He showed S. the image of a miner wounded and in rags, who was opening a passage with his pickaxe in a collapsed tunnel.

'This man was alone, wounded, starved, cut off from the world, plunged in darkness. It would have been easy for him to die: for him it would have been nothing but passing from one darkness to another darkness. He did not even know in what direction he might find salvation; but he dug at random, for twelve days, and saw the light again. And this other one, whom you see here? This is a famous case, agreed, but how many others would not have acted as he did, young or old, men or women, if only they had the technical abilities? His name was Robinson Crusoe: he lived in solitude for twenty-eight years without ever losing hope and the joy of life; he was rescued, and being a sailor he went back to sea. Now this is a less dramatic, but much more general case.'

The image was subdivided into four squares. In it one saw, respectively, a man in a dusty, dimly lit office in front of a pile of forms, all the same; the same man at a table, with a newspaper resting against a bottle, while in the background his wife telephoned and turned her back to him; the same man in front of the door of his house, heading for work on foot, while his son left on a motor bike with a flashy girl; the same man in the evening, alone, looking bored in front of the TV set. Unlike all the others these figures were static; they did not even vibrate.

'The man you see,' G. resumed, 'is forty years old here: his daily work is an immutable well of boredom, his wife despises him and probably loves someone else, his children are grown up and look at him without seeing him. And yet he endures, and he will endure for a long time, like a rock: every day he will wait for its tomorrow, every day he will hear a voice that for tomorrow promises him something beautiful, great and new. Go ahead, take this,' he adds, addressing R., 'put them away, please.'

S. was perplexed. 'But you'll have to admit, someone who's born sick, or from undernourished parents . . .'

R. intervened in a didactic manner. 'If you're alluding to the problem of hunger, you should realize that it has been vastly exaggerated. That a good part of the human species is acquainted with hunger may even be true, but it is not true that they die from it. You certainly understand that in order to live one must eat, and that in order to eat one must desire food: now, what is hunger if not a desire for food? It is not at all proven that satiety is good: mice allowed to eat at will have a briefer life that those kept to a controlled diet – these are irrefutable facts.'

While R. was speaking, G. had risen to his feet and was pacing up and down in the small room; then he halted and said to his colleagues, 'Would you leave the room for a moment, please? I would like to speak to this gentleman alone for two minutes.' Then he addressed S. in a low, confidential voice, and continued, 'I think that you've sensed this: someone somewhere has made a mistake, and the terrestrial plans present a fault, a procedural error. For about forty years they pretended they didn't notice, but now too many problems are coming to the surface, and we cannot wait any longer; we must find remedies, and we need people like you. Are you surprised? I did not reveal this at the beginning, because I didn't know you yet and I wanted to verify certain things, but now I can tell you: we did not come to you as we go to everyone else, we did not show up here by chance. You were singled out to us.'

'I was?'

'Yes. We have an urgent need for serious, prepared people, honest and courageous: that's why we've persisted, and are still persisting. We are not interested in quantity but in quality.'

'Am I to understand then that . . . I'll not be born just at random, that my fate is already set down, as in a book?'

'Actually written page for page, with all the details worked out? – no, I can't affirm that: you know, we believe in free will, or at least we are expected to behave as though we believe in it, and therefore, for our purposes, every man is to a great extent exposed to chance and to the consequences of his own actions; but we can offer you excellent possibilities, give you good initial advantages, that we can do. Would you like to take a look? . . . This is you, you see? We will give you a limber, healthy body and we will place you in fascinating surroundings: in these silent places the world of tomorrow is being built, or the world of yesterday is being scrutinized, with new and marvelous instruments. And this is you again, here where wrongs are set aright and justice is done swiftly and at no expense. Or also here, where pain is assuaged and life is made more tolerable, safer and longer. The true masters are these, they are you: not the heads of state or the chiefs of armies.

'And now that we are alone, I can, indeed I must, show you the rest also, the confidential material, the material that you, and rightly so, tried to tear from my hands several times.'

These images required no comments, nor the flattery of living movement: they spoke in extremely clear language. One could see a multiple cannon shoot into darkness, lighting up with its glare collapsed houses and factories in ruins; then mounds of skeletal corpses at the foot of a bonfire, within a gloomy frame of smoke and barbed wire; then a hut made of cane beneath a tropical rain and inside on the bare earthen floor a child dying; then a squalid expanse of uncultivated fields reduced to swamp, and of forests without leaves; then a village, and an entire valley, invaded and buried by a gigantic tide of mud. There were many others, but G. pushed them aside and went on:

'You see? There are still many things that need to be put aright; but none of these sufferings will be for you. You will not have to undergo evil like a passive object: you, and many with you, will be called to fight it in all of its forms. You will receive, together with your human guise, the weapons that you will need, powerful and subtle weapons: reason, compassion, patience, courage. You will not be born as everyone else is born: the life before you will be smoothed out, so that your good qualities will not be wasted. You will be one of us, called to finish the work that was begun billions of years ago, when a certain fiery sphere exploded, and the pendulum of time began to beat. You will not die: when you put aside your human costume, you will join us and become a hunter of souls like us – provided that you'll be satisfied with a modest commission, besides the reimbursment of all expenses.

'There, I've finished. I wish you good luck in your choice and afterward. Think about it, and give me an answer.' Having said this, G. put away the last images in the case and closed it.

S. was silent for a long time: so long that G. was on the point of prodding him for an answer; finally he said, 'I wouldn't like to set out with an advantage. I'm afraid I would feel like a profiteer, and I would have to bow my head throughout my life before each of my unprivileged companions. I accept, but I would like to be born at random, like everyone: among billions of beings to be born without a fate, among the predestined to servitude or contention from the cradle on, if in fact they have a cradle. I prefer to be born black, Indian, poor, without indulgences and without pardons. You understand me, don't you? You yourself said that each man is his own maker: well, it is best to be so fully, build oneself from the roots. I prefer to be the only one to fabricate myself, and I prefer the anger that I will need if I will be capable of it; if not, I will accept everyone else's destiny. The path of defenseless and blind humanity will be mine.'

Small Red Lights

His was a quiet job: he had to spend eight hours a day in a dark room, in which at regular intervals the small red lights of the indicators lit up. What they meant he didn't know, and this was not part of his task. He had to react to each flash by pushing certain buttons, but he did not know the meaning of these either; nevertheless, his job was not mechanical, he had to choose the buttons rapidly and on the basis of complex criteria, which varied from day to day, and furthermore were determined by the order and rhythm with which the lights went on. In short, it was not stupid work, it was work that could be performed well or badly; sometimes it was also quite interesting, one of those jobs that offer an opportunity to be pleased with one's promptness, inventiveness and logic. But of the ultimate effect of his actions he had no precise idea; he only knew that there were hundreds of dark rooms, and that all decisional data converged somewhere, in a selection center. He also knew that somehow or other his work was judged, but he did not know whether singly or cumulatively with the work of the others: when the siren sounded other red bulbs lit up on the lintel of the door, and their number was both a judgment and a summary. Often seven or eight of them would light up; ten had lit up only once and never less than five, so he was under the impression that things weren't going too badly.

The siren sounded, seven bulbs lit up. He went outside, and stopped for a minute in the hallway to accustom his eyes to the light, then he descended to the street, got into his car and started the engine. Traffic was already very heavy, and he found it difficult to enter the flow that traveled down the avenue. Brakes, gear, shift to first. Gas, gear, second, gas, brakes, first, brakes again, the light is red. It's forty seconds and it seems forty years, who knows why: there is no longer time than the time spent at traffic lights. He had no other hope or desire than that of getting home.

Ten traffic lights, twenty. At each one an ever longer line, three reds long, five reds long; then a little better, the traffic more fluid on the outside lane. You look in the rearview mirror, to confront briefly the anger and malicious impatience on the face of the fellow who's behind you and wishes you weren't there; then signal left; when you turn left you always feel a bit guilty. You turn left, cautiously: there's the door, there's a free space, shift, brakes, ignition key, hand brake, burglar alarm, for today it's over.

The small red light of the elevator gleams: wait till it's free. It goes off: press the button, the small light goes on again, wait till it comes down. To wait half of one's leisure time, is that leisure time? In the end the lights of the third, second and first floor lit up in the correct order, the word PRESENT flashed on and the door opened. Again small red lights, first, second, all the way to the ninth floor, here we are. He pressed the doorbell, no need to wait here: he waited very little in fact, heard Maria's placid voice say 'Coming,' her footsteps, then the door opened.

He was not surprised to see the small light lit up between Maria's clavicles, it had been burning for six days now, and it was to be expected that its melancholy light would shine for a few more days. Luigi would have liked Maria to hide it, to mask it somehow; Maria said she would, but often she forgot about it, especially at home; or at other times she didn't hide it well and one could see it glimmer under her scarf, or at night through the sheets, and that was the saddest thing. Perhaps, deep down and without admitting it even to herself, she was afraid of the inspections.

He made an effort not to look at the bulb, indeed, to forget it: at bottom he also asked other things of Maria, many other things. He tried to talk about his job, about how he had spent the day; he asked her about herself, about her hours of solitude, but the conversation did not take on life, it flashed for a moment and then was doused, like a fire made with damp wood. But the small light was different: it shone firmly and constantly, the most burdensome of prohibitions because it was there, in their house and in everyone's, minuscule yet stable like a barrier, on all fertile days, erected between every married couple that already had two children. Luigi kept silent for a long time, and then he said, 'I'll . . . I'll go and get the screwdriver.'

'No,' Maria said, 'you know we can't, it always leaves a mark. And besides . . . what if a baby were to be born afterward? We already have two, don't you know how much they would tax us for it?'

It was clear that once again they would not be able to speak of anything else. Maria said, 'Do you know Mrs Mancuso? You remember, don't you? – the lady who lives below, the elegant one, on the seventh floor? Well, she's made an application to exchange the Government model with the new IBM 520: she says it's something else altogether.'

'But it costs an arm and a leg, and the calculation is the same anyway.'

'Sure, but you don't even know you're wearing it, and the batteries last a year. And she's also told me that in Parliament there's a subcommittee that's discussing a model for men.'

'What nonsense! With men the red light would always be on.'

'Oh no, it's not that simple. The woman is always the guide, and she too wears the light, but the locking device is worn also by the man. There's a transmitter, the wife transmits and the husband receives, and during the red days it remains blocked. After all, it seems only right: it seems much more moral.'

Luigi suddenly felt submerged by weariness. He kissed Maria, left her in front of the TV and went to bed. He had no trouble falling asleep, but in the morning he woke up long before the red indicator of the silent alarm clock lit up. He got out of bed and only then, in the dark room, did he notice that Maria's light had gone out: but by now it was too late, and he didn't like to wake her up. He checked the red indicator of the water heater, and those of the electric razor, the toaster, and the security lock; then he went down into the street, got into his car and watched the red indicators of the generator and hand brake light up. He activated the left blinker, which meant that a new day was beginning. He headed for work, and along the way he calculated that the red lights of one of his days came on the average to about two hundred; seventy thousand in one year, three and a half million in fifty years of active life. At that it then seemed to him that the top of his cranium was hardening, as though covered by an enormous callus, excellent for being beaten against walls, almost the horn of a rhinoceros, but flatter and more obtuse.

For a Good Purpose

Anyone who has to punish himself finds opportunities everywhere. Masoero, the engineer, opened his newspaper and felt overcome by disgust: once again, on the second page, the usual mawkish ironic item, which denounced the inefficiency, the always busy long-distance lines, the poor acoustic quality of the connections. The truth, he knew, the gospel truth: but what in the name of heaven could he do about it? So he was district manager, but if funds are lacking, or they are there but allotted for other work; and if the Ministry, instead of giving you a hand, inundates you with prolix, futile and contradictory memos, what can you do? Just about nothing: you go to the office full of poison, ask the heads of the various branches to report to you, the head of new installations, the head of preventive maintenance and the head of repairs, all fine people, and you give them a lecture, and when they leave you know very well that as soon as they're outside the door, they'll shrug their shoulders, and everything will remain the same as before, and you will feel as miserable as ever.

He prepared to write a forceful report for the Ministry; it wasn't the first, but a nail doesn't go in at the first blow of the hammer. Who could say whether, by dint of banging away, they wouldn't end up listening to him? This is how he spent the day: he finished the report, reread it, cut out a few too virulent adjectives, and handed the manuscript to the typist.

The next day he found on his desk not one but two memos from the Complaints Office. No doubt about it, they had been written by Rostagno, two doors down: it was his style, precise, circumstantiated and nasty. This time, however, instead of the usual customers' generic complaints, two mint-new problems were being reported with unusual anecdotal abundance. In the first memo it was said that various subscribers when lifting the receiver had heard for hours on end a musical program broadcast by a radio station, and had not been able to get a line in or out. The second memo described the disappointment and astonishment of other subscribers, about fifty of them, who had dialed some number or other of the network, and instead were obstinately answered always by the same wrong number, precisely the number of someone with whom they habitually exchanged long and frequent calls: the number of their in-laws or their fiancée or their branch office or the kid who shared their son's bench at school.

Well, the first complaint wasn't catastrophic: it didn't seem too difficult to be handled. But as for the second, Masocro read it, reread it, and became convinced that there was something behind it. Rostagno was a pirate. He'd been expecting a promotion for some time, and it would not have been incredible if he had chosen that method to step into his shoes. He meant to provoke him: force him to take useless measures, trip him up. Because a telephone network isn't a simple thing, everyone knows that; it breaks down easily, is sensitive to wind, rain, and freezing temperatures, is subject to certain illnesses—but they are few, well known, and above all plausible: that illness instead was an impossible one. He put away the two memos and turned his mind to something else.

But that very evening Silvia, quite offhandedly, told him that all day long she had not been able to telephone the greengrocer, nor her hairdresser, nor Lidia, not even himself at the office: the only number that had answered was her mother's, to whom, as a matter of fact, she had nothing to say that day. He realized that Silvia had not the least intention of wounding him with that remark, which at any rate had been enunciated in a careless, jaunty tone;

yet he couldn't help thinking that his wife knew him quite well, knew that he had a difficult character, and that he cared a lot about his work; or, more precisely, that he didn't care all that much, but that being caught in error under whatever circumstances, and especially on the job, stung him like a burn and kept him awake at night. In short, Silvia might have spared him that displeasure; he already had so many, telephonic and otherwise.

So then it meant that Rostagno hadn't made up the whole thing; never mind, he was a pirate all the same, a malingerer. As he thought about it, that memo seemed to him a distillate of viciousness, every line full of *Schadenfreude*. A dishonestly ambitious man, a social climber, that's what he was: he was at his proper place in a Complaints Office, because he was the kind of person who lives by catching other people in mistakes, feeds on his neighbors' mistakes, and prospers on their troubles, and enjoys their miseries. He took two tranquilizers and went to sleep.

Twenty days passed and a third memo arrived. This time, Masoero thought, it was quite clear that Rostagno had fun writing it: more than an office document it was a lyric, a ballad. It was a case history of dialing errors: apparently, thousands of subscribers had complained, in the first place because the number of errors was abnormally high, and in the second because the nature of these errors was irritating. Irritating above all for him, Masoero, but Rostagno seemed to gloat over them; he had gone to the trouble of compiling a long tabulation in three columns: the first contained calling numbers, the second the numbers called, the third the numbers that had answered instead of those called. Between the first and second columns there obviously existed no correlation. But Rostagno pointed out (and, damn it, rightly so!) that there was a correlation between the first and third columns. That was all: Rostagno did not formulate explanatory hypotheses, he confined himself to indicating a curious regularity. Nevertheless, when he was through reading, Masoero felt the blood rise to his head from anger, and immediately after from shame at having experienced anger: he mustn't, he forbade himself to entertain such abject envy and jealousy. If your neighbor makes an ingenious discovery (by chance, by chance, a tiny voice hissed inside him) you must recognize his merits and admire him, instead of foaming with rage and hating him. He did his best to get hold of himself; but, damn it, that fellow beyond the wall, ingenious as you please, was building a reputation based precisely on the errors and failings or rather the misfortunes of himself, Masoero – from any angle, that's how it is, what's your poison is his food, they are all steps to his ascent, to his catching up with you and taking your place. He touched the armchair on which he was sitting, which never seemed to have meant anything special to him, and it suddenly felt like a part of his body, upholstered with his own skin: if they were to tear it away from him it would have been tantamount to flaying him, he would die in atrocious torment. And if later on someone else were to be installed in it, especially Rostagno, it would be as though the fellow had crept into his conjugal bed. He thought about it seriously, trying to be honest with himself, and he concluded that it would be even worse. Too bad, but that was how he was, and he couldn't change, and he didn't want to either: like it or not, he was too old to move, he could if necessary feel ashamed, but he could not be different.

In any case, go on raving, scramble, limp along, but the memo lies there in front of you, it is an official act and you must drain the cup, there's no way out. Rostagno had noticed that between the calling numbers and the numbers that had answered there was a correlation: extremely simple in some instances, less obvious in others. At times the two numbers differed only by one unit plus or minus: 693 177 had been unduly answered by 693 178 or 693 176. At other times the second number was a multiple of the first, or was the first read backward; and at others yet, the two numbers added up to 1,000,000. In fifteen instances out of the 518 studied, one number was with fine approximation the natural logarithm of the other; in four instances their product, less decimals, was a power of 10; in only seven instances it hadn't been possible to establish any correlation, and the seven that hadn't been clarified were the last ones called.

Masoero felt he was on the ropes. One could sense, also from the fluent, satisfied style of the brief comment accompanying the table, that Rostagno was not sitting on his hands. He had made a brilliant observation, but he was not the kind of person to be content and rest on his laurels: indeed, as he attentively reread the concluding sentence, it seemed to Masoero that in it he detected a barb, an attack; perhaps Rostagno was already preparing a diagnosis, if not actually a therapy.

It was definitely time for him, Masoero, to wake up. He could do one of two things: throw himself into pursuit and try to beat him to the punch, or summon him into his office and get him to talk, in the hope of getting him to put his cards on the table, possibly against his will or without his knowledge. Rostagno was a better technician than he, but he wasn't born yesterday either, and during a career of twenty-four years he had after all learned a thing or two, not only pertaining to the theory of communications. He thought about it again, and discarded the second choice. Did he love his armchair? Did he want to hold on to it? Well, he had all that was needed: time, brains, archives, rank, an old and accepted authority that could be used as the basis for operations and as a stake in the gamble to remain on target. Rostagno had the advantage of being the first to receive the daily reports on complaints, but the time had come to find a remedy. Take heart, man, strip for action: hit above or below the belt, any old way. He dictated a memo with precise instructions to send the daily reports to him personally: all of them, from all sections. This is how we'll begin, then we'll see.

He picked up the inside telephone, told his secretary not to disturb him except for important matters, and set himself to meditate for a few days. He could already hear the huge hypocritical question ring in his ears, the question that comes from above, from someone who has by now interposed a solid desk between orders and their execution, the question so easy to formulate and so difficult to answer: 'What on earth did you change? What's been done that's new? Why did everything work well until two months ago?'

What's been done that's new? Nothing and everything, as usual. The supplier of one-millimeter cable was changed, because his deliveries were late. The shape of the 12–22 panels had been changed due to standardization. Three of the zone assembly men go to work in the factory, earn more and aren't exposed to the cold. The tolerances of carrying frequency were changed, but you gave orders to do that, Mr General Director, sir. And so, my dear General Director, sir, you can go on saying don't rock the boat, but if you don't change you don't live, and if you change you make a mistake. Be patient, sir, and let's see where we went wrong. Suddenly, it occurred to him that the most conspicuous change was the one that had been planned for many years and realized three months earlier: the merger of the long-distance network with the German and French networks, and so, potentially, the establishment of a single network that took in all of Europe. Could that be relevant? And here the most obvious of questions came to his mind: how were things going in the other districts, in Italy and Europe? Was everything in good health?

Three days later Masoero felt like a different man: perhaps uniquely in the history of telecommunications, from a total of tens of thousands of accidents a felicitous result was born. Not the solution, not yet: but a broader and better-defined picture, and above all a nice quail hop over Rostagno's head. Yes, Mr General Director, it's not that things are going well, but they're going badly everywhere in the same way, from Cape North to Crete, and from Lisbon to Moscow: it's the same illness everywhere. The undersigned, if it please your Honor, has nothing whatever to do with it, or is not involved at all, or is involved only because in his district the problem was identified and described before the others did so. The merger of the networks is involved and it isn't, we don't know, but it was part of the plan and in any case what's done is done: what's urgent now is to compile a handsome report, have it translated and distributed to all the capitals with which we are connected.

There followed a period of complicated, anguished accusations and counteraccusations: each of the connected countries rejected every charge of inefficiency and blamed another country, almost always the one on its borders. It was decided to convene a congress and a date was set, but it immediately had to be postponed until further notice due to a new wave of disturbances. Suddenly throughout Europe a high number of 'blank calls' were recorded: two pieces of equipment often in different countries rang simultaneously and the two subscribers were connected without either one's having called. In the few cases in which language differences brought about the beginning of a conversation, the two people usually learned from each other that their numbers were the same, except of course for the prefix. This fact was confirmed by surveys initiated at headquarters, which showed that when the numbers were the same, they were linked by one of the correlations that had been pointed out in Rostagno's second memo. Strangely, people began to talk about Masoero and Rostagno in the same breath: about the first for having highlighted the European character of the malfunction, about the second for having described its characteristics; from this pairing Masoero derived at once unease and satisfaction.

It seemed to him that by now the sting of company jealously had lost its poison, when, suddenly, with the morning paper he felt it penetrate his flesh as burning and brutal as never before. The monster had given an interview! Masoero gulped down the article two, then three times, flabbergasted at first, then furiously searching for the weak point, the crime, the divulgence of office documents; but he'd been skillful, that fellow, there wasn't a single sentence that could be incriminating. He had known how to deliver the haymaker with painstaking cleverness, outside the bureaucratic maze, with elegance, simplicity, and under the guise of a hypothesis: but it was a fulminating hypothesis.

Vague in its mathematical treatment, which for the rest was barely hinted at in the interview, the explanation that Rostagno proposed was simple: by its extension to all of Europe, the telephonic network had surpassed in complexity all the installations realized until then, including those in North America, and had without transition reached such a numerical volume that it behaved as a nerve center. Not like a brain, of course – or at least not like an intelligent brain; nevertheless, it was able to make some elementary choices, and to exert a minuscule will. But Rostagno did not stop at that. He had asked himself (actually he had gotten them to ask him) what the choice and will of the Network were, and he had advanced the hypothesis that the Network was animated by substantially good will; i.e., that, in the abrupt leap by which quantity becomes quality, or (in this case) in which the brute entanglement of cables and selectors becomes organism and consciousness, the Network had preserved all and only the purposes for which it had been created; in the same manner in which a superior animal, even though acquiring new faculties, preserves all the purposes of its simpler precursors (to remain alive, avoid pain, reproduce), the Network in crossing the threshold of consciousness, or perhaps only that of autonomy, had not rejected the original aims for which it had been planned – to permit, facilitate and accelerate communications among subscribers. This exigency must be a moral imperative for it, a 'reason for being,' or even an obsession.

To 'cause communication' one could follow, or at least attempt, various paths, and the Network seemed to have tried them all. Naturally, it did not possess the patrimony of information needed to connect unknown individuals apt to become friends or lovers or business partners, because it knew their individual characteristics only through their brief and sporadic communications: it knew only their telephone numbers, and seemed anxious to put numbers somehow correlated with one another in contact – and this was the single type of affinity it knew. It had pursued its aim at first by 'errors,' then through the artifice of blank calls.

In sum, according to Rostagno, in a certain inefficient and rudimentary manner there was a mind moving the mass; unfortunately the mind was infirm and the mass boundless, and thus the qualitative leap for the moment turned into a frightful accumulation of failures and disturbances – but undoubtedly the Network was 'good': one mustn't forget that it had initiated its autonomous life by administering cabled music (certainly good music in its judgment) even to the subscriber who didn't request it. Without insisting on a preferable approach, whether electronic, or neurological, or pedagogical, or fully rational, Rostagno maintained that it would be possible to harness the Network's new capacity. It would be possible to teach it a certain selectivity; for instance, once it was supplied with the necessary information, it would be able to change into a vast and speedy human relations organism, a sort of huge agency which through new 'errors' or blank calls could supplant all the personal ads in all the newspapers of Europe, combining with lightning speed sales, marriages, commercial agreements and human relations of all sorts. Rostagno stressed that something different and better than what a computer can do would thus be obtained: the Network's kind temperament would have spontaneously favored the deals most advantageous to the general run of subscribers and discarded insidious or deciduous propositions.

Masoero's and Rostagno's offices were a few meters apart; they respected each other and at the same time they detested each other, they did not say hello when they met in the hallway and they carefully avoided any meetings. One morning both their telephones rang simultaneously. It was a blank call: each of them was surprised and irritated at hearing the other's voice in the earpiece. They understood, almost at the same time, that the Network had remembered them with gratitude perhaps, and was trying to reestablish between them the human contact that had been missing for too long. Masoero felt absurdly moved, and thus inclined to surrender; a few moments later they were shaking hands in the hallway, and a few minutes later yet they were together at the bar in front of an aperitif, and observing that they could have lived better by joining forces instead of wasting them against one another, as they had done until then.

Indeed other problems were pressing: during recent months various services of New Installations had signaled an absurd condition. Several crews had noticed the presence of stretches of line that did not exist on any of the local maps, and had never even been planned: they departed from functioning trunk lines, and extended like plant stolons toward small population centers not yet connected to the Network. For several weeks they were unable to discover how this growth took place, and Masoero and Rostagno had already racked their brains for many hours over the subject, when they received an interoffice report from the Pescara district. Matters were much simpler: a rural constable had by chance noticed an assembly crew stretching an aerial line. When questioned, they had answered that they had received over the phone the order to do this, along with instructions to obtain the necessary materials from the area warehouse; the warehouse manager in turn had received telephone orders to release the material. Both the assembly crew and the warehouse manager declared themselves somewhat surprised at the unusual procedure; on the other hand, they were not in the habit of discussing orders. Was the voice that had given the instructions that of the section head? Were they certain? Yes, it was, they knew it well; it just had a slightly metallic ring.

At the beginning of July, things came to a head: the new incidents accumulated at such a pace that the two new friends were overcome, and with them all the other specialists who followed the situation in Europe. It seemed that now the Network intended to control not only some but all communications. By now it spoke fluently all the official languages and various dialects, evidently drawing vocabulary, syntax and inflections from the innumerable conversations that it intercepted incessantly. It would butt in to give unasked-for advice even on the most intimate and confidential subjects; it repeated to third parties data and facts it had casually learned; it tactlessly encouraged the shy, reproached the violent and those who cursed, gave the lie to liars, praised the generous, laughed uproariously at jokes, cut off communications without warning when they seemed to degenerate into altercations.

By the end of July, the violations of the telephonic confidentiality had become the rule rather than the exception; every European who dialed a number felt he was on public display, no one was sure any longer that his equipment, even after a call was interrupted, did not continue to eavesdrop, making his private affairs part of a complex and gigantic stream of gossip.

'What shall we do?' Rostagno said to Masoero. Masoero had thought about it at length and made a simple, sensible suggestion. 'Let's make a deal; we have a right to, don't you think? We were the first to understand it. We'll talk to it, and we'll tell it that if it doesn't stop it will be punished.'

'Do you think . . . that it can feel pain?'

'I don't think anything: I believe that it is essentially a simulator of average human behavior, and if that is so, it will imitate men also in showing itself sensitive to threats.'

Without further ado, Masoero lifted the receiver and instead of the expected signal he heard the well-known metallic voice declaiming proverbs and moral maxims: that's what the Network had been doing for three or four days. He did not dial any number but shouted 'Hello!' until the Network answered; then he began to speak. He spoke at length: in a stern and persuasive tone he said that the situation was intolerable and that numerous cancellations had already been recorded, something that the Network itself obviously could not be unaware of; that interventions in private conversations were detrimental to the service, besides being morally inadmissible; and that, finally, if the Network did not immediately suspend all arbitrary initiatives, all the European central stations would at the same time hit its body with twenty-five high-tension and frequency impulses. Then he hung up.

'Aren't you waiting for an answer?' Rostagno asked.

'No: perhaps it's best to wait a few minutes.'

But no answer came, then or later. After about half an hour the bell on the apparatus gave a long convulsive ring, but no sound came from it when the receiver was lifted; that same day they learned, from telex and radio, that all of Europe's telephones, approximately a hundred million, had rung and gone mute at the same instant. The paralysis was complete and lasted several weeks: the emergency crews who had immediately been sent out found that all the lead contacts in the contact boxes were fused and that in all coaxial cables there had appeared conspicuous perforations of the dialectrics, both internal and peripheral.

Psychophant

We are a rather exclusive group of friends. We are men and women tied by a bond that is serious and profound, yet old and rarely renewed, a bond that consists in having lived through important years together, and having lived them without too many weaknesses. Since then, as often happens, our paths have diverged, some of us have made compromises, some have wounded each other intentionally or not, some have forgotten how to speak or lost their antennae. Nevertheless, we enjoy getting together: we trust each other, we respect one another, and whatever subject we may be discussing, we realize with joy that despite everything we still speak the same language (some call it a jargon), even though our opinions don't always coincide. Our children show a precocious tendency to move away from us, but they are bound among themselves by a friendship similar to ours, and this seems to us strange and beautiful, because it happens spontaneously, without our having meddled. Now they constitute a group that in many aspects reproduces our group when we were their age.

We profess to be open, universalist, cosmopolitans; we feel like this in our innermost beings, and we despise intensely all forms of segregation due to wealth, caste or race. And yet, in actuality, our group is so close that, even though it is generally held in esteem by the 'others', over the course of thirty years it has accepted only a few recruits. For reasons that I find difficult to explain to myself, and of which in any case I am not proud, it would seem unnatural to us to welcome someone who lives north of Corso Regina Margherita or west of Corso Raconigi. Not all of us who have married have seen our spouses accepted; in general the endogamous couples, who are not few, seem to be favored. Every now and then, someone makes an outside friend and brings him along, but it is rare for this friend to become part of the group; most often, he's invited once, twice, and treated benevolently, but the next time he's not there, and the evening is devoted to studying, discussing, and classifying him.

There was a time when each of us would occasionally invite all the others to visit. When the children were born, some of us moved to the country, others had their parents living in their home and did not want to disturb them, so at present, there's only Tina who has people in. Tina likes to have people in, and so she does it well; she has good wine and excellent stuff to eat, she's lively and curious, she always has new things to tell and she tells them gracefully, she knows how to put people at their ease, she's interested in other people's affairs and remembers them with precision, she judges with severity but is fond of almost everyone. She is suspected of entertaining relations with other groups, but she (and only she) is willingly forgiven for this infidelity.

The bell rang and Alberto entered, late as usual. When Alberto enters a house the light seems to grow brighter: everybody feels in a better mood, and in better health too, because Alberto is one of those doctors who can heal patients simply by looking at them and talking with them. From patients who are friends (and few people in this world have as many friends as Alberto) he does not accept payment, and therefore every Christmas he receives an avalanche of presents. That evening in fact he had just received a gift, but different from the customary bottles of precious rare wines and the usual useless accessories for his car: it was a curious present, one he couldn't wait to try out, and he had decided to inaugurate it with us, because apparently it was a sort of parlor game.

Tina did not say no, but you could easily tell that she wasn't fond of the idea; perhaps she felt her authority threatened, and feared that the reins of the evening might slip from her hands. But it is difficult to resist Alberto's wishes, which are quite numerous, unpredictable, amusing and compelling: when Alberto wants something (and this happens every fifteen minutes), he manages in an instant to get everyone else to want it, and so he always moves at the head of a swarm of followers. He takes them to eat snails at midnight, or to ski on the Breithorn, or to see a risqué film, or to visit Greece in the mid-August holidays, or to drink at his house while Miranda is asleep, or to call on someone who isn't at all expecting it but welcomes him with open arms all the same, him and all his friends, and the other men or women he has picked up on the way.

Alberto said that in the box there was an instrument called a Psychophant and that confronted by a name like that there could be no hesitation.

In the blink of an eye, a table was cleared, we all sat down around it, and Alberto opened the box. From it he extracted a broad, flat object formed by a rectangular tray of transparent plastic that rested on a black enameled metal base; this base projected approximately thirty centimeters beyond one of the short sides of the tray, and on the projection was a shallow mold in the shape of a left hand. There was an electric wire with a plug; we inserted it in the socket, and while the apparatus was warming up, Alberto read aloud the instructions. They were very vague and written in abominable Italian, but in substance they told us that the game, or pastime, consisted in putting one's left hand into the mold: on the tray would then appear what the instructions clumsily defined as the players' 'inner image.'

Tina laughed 'It's probably like those tiny cellophane fish they used to sell before the war: you put them on the palm of your hand, and depending on whether they rolled up or vibrated or fell to the floor, they could tell your character. Or the same as doing "he loves me, he loves me not" with a daisy.' Miranda said that if this was the case she would take the veil rather than put her hand in the mold. Others said other things, there were noisy exchanges. I said that if you wanted to see cheap miracles, you might as well go down to the fair on Piazza Vittoria; however, some people competed for the first try, others designated this or that person to do it, and this or that person refused with various excuses. Little by little the victory went to the party who proposed to send Alberto on reconnaissance. Alberto was delighted: he settled in front of the apparatus, put his left hand in the mold, and pressed a button with his right.

There was a sudden silence. At first a small, round, orange spot like the yolk of an egg formed on the tray. Then it swelled, stretched upward, and the upper extremity dilated, taking on the appearance of the cap of a mushroom; spread over its entire surface there appeared many small polygonal spots, some emerald green, some scarlet, some gray. The mushroom grew rapidly, and when it was about a hand's breadth tall it became weakly luminous, as though inside it had a small flame that pulsed rhythmically: it emitted an agreeable but pungent odor similar to the scent of cinnamon.

Alberto removed his finger from the button, and at that the pulsation stopped, and the luminescence slowly dimmed. We were uncertain as to whether we could touch the object or not; Anna said it was better not to do so, because it would certainly dissolve right away – indeed, perhaps it didn't even exist, was a purely sensory illusion, like a dream, or a collective hallucination. There was nothing in the instructions about what one could or should do with the images, but Henek wisely observed that it was certainly necessary to touch it, if only to clear the tray: it was absurd to think that the apparatus could be used only once. Alberto detached the mushroom from the tray, examined it carefully, and declared himself satisfied; in fact, he said that he had always felt orangeish, even as a child. We passed it around: it had a firm and elastic consistency, it was tepid to the touch. Giuliana said she wanted it; Alberto gladly let her have it, saying that he had plenty of time to make more of them for himself. Henek pointed out to him that they might turn out differently, but Alberto said he didn't care.

Several people insisted that Antonio should try. By now Antonio is only an honorary member of our group, because he's been living far away for many years, and he was with us that evening only because of a business trip: we were curious to see what he would cause to grow on the tray, because Antonio is different from us, more resolute, more interested in success and gain; these are virtues that we obstinately deny possessing, as if they were shameful.

For a good minute nothing happened, and some were already beginning to smirk, and Antonio was beginning to feel uncomfortable. Then we saw a small square metal bar push up on the tray: it grew slowly and steadily, as though coming from below already perfectly formed. Soon another four appeared, arranged in the shape of a cross around the first; four small bridges joined them to it; and then one after another, more small bars appeared, all of them with the same cross-pieces, some vertical and others horizontal, and in the end on the tray there stood a small, graceful, shiny structure that had a solid and symmetrical appearance. Antonio tapped it with a pencil, and it rang out like a tuning fork, emitting a long pure note that slowly faded away.

'I don't agree,' Giovanna said.

Antonio smiled quietly. 'Why?' he asked.

'Because you're not like that. You're not all straight corners, you're not made of steel, and you have a few cracked weldings.'

Giovanna is Antonio's wife and she is very fond of him. We thought that she shouldn't have expressed all those reservations, but Giovanna said that no one could know Antonio better than she, who had lived with him for twenty years. We didn't really listen to her because

Giovanna is one of those wives who are in the habit of denigrating their husbands in their presence and in public.

The Antonio-object seemed rooted to the tray, but a weak tug detached it cleanly, and it wasn't even as heavy as it looked. Then it was Anna's turn, who squirmed on her chair with impatience and kept saying that she always wanted such an apparatus, and that several times she had even seen it in her dreams, but hers created life-size symbols.

Anna placed her hand on the black slab. We were all watching the tray, but you couldn't see a thing on it. Suddenly, Tina said, 'Look, it's up there!' In fact, at the height of about half a meter above us we saw a purple-pink cloudlet of vapor, the size of a fist. Slowly, it unwound like a ball of yarn, and lengthened downward emitting many transparent vertical ribbons. It continually changed shape: it became oval like a rugby ball, although always preserving its diaphanous and delicate appearance; then it divided into rings set one on top of the other, from which shot out small crepitating sparks, and finally it contracted, shrank to the size of a nut, and disappeared with a sputter.

'Very beautiful, and accurate too,' Giuliana said.

'Yes,' said Giorgio, 'but the trouble with this gadget is that one never knows what to call its creations. They're always hard to define.'

Miranda said it was best that way: it would have been unpleasant to find oneself represented by a soup ladle or a fife or a carrot. Giorgio added that, come to think of it, it could not have been otherwise: 'These . . . these things, in short, have no name because they are individuals, and there is no science, that is, no classification of the individual. In them just as in us, existence precedes essence.'

Everyone had liked the Anna-cloud, but not Anna herself, who had actually been rather disappointed. 'I don't think I'm so transparent. But perhaps it's because I'm tired tonight and my ideas are confused.'

Hugo caused the growth of a sphere of polished black wood, which upon closer examination turned out to be made up of about twenty pieces that fit into each other perfectly; Hugo took it apart and was unable to put it together again. He wrapped it up in a small parcel and said he would try again the next day, which was a Sunday.

Claudio is shy, and he agreed to the test only after much insistence. At first – and nothing could yet be seen on the tray – there hung in the air a familiar but unexpected smell: we had trouble defining it there and then, but it was unquestionably a kitchen smell. Immediately thereafter we heard a frying sound, and the bottom of the tray was covered by a liquid that bubbled and smoked; from the liquid emerged a flat beige polygon which beyond all reasonable doubt was a large Milanese cutlet with a side dish of fried potatoes. There were surprised comments because Claudio is neither a gourmet nor a voracious man; on the contrary, about him and his family we always say that they lack a digestive system.

Claudio blushed, and looked this way and that, embarrassed. 'You've turned real red!' Miranda exclaimed, so that Claudio turned almost purple; then, addressing us, she added, 'What are you talking about, symbols! It's very clear that this thing here has absolutely no manners, and intended to insult Claudio: to say that somebody is a cutlet is an insult. These things are to be taken literally! I knew that sooner or later it would show its hand. Alberto, if I were you I would return it to the person who gave it to you.'

In the meantime, Claudio had managed to recover enough breath to speak, and he said that he had turned red not because he felt insulted, but for another reason, so interesting that he almost felt like telling us about it, even though it was a secret he had never confessed to anyone before, not even to Simonetta. He said that he had, not a vice really, or a perversion, but, let's say, a singularity. He said that ever since he was a young boy, women, all of them, have always felt distant to him: he does not feel their closeness and attraction, he does not perceive them as creatures of flesh and blood, unless he has seen them at least once in the act of eating. When this happens, he feels intense tenderness for them, and almost always falls in love with them. It was clear that the Psychophant had meant to allude to this: in his opinion it was an extraordinary instrument.

'Did you fall in love with me that way too?' Adele asked, seriously.

'Yes,' Claudio answered. 'It happened the evening that we had dinner at Pavorolo. We had fondue with truffles.'

Adele too was a surprise. As soon as she placed her finger on the button, we heard a sharp 'pop,' as when a cork pops out of a bottle, and on the tray there appeared a tawny, shapeless, squat, vaguely conical mass made of a rough, friable material, dry to the touch. It was as large as the entire tray; actually it even protruded a bit. In it were set three white-and-gray spheres: we immediately realized that they were three eyes, but no one dared to say so, or comment in any way because Adele has had an irregular, painful and difficult existence. Adele was dismayed. 'That's me?' she asked, and we noticed that her eyes (I mean the real ones) had filled with tears. Henek tried to come to her help.

'It's impossible for an apparatus to tell you who you are, because you aren't any one thing. You and everyone, change from year to year, from hour to hour. Anyway: who are you – what you think you are, the one you'd like to be? Or the one others think you are – and which others? Everyone sees you differently, everyone gives his personal vision of you.'

Miranda said, 'I don't like this gismo, because it's a kibitzer. As for me, what counts is what one does, not what one is. One is one's actions, past and present: nothing else.'

I, however, like the device. It didn't matter to me whether it told the truth or it lied, but it created from nothing, invented: *found*, like a poet. I placed my hand on the plate and waited without distrust. On the tray appeared a small shiny grain, which grew to form a cylinder the size of a thimble; it continued to grow, and soon it reached the dimensions of a tin can, and then it became clear that it was in fact a can and more precisely a can of varnish, lithographed on the outside with lively paint colors; nevertheless it did seem to contain paint because when shaken it rattled. Everyone urged me to open it, and inside there were several things that I lined up in front of me on the table: a needle, a seashell, a malachite ring, various used tickets from streetcars, trains, steamers and airplanes, a compass, a dead cricket and a live one, and a small ember, which however, died out almost immediately.

Recuenco: The Nurse

Sinda had risen at the first light to take the goats to pasture. Around the village, for many years not a blade of grass had grown over a radius of two hours' walking: only brambles and cactus so harsh that even the goats would not have them. Sinda was only eleven years old, but by now he was the only one in the village who could go to pasture; the others were children, or too old, or sick, or so enfeebled that they barely managed to drag themselves as far as the stream. He took with him a gourd filled with an infusion of watercress and two slices of cheese that had to last him until evening. He had already gathered together the goats on the piazza when he saw Diuka, his sister, coming out of the hut rubbing her eyes: she wanted to go to the pasture with him. He thought that the cheese was scant, but he also thought that the day was long, the pasture far away, and the silence up there too deep; so he took her along with him.

They had been climbing for an hour when the sun rose. The goats were only twenty-eight, all that there were in the village. Sinda knew this, and he also knew how to count them: he kept an eye on them so that they wouldn't get lost and wouldn't lame themselves as they went down the rocky precipices. Diuka followed him in silence; every so often they stopped to pick blackberries and a few snails awakened by the night's dew. One mustn't eat snails, but Sinda had already tried them several times and he had never gotten a bellyache; he had taught Diuka how to pry them from the shell, and he was certain that Diuka would not betray him.

There wasn't a cloud in the sky, but in it there stagnated a dazzling haze: there was no wind (there never was any wind) and the air was damp and hot like that of a bread oven. They followed the path, went over the ridge that bordered the valley and saw the sea, veiled in mist, gleaming, still and distant. It was a sea without fishes, good only for salt: the salt-works basin had lain abandoned for ten years now, but one could still extract salt from it, though mixed with sand. Sinda had been there once with his father, many years before; then his father had left to go hunting and had never returned. Now the salt was sometimes brought by the traders but, since at the village there was nothing to barter for it, they came less and less frequently.

In the sea Sinda saw something he had never seen before. At first, precisely on the line of the horizon, he saw a small luminous round and white bump; like a tiny moon, but it could not be the moon: he had seen the real moon, almost full and with clear edges, set only an hour before. He pointed it out to Diuka, but without much interest: in the sea there are many things that both had heard described around the hearth – ships, whales, monsters, plants that grow from the bottom, ferocious fish and also the souls of those who died by drowning. Things that come and go and don't concern us, because the sea is vanity and malign appearance: it is an immense clearing that seems to take you everywhere and does not take you anywhere; it seems smooth and solid like steel armor and instead it does not support the foot, and if you venture upon it you sink. It is water and you cannot drink it.

They continued walking: by now the climb was ended and the pasture was visible, not far above them, about an hour's walk. The two children and goats advanced along a well-trodden track amid a cloud of yellow dust, horseflies and the smell of ammonia. At intervals, Sinda observed the sea on his left, and he noticed that the thing kept changing in appearance. Now it was completely away from the horizon, now it was closer, and it looked like one of those globe-shaped mushrooms that you find at the edge of paths, that if you touch them break open and blow out a breath of dark brown powder; but in reality it must be very large, and if you looked carefully you saw that its contours were shaded like those of the clouds. In fact it seemed to be boiling within, to be continually changing in shape, like the foam of milk about to brim over; and it kept getting larger and closer. Just before they reached the pasture, and when the goats were disbanding to browse on certain blossoming thistles, Sinda realized that the thing was traveling directly toward them. At that he then remembered certain stories he had heard from the old people, and had only half believed as you believe fairy tales: he entrusted the goats to Diuka, promised her that he or someone else would come before evening to take them back, and took off at a run for the village. In fact from the village the sea couldn't be seen: it was separated from it by a chain of jagged cliffs, and Sinda ran because he hoped-feared that the thing was the Nurse, who comes every hundred years and brings abundance and slaughter; he wanted to tell everyone, so they should prepare, and he also wanted to be the first to bring the news.

There was a shortcut that only he knew, but he did not take it because it would have deprived him too soon of the view of the sea. Shortly before Sinda reached the ridge, the thing appeared enormous, enough to take his breath away: the top reached high into the sky and from the peak torrents of water streamed toward the base, and other water hurled itself toward the peak. He could hear something like continuous thunder, a rumble-whistle-crash that froze the blood in his veins. Sinda stopped for a second and felt the need to throw himself to the ground and worship; but he controlled himself and plunged down the incline, getting scratched by the brambles, tripping over the rocks, falling and getting up again. Now he could no longer see anything, but he could hear the rumble, and when Sinda reached the village they were all hearing it but did not know what it was, and he, Sinda, did know, and he stood in the middle of the square, intoxicated and bloodied, waving his arms for everyone to come and listen, because the Nurse was arriving.

At first only a few came, then all of them. The many, the too many children came, but they weren't the ones who were needed. The old women, and the young women who seemed old, came to the thresholds of their huts. The men came from the kitchen gardens and the fields with the slow, enervated gait of those who know only the mattock and plow; and finally also Daiapi came, the one Sinda most awaited.

But even Daiapi, although he was the oldest in the village, was only fifty and so he could not know from his own experience what must be done when the Nurse comes. He had only vague memories, drawn from the hardly less vague memories transmitted to him by who-knows-what other Daiapi, and then consolidated, cemented and distorted by innumerable repetitions around the fire. The Nurse, of this he was certain, had already come to the village at other times: two times, or perhaps even three or more; but of the most ancient visits, if there had been any, all memories were lost. But with certainty Daiapi knew, and with him everybody knew, that when she came, this was how she came, suddenly, from the sea, in the midst of a whirlwind, and she stopped only a few seconds, and flung down food from on high, and one must be somehow ready so that the food did not get lost. He also knew, or it seemed to him he knew, that she crossed the mountains and the sea like a lightning bolt, attracted to places where there was hunger. Because of this she never stopped: because the world was boundless and hunger existed in many places far from each other, and as soon as it was satiated, it was reborn like the sprouts of noxious plants.

Daiapi had little strength and little voice, but even with the voice of the monsoon he would not have been able to make himself heard in the clamor that came from the sea and that by now had filled the valley, so much so that each person felt he was deaf. By his example and by gesturing, he got everyone to bring into the open all the receptacles they had, small and large; then, as the sky was already growing dark, and the plain was swept by a wind such as never seen before, he seized a pick and shovel and began digging feverishly, imitated immediately by many others. They dug with all their might, their eyes filled with sweat and their ears filled with thunder: but they had barely managed to excavate a ditch the size of a grave on the square, when the Nurse came across the hills like a cloud of iron and uproar, and hovered there directly over their heads. She was larger than the entire village, and covered it with her shadow. Six steel trumpets, pointed at the ground, poured out six hurricanes on which the machine was supported, almost immobile; but the air blasting to earth swept up dust, stones, leaves, fences, the roofs of the huts, and dispersed them on high and in the distance. The children fled, or were blown away like chaff; the men held on, clinging to trees and walls.

They saw the machine slowly descend: some maintained that in the midst of the maelstrom of yellowish dust they caught a glimpse of human figures leaning down from above to look; some said two, some three. One woman declared that she had heard voices, but they weren't human, they were metallic and nasal, and so loud that they could be heard over the uproar.

When the six trumpets were a few meters above the tops of the huts, from the belly of the machine issued six white pipes that remained dangling in the void: and suddenly the nourishment, the celestial milk, poured in white spurts from the pipes. The two central pipes poured into the ditch, but meanwhile a deluge of nourishment fell at random over the entire village and also outside it, swept along and pulverized by the wind of the trumpets. Sinda, in the midst of the uproar, had found a trough that in the past had been used to water the animals: he dragged it under one of the pipes, but in an instant it was full, and the liquid brimmed over, fell to the ground and stuck to his feet. Sinda tasted it: it seemed like milk, cream actually, but it wasn't. It was dense and insipid, and killed hunger in an instant. Sinda saw that everyone was swallowing it avidly, gathering it from the ground with their hands, shovels and palm leaves.

A noise resounded from the sky, perhaps the sound of a horn, or perhaps a command pronounced by that cold mechanical voice, and the flow ceased abruptly. Immediately after, the roar and the wind swelled beyond measure, and Sinda was blown away, rolling through the viscous puddles; the machine rose, at first perpendicularly, then obliquely, and in a few minutes it was hidden behind the mountains.

Sinda got to his feet and looked around: the village no longer seemed his village. Not only had the ditch overflowed, but the milk poured thickly down all the inclined alleys and streamed from the few roofs that had not collapsed. The lower part of the village was flooded: two women had drowned, and so had many rabbits and dogs, and all the chickens. Floating on the liquid were found hundreds of sheets of printed paper, all the same: on the upper left-hand corner they bore a round mark, which perhaps represented the world, and then there followed a text divided into paragraphs, and repeated in various characters and various languages; but no one in the village knew how to read. On the back of the sheet there was a ridiculous series of drawings: a thin naked man, next to him a glass, next to that the man drinking from the glass, and finally the same man but no longer thin; further down, another thin man, next to him a bucket, then the man drinking from the bucket, and finally the same man lying on the ground, his eyes wide open, his mouth agape, and his belly burst.

Daiapi immediately understood the meaning of those drawings and summoned the men into the square, but it was too late: during the following days eight men and two women died, livid and bloated; an inventory was made, and it became clear that, without counting the milk that had been lost or had become mixed with earth or manure, there was still enough left to feed the entire village for a year. Daiapi gave instructions to bake some earthenware jars and sew goatskin bottles as soon as possible, because he feared that the milk in the ditch would become contaminated in contact with the ground.

Only when night had come did Sinda, dazed by all the things he had seen and done, and numbed by the milk he had drunk, remember Diuka left at pasture with the goats. He departed at dawn the next day, carrying with him a gourd full of food, but he found that the goats were dispersed and four of them were missing, and Diuka was also missing. He found her a little later, wounded and frightened, at the foot of a bluff together with the four dead animals: the Nurse's wind had blown them down there, when she had flown over the pasture.

A few days later, an old woman, while removing from her courtyard the crusts of milk dried by the sun, found an object never seen before. It was as shiny as silver, harder than flint, a foot long, narrow and pointed; at one extremity it was rounded, forming a disk with a large hexagonal notch; the other extremity was rather like a ring, and its hole, two inches wide, had the shape of a star with twelve blunt points. Daiapi gave orders for a stone tabernacle to be built on the stray boulder that stood near the village, and for the object to be preserved there forever in remembrance of the day of the Nurse's visit.

Recuenco: The Rafter

Suspended a few meters above the waves, the platform was gliding swiftly, vibrating and humming weakly. In the cabin, Himamoto was asleep, Kropiva was attending to the radio and writing, and Farnham was at the controls. Farnham was the one who got bored the most, because to pilot a 'rafter' means to pilot a big nothing: you are at the wheel but you mustn't touch it, you watch the altimeter and the needle doesn't move by a hair, you watch the gyrocompass but it is steady as a stone; when there is a change of route (which rarely happens, because a rafter always travels in a straight line) the other guys down there take care of it. All you have to do is be careful that one of the yellow emergency lights does not go on, and he had never heard anyone at the pilots' mess say that a yellow light had ever lit up. In short, it is like being a night watchman. It's not a man's job; it's a job as boring as knitting. So as not to fall asleep, Farnham smoked cigarette after cigarette, and recited a poem under his breath. Or rather, it was a little song, in which, in verses easy to remember, were condensed all the instructions to be followed in the unlikely, almost comical circumstance that a yellow light actually did flash on. All the pilots were expected to know the little emergency song by heart.

Farnham came from the jets, and on board a rafter he felt almost as though retired, and he also was somewhat humiliated and ashamed. Agreed, that too was a useful service, but how could he forget certain missions over the jungle with the B-28's, two, three trips a day, and sometimes also at night with the fires of the rebels winking amid the foliage, six flame-spitting machine guns and twenty tons of bombs on board? But, precisely, he was fifteen years younger then: when your reflexes slow down a bit, they dump you on the rafters.

If only Himamoto would wake up; but no, that fellow always slept his full eight hours. With the excuse that he suffered from nausea, he stuffed himself with pills, and as soon as he got off his four-hour shift, he fell asleep like a rock. It must be kept in mind that the rafter after all isn't that fast: it takes a good thirty-five or forty hours to cross the Atlantic, and when it is fully loaded, that is, with two hundred and forty tons of milk, it handles as well as a streetcar during the rush hour.

Also, looking out wasn't much fun. It was still deep night, the sky was covered; in the gleaming swathes of lights, front and back, all you could see were swollen, lazy waves and the endlessly repeated deluge of water raised by the six blowers which fell with a crash onto the platform, the size of a tennis court, and onto the absurdly small cabin.

You could hear Himamoto snore. He snored in an irritating way: at first very, very lightly, almost like a sigh, then suddenly he shot out a dry, obscene grunt, and stopped as if he had died; but no, after a minute of anguished silence he began all over again. This was the first trip Farnham had taken with Himamoto and he found him polite and pleasant when awake and unbearable when asleep. When awake, Himamoto was likeable because he was young, didn't have much navigational experience and was willing to play the learner role with diligence and naiveté: now, since Farnham in fact set great store in showing off his experience, the two got along quite well, and the best four-hour shift was the one when Kropiva slept. That's why Farnham couldn't wait for six o'clock to arrive.

Unlike Himamoto, he found Kropiva likeable when asleep and quite annoying when awake. When awake, he was a monster of meticulousness: Farnham, who had seen a lot of the world, had never met a Russian like him, and he asked himself where the Organization could have dug him up. Perhaps in some administrative office lost in the tundra, or from among railroad or penetentiary personnel. He didn't drink, didn't smoke, spoke only in monosyllables, and made calculations all the time. On a few occasions, Farnham had glanced at the pieces of paper that Kropiva left strewn about, and he saw that he counted everything: how many years, months and days he lacked for his pension; how many dollars they were going to give him, down to the cents and hundredths of cents, and how many rubles and kopecks those dollars amounted to, on the illegal exchange and the official one. How much every minute and every mile of the rafter's voyage cost in fuel, salaries, maintenance, insurance, amortization – as though he owned the rafter. How much pay he would draw the coming month: that vertiginous list of items that he, Farnham, stuffed into his pocket without even looking at it, fascinated Kropiva, who took delight in calculating it in advance, everything included, family allowances, reimbursement for mess expenses at their stopovers, the increment for crossing the dateline, indemnity for night watches, for overtime, for hardship, for tropical and arctic climates, for official holidays; and with all the deductions, for taxes, health insurance and pensions. All wonderful and proper things, but to Farnham it seemed foolish and petty to spend the whole day on them, as though the computerized center didn't exist or functioned improperly. It was lucky that Kropiva didn't talk, but even so his presence filled Farnham with confused discomfort.

At six on the dot Farnham awakened Himamoto, and Kropiva went to his berth without even a by-your-leave. At the poop, through the rain from the blowers, he saw the sky turn clear and light up with a tenuous green that announced the day. Farnham went to the radio and Himamoto, still heavy with sleep, sat at the wheel. At least now they could exchange a few words.

'How soon will we arrive?' Himamoto asked.

'In three or four hours.'

'And . . . what's the name of that place?'

'Recuenco. It's the third time that you ask me.'

'I know, but I always forget it.'

'No problem: one place is as good as another. Over Recuenco we're supposed to release fifty tons.'

'Shall I set the counter on zero?'

'Already done, while you were sleeping. By the way, you know that you snore like a devil?'

'Not true,' Himamoto protested with dignity. 'I don't snore at all.'

'Next time I'll bring along my recorder,' Farnham threatened good-naturedly. Himamoto washed up, shaved with a splendid old-fashioned razor (apparently that's what people used in his country) and went to get a hot coffee and bun from the machine. He threw a glance at Kropiva. 'He's already asleep,' he remarked with a shade of satisfaction in his voice.

'He's a bit strange,' Farnham said. 'But it doesn't matter; I've seen so many of them and he's better than those who drink or take dope or go on binges at every stop. There's no one like him when it comes to overseeing the loading and unloading of the milk and kerosene, all those custom nuisances, and the final report to base. Because, you know, sometimes we get back with five or six different currencies, and we're expected to account for every last penny; and when it comes to such things he's extraordinary, as good as three computers.'

Harmony and mutual esteem above all on board, he was thinking meanwhile.

The sun was rising behind them, and immediately resplendent concentric rainbows appeared. 'How beautiful! Very beautiful!' Himamoto cried. His English was fluent and correct, but he lacked the words to express the soul's movements.

'Yes, it is beautiful,' Farnham answered. 'But it is always the same, at every dawn and at every sunset; you get used to it. It comes from the water stirred up by the engines. Also the sunset seems wet, do you see?'

There was silence for half an hour. Himamoto, precisely because he knew that he was absentminded, watched the route and the instruments with concentrated attention. A trace appeared on the radar screen, twenty miles off the prow: Himamoto instinctively seized the wheel.

'Don't worry,' Farnham said, 'it does everything by itself.' And indeed, without jolts and without jerks, the rafter spontaneously swerved to the right, gave a wide berth to the ship or wreck or iceberg, whatever it was, then ponderously returned to its course.

'Say,' Himamoto asked, 'did you ever taste it?'

'It doesn't taste like anything,' Farnham answered.

After a few minutes, Himamoto insisted, 'I'd like to taste it anyway; they'll ask me at home later.'

'No problem: but try it now, if you must then, while he's asleep, or else he's capable of writing you up a withdrawal slip.'

'From where do you draw it?'

'From the spigot under the purifier. But it's no fun, I tell you: it tastes like blotting paper. Go ahead, I'll stay at the controls.'

Himamoto extracted a plastic glass from the distributor and went to the spigot, tripping among pipes and valves painted in bright colors.

'Well, it's neither good nor bad. But it fills your stomach.'

'Of course; it isn't stuff for us, it's good for those who are hungry. You feel sorry for them, especially the children: you too must have seen them, on film, during the training course. But at bottom they are people who don't deserve better, because they are lazy, improvident and good for nothing. You wouldn't expect us to bring them champagne.'

A buzzer went off, and a green screen lit up in front of Farnham. 'Damn it! I had a feeling. Another urgent request: Shangeehaydhang, Philippines: who the hell knows how it's pronounced. Twelve degrees five minutes forty-three seconds north, one hundred twenty-four degrees forty-eight minutes forty-six seconds east. Take heart: no weekend in Rio. It's at the other end of the world.'

'So why do they send a signal to us?'

'I guess that, despite everything, we're the closest, or the least loaded, or the other three are refueling. The fact is they always keep us on the move: and that's understandable because a rafter costs more than a mission to the moon and the milk costs almost nothing. It's because of this that they give us only three minutes to unload: even if a bit of it is wasted, it doesn't matter; what's essential is that no time is lost.'

'It's a pity that any should be wasted. When I was a child I did go hungry.'

'Some of it always gets wasted. Sometimes we manage to alert them by radio, and the job is quick and clean; but in the majority of cases they don't even know what a radio is, just like the people we are on our way to supplying now, and then in such cases we manage as best we can.'

A cloud bank was forming to their left, behind which they glimpsed a chain of mountains: a high, conical peak covered with snow stood out.

'I once went where they make it; it isn't very far from here. There is an enormous forest, as large as all of Texas, and a super-rafter that travels back and forth. Gradually as it proceeds it cuts down all the plants in front of it and leaves behind it a thirty-meter-wide empty wake. The plants end up in the hold, are chopped up, cooked, washed with acid, and from it are extracted the proteins which are in fact the milk – that's what we call it, but its official name is FOD. The rest of the plant is used to supply energy to the machine itself. It's quite a job: it's worth going to look at, and it isn't difficult either; every two years a trip is organized as a reward for the pilots without penalties. I also took photographs – I'll show them to you at the base. It is a guided trip, they explain everything, also the business of the detectors that sense the acetone in the atmosphere, near the towns where people are starving, and transmit the signals to the computers at the base.'

A few minutes later they both saw a large barrier taking shape on the radar screen: it was only seven miles away but the haze that covered the sea prevented them from seeing it. 'Here we are,' Farnham said. 'Perhaps it's better if I take the controls; you go and wake up Kropiva.'

They felt the vibration of the platform increase; at the same moment the deluge around them ceased abruptly, and was replaced by a whirling cloud of yellowish dust, sand and tatters of foliage. A chain of jagged crags became visible: Farnham raised the rafter to a safe elevation and a few instants later, in a short barren plain, there appeared the village of Recuenco, about fifty huts made of mud and gray stone, with palm-leaf roofs. Tiny human figures crawled in all directions, like ants in a decapitated anthill: some of them fumbled about with shovels and picks. Farnham stopped the rafter directly above the square: the shadow of the platform entirely covered the village. 'Let's go outside,' he said.

They slipped into their coveralls and goggles and the three of them went outside: the heat, the uproar and wind struck them like the blow of a cudgel. They could communicate with each other only by gestures or through the loudspeakers; despite their coveralls, they felt stones and splinters hit them like hail. Clinging to the rail, Farnham dragged himself to the outside controls, and noticed that the nuts that attached the panel to the deck were loose; he shouted to Himamoto to get the 24 wrench and to Kropiva to get ready to launch the milk and leaflets. He lowered the machine until the six blowers were a few meters above the huts, then he made the pipes project from their housings. Looking down from the railing, through the vortices of stifling dust, he saw that a ditch had been dug at the center of the square, and he guided the machine in such a way that at least the two central parts were placed perpendicularly above it;

then he told Himamoto to tighten the bolts on the panel, and Kropiva to begin the unloading operation.

In less than two minutes the counter marked 50,000 liters; Kropiva halted the flow and flung out the leaflets with the instructions, which scattered in all directions like frightened birds. Farnham revved up the blowers; the rafter rose first vertically, then obliquely, a bit lighter and more docile than before, and began to cross a barrier of desolate mountains. In the middle of the rocky wastes Farnham saw a small green plateau, where a flock of goats was grazing: there was nothing alive or green for tens of miles in all directions.

Kropiva filled out the unloading form, stamped it, signed it and got the other two to sign it, then he went back to sleep; Himamoto returned to the controls, but he immediately slapped a hand against his forehead. 'The wrench!' he said, and without coveralls or glasses he flew out onto the platform. He came back soon after. 'It's not there, it must have fallen off.'

'It doesn't matter,' Farnham said, 'we have a spare.' Kropiva said, 'We'll have to file a report on the loss. I'm sorry, but I'll have to dock it from your salary.'

His Own Blacksmith

To Italo Calvino

It will be best to be clear from the start: I who am talking to you today am a man, one of you. I am different from you living beings in only one regard: my memory is better than yours.

You forget almost everything. I know, there are those who maintain that nothing is really erased, that every notion, every sensation, every leaf of every tree you have seen since childhood lies inside you, and can be summoned up under exceptional circumstances, after a trauma, say, a mental illness, perhaps even in dreams. But what remembrances are those that do not obey your summons? What good are they to you?

More solid is that other memory, the memory that is inscribed in your cells, so that your blond hair is the memory (yes, the 'souvenir,' memory become matter) of innumerable other blond hairs, all the way back to the remote day on which the seed of an unknown ancestor of yours mutated inside him, without him, without his knowing it. You have registered these things, 'recorded them': you remember them well, but, I say again, what good is remembering without the summoning up? That is not the meaning of the verb 'to remember,' as it is commonly pronounced and understood.

For me it's different. I remember everything – I mean everything that has happened to me since childhood. When I wish to I can kindle the memory of it in me and tell it. But also my cellular memory is better than yours, indeed it is full: I remember everything that has happend to every one of my ancestors, in direct lineage, back to the most remote times. Until the time, I believe, in which the first of my ancestors received the gift (or gave himself the gift) of a differentiated brain. Therefore, my saying 'I' is richer than yours, and sinks its roots in time. You, my reader, must certainly have known your father, or at any rate known a lot about him. Perhaps you even knew your grandfather; less probably your great-grandfather. A few among you can go back in time for five or ten generations, through documents, testimonials, or portraits, and there find men who are different from yourselves, in habits, character and language, and still are men. But what about ten thousand generations? Or ten million generations? Which of your ancestors of the male line will no longer be a man but a quasi-man? Put them in a row and look at them: which of them is no longer man but something else? Which no longer a mammal? And what was his appearance?

'I' know all of this, I've done and suffered all that my ancestors have done and suffered, because I've inherited their memories and so I am they. One of them, the first, after being felicitously mutated acquired this virtue of hereditary memory, and has transmitted it all the way down to me, so that today I can say 'I' with such unequaled scope.

I also know the how and why of every variation, whether small or large. Now, if I know that a thing must be done, that I want to do it, and it is done, is this not as though I had done it, did I not do it? If sunrise dazzles me, and I want to close my eyes, and my eyes close, did I not close my eyes? But if I need to detach my belly from mother earth, if I want to detach it, and through the millennia it detaches itself, and I no longer crawl but walk, is that not my own work? I'm the forger of myself, and this is my diary.

-10^9 Yesterday the water sank another two millimeters. I cannot really remain in water permanently: I've known this for a long time. On the other hand, getting equipped for aerial life is a job. It's easy to say: 'Practice, go ashore, pull in your gills'; there's a slew of other problems. The legs, for example: I'll have to calculate them with good safety margins, because in here I don't weigh anything, or almost, or rather, more accurately, I weigh as much as I want, but once ashore I'll have to handle my entire weight. And what about my skin?

-10^8 My wife has gotten it into her head to keep the eggs inside her body. She says she's studying a system to raise the little ones in some cavity of her own organism, and then put them outside once they're autonomous. But she doesn't feel up to separating from them all of a sudden: she says she would suffer too much, and that she is thinking about a complete alimentation, sugars, proteins, vitamins, and fats, and she plans to manufacture it herself. It's clear that she will have to restrict very much the number of little ones, but she has explained to me that, in her opinion, it would be better to have five or ten children instead of ten thousand or one hundred thousand, and to raise them properly, until they really know how to take care of themselves. You know how females are: where the little ones are concerned, they won't listen to reason; they would jump into the fire for them, or let themselves be devoured. Indeed, they actually let themselves be devoured: recently I've been told about a beetle of the late Permian age; well, the larvae's first food is precisely their mother's corpse. I hope that my wife will not give in to such excesses, but meanwhile this business, which she tells me about a little at a time so as not to shock me, when all is said and done comes to pretty much the same. Tonight she informed me that she has been able to modify six epithelial glands and press from them a few drops of a white liquid that she thinks will fit the purpose.

-5×10^7 We have landed: there wasn't much choice, the sea is getting colder and saltier, and besides it is filling up with animals that I don't like too much, fishes with teeth, more than six meters long, and others that are smaller but poisonous and extremely voracious. However, my wife and I have decided not to burn our bridges; you never know, perhaps one day it will be convenient to go back into the water. So, I've thought it a good idea to maintain the same specific weight as seawater; in order to do this I had to put on a bit of fat to compensate for the weight of the bones. I also tried to keep the plasma at the same osmotic tension as seawater, and more or less with the same ionic composition. Also my wife has recognized the advantages of doing this: when we get into the water to wash or to keep in practice, we float without difficulty, we can immerse ourselves without effort, and our skin does not shrivel.

Staying on dry land entails something good and something less good. It is more uncomfortable, but also more amusing and more stimulating. As for locomotion, I may well say that the problem is solved by now: I first tried to glide on the sand as if swimming; then I went so far as to reabsorb the fins, which were a nuisance more than anything else. It might even have worked, but the speed obtained was not satisfactory, and it was difficult, for instance, to move about on smooth rock. For the time being I still walk by crawling on my belly, but I'm planning on making myself a couple of legs soon, though I don't know yet whether they'll be two or four or six.

More stimulating, I was saying: you see and hear more things, smells, colors, sounds; you become more versatile, more prompt, more intelligent. It is precisely because of this that sooner or later I want to carry my head erect: from on high you can see farther. Besides, I also have a project that regards the front limbs, and I hope to be able to concentrate on it soon.

As for the skin, I've been forced to acknowledge that it is too short to be used as a respiratory organ; more's the pity, I was counting on it. But it came out well anyhow: it is soft, porous, and at the same time almost impermeable, it stands up magnificently to the sun, to water and aging, it is easily pigmented, and it contains a quantity of glands and nerve endings. I don't believe that I'll have to go on changing it as I had to until a short while ago; it's no longer a problem.

There is a problem, however, and a big and idiotic one, when it comes to reproduction. It's easy for my wife to say: few children, pregnancy, breast-feeding. I tried to go along with her because I'm fond of her, and also because the major part of the work falls to her; but, when she decided to convert to mammalism, she definitely did not realize what an upheaval she was causing.

I had told her so. 'Now, listen, I don't care whether the children are three meters long or weigh half a ton, or are able to crush a bison's femur with their teeth; I want children with prompt reflexes and well-developed senses, and above all alert and filled with imagination, who in due time will perhaps be able to invent the wheel and the alphabet. So they'll have to have quite a lot of brain, and therefore a large skull, and so how will they manage to come out when the moment arrives to be born? It'll end up that you will have to give birth in pain.' But when she gets an idea in her head, nobody can budge her. She got busy, tried various methods, and also had several failures, and in the end she has chosen the simplest: she has broadened her pelvis (now it's larger than mine), and she's made the kid's skull soft and sort of supple; in short, with a little help maybe, now she can manage to deliver at least nine times out of ten. In pain, however: when it comes to this, she admits it herself, I was right.

-2×10^7 Dear diary, today I had a close call: an enormous beast, I don't know what it's called, came out of the swamp and pursued me for almost an hour. As soon as I got my breath back, I made up my mind: in this world it is imprudent to go about unarmed. I thought about it, I made a few sketches, then I made my choice. I built myself a beautiful armor of bony shields, four horns on the forehead, a nail on every finger, and eight poisonous stingers on the tip of my tail. You won't believe me, but I did all this using only carbon, hydrogen, oxygen and nitrogen, besides a pinch of sulfur. It may be a fixation of mine, but I don't like novelties when it comes to construction materials: metals, for instance, don't seem reliable to me. Perhaps it's because I'm not well versed in inorganic chemistry; I'm at greater ease with carbon, the colloidals, and macromolecules.

-10^7 On land, among other novelties, there are the plants. Grasses, bushes, algae, thirty- or fifty-meter-tall trees, everything is green: everything sprouts and grows, and displays itself to the sun. They seem stupid, and yet they steal energy from the sun, carbon from the air, salts from the earth, and they grow for a thousand years without spinning or weaving or disemboweling each other as we do.

There are those who eat plants, and those who watch this and then eat those who eat plants. On the one hand this is more convenient, because with the latter system you can quickly stuff yourself with well-developed molecules without wasting time on syntheses that not everyone is able to perform; on the other, it is a hard life, because no one likes to be eaten, and so everyone protects himself as best he can, both with classical means (as I do) and with more imaginative methods, for instance by changing color, delivering a shock, or by stinking. The simpler ones train at making their escape.

As for me, I had a lot of trouble getting used to grass and leaves: I was forced to lengthen my intestine, double my stomach, then I even made a contract with certain protozoa I had met along the way: I keep them warm in my belly, and they demolish the cellulose on my behalf. When it comes to wood, I wasn't able to get used to it at all, and that's a pity, because there's an abundance of it.

I was forgetting to tell you that for some time now I have owned a pair of eyes. That wasn't actually an invention, but a chain of little ruses. At first I made myself two small black spots, but I could only distinguish light from darkness: I clearly needed lenses. In the beginning I tried to make them out of horn or of some polysaccharide, but then I changed my mind and decided to make them of water, which at bottom was the great discovery: water is transparent, costs little, and I know it very well; indeed, I myself, when I issued from the sea (I don't remember whether I have already written about this here), carried with me a good two thirds of water – and this seventy percent of water that feels, thinks, says 'I' and writes a diary, even makes you laugh a bit. Anyway, to make it short, I was very successful with the lenses made of water (I only had to add a bit of gelatin); I was even able to make them with a variable focus and to complete them with a diaphragm, and I didn't even use one milligram of elements different from the four of which I've become fond.

-5×10^6 Speaking of trees, by dint of living among them, and occasionally also on top of them, we've begun to like them, my wife and I: I mean to say like them not only as a source of food, but from several different aspects. They are absolutely beautiful structures, but about this we'll talk some other time; they are also a marvel of engineering, and besides they are almost immortal. Those who say that death is incised in life did not think of them: every spring they become young again. I must think about this at my leisure: might they not be the best model? Just think, as I'm writing, I have an oak here before me, thirty tons of good compact wood; well, it's been standing on its feet and growing for three hundred years, it does not have to hide or flee, no one devours it and it has never devoured anyone. There's more: they breathe for us, I've become aware of it recently, and one can live safely on them.

Yesterday in fact a funny thing happened to me. I was looking at my hands and feet, just like that, idly: by now, just so we understand each other, they are shaped more or less like yours. Well, they're made for the trees. With index and thumb I can form a circle suited to grasping a branch up to five centimeters thick; if it is up to fifteen centimeters thick I can manage with both hands, thumb against thumb, fingers against fingers, and they form a perfect circle. For still bigger branches, up to fifty or sixty centimeters, I manage like this, with both arms before my chest. The same, approximately more or less, can be said for the legs and feet: the arch of my foot is the mold of a branch.

'But you're the one who wanted it!' you will say. Certainly; but I hadn't noticed, you know how it happens sometimes. Because, it's true that I made myself by myself, but I tried various models, I made several experiments, and at times it happens to me that I forget to cancel certain details, above all when they don't bother me; or I might even preserve them deliberately, as you do with the portraits of ancestors: for instance, in the pinna of my ear I have a small bone that no longer serves any purpose, because it's a long time since I needed to orientate my ears; but I care very much for it, and would not let it atrophy for all the gold in the world.

– 10^6 For quite a while now my wife and I have realized that walking is a solution, but walking on four legs is only a semisolution. It's clear: a tall person like me, who stands erect, dominates the horizon with a radius of a dozen kilometers; that is, such a person almost is its master. But there's more: the hands remain free. I already have them, but until now I hadn't yet thought of using them for anything but climbing trees; well, now I've become aware that with a small modification they'll be useful for a host of other small jobs that I've had in mind for some time.

I like comforts and novelties. For example, it is a matter of tearing up branches and leaves, and making myself a pallet and a roof from them; of sharpening a shell against a slab of slate, and with the sharpened shell polishing an ash branch and with the well-smoothed, pointed branch killing an elk; and out of the elk's skin making myself a garment for the winter and a cover for the night; and from its bones a comb for my wife, and an awl and an amulet for myself and a small elk for my son, so that he can play with it and learn how to hunt. I've also noticed that, as you do things, other things come to your mind in a chain: I often have the impression that I'm thinking more with my hand than with my brain.

With your hands – not that it is easy – but with your hands you can also chip a flint and tie the chip to the end of a stick, in short make yourself an axe, and with that axe protect your territory or perhaps even enlarge it.

In other words, bash in the heads of certain other 'I's that are in my way, or court my wife, or are even only whiter or blacker or hairier or less hairy than me, or speak with a different accent.

But here this diary might as well end. With these last transformations and inventions of mine, the major part of the job is now accomplished: since then, nothing essential has happened to me, nor do I think is going to happen to me in the future.

The Servant

In the ghetto, knowledge and wisdom are cheap virtues. They are so widespread that even the shoemaker and the porter could boast of them, and in fact do not boast of them: they are almost no longer virtues, just as it is not a virtue to wash one's hands before eating. Therefore, even though he was more knowledgeable and wiser than anyone else, Rabbi Arié of Prague did not owe his fame to these qualities, but to another, much more rare, and that was his strength.

He was as strong as a man can be, in spirit and in the flesh. It is said about him that he protected the Jews from a pogrom, without weapons but only with the power of his large hands; it is also said that he got married four times, that four times he became a widower, and that he procreated a great number of sons, one of whom was the progenitor of Karl Marx, of Franz Kafka, of Sigmund Freud and of Albert Einstein, and of all those who in the old heart of Europe pursued truth down daring and new paths. He got married for the fourth time at the age of seventy; he was seventy-five years old and was rabbi of Mikulov in Moravia, a holy place, when he accepted the appointment as rabbi of Prague; he was eighty when, with his own hand, he sculpted and erected the sepulchre that even today is the goal of pilgrimages. On the top of the ark this sepulchre has a slit: anyone who drops into it a slip of paper with a wish written on it, whether he be Jew, Christian, Moslem, or pagan, will see it fulfilled within the year. Rabbi Arié lived to the age of one hundred and fifty, in full vigor of body and spirit, and he was ninety when he undertook to build a golem.

To build a golem is in itself not an enterprise of great account, and many have attempted it. In fact, a golem is little more than a nothing: it is a portion of matter, or rather of chaos, enclosed in human or animal semblance; it is in short a simulacrum, and as such it is good for nothing – indeed it is something essentially suspect and to stay away from, for it is written that 'you shall not make graven images and shall not worship them.' The golden calf was a golem: so was Adam, and so are we.

The difference between golems resides in the precision and completeness of the instructions that guided their construction. If one just says, 'Take two hundred and forty pounds of clay, give them the shape of a man, and take the simulacrum to the kiln so that it becomes fixed,' the result will be an idol, as the gentiles make them. To make a man, the path is longer because the instructions are more numerous: but they are not infinite, being inscribed in each of our minuscule seeds, and Rabbi Arié knew this, because he had seen numerous sons born and grow around him, and had observed their features. Now, Arié was not a blasphemer, and had not set himself the task of creating a second Adam. He did not intend to build a man, but rather a *po'el*, or shall we say a worker, a strong, faithful servant and not too discerning: in short, what in his Czech language is called a robot. In fact, man can (and at times must) labor and fight, but these are not properly human works. These are the sort of enterprises that a robot is good for, precisely: something a bit more and bit better than the bell-ringing automatons, and those who march out when the hours ring on the façade of Prague's City Hall.

A servant – but he must be as strong as he was, heir to his strength, a servant who must defend and help the people of Israel when his, Arié's, days came to end. To achieve this, more complex instructions were therefore needed than those required to make an ideal which grimaces immobile in its niche, but not as complex as those which are needed to 'be like God' and create the second Adam. These instructions – and there is no need to look for them in the vortex of the starry sky, nor in a crystal ball, nor in the ravings of the spirit of Python – they are already written, they are hidden in the books of the Law; all you need do is choose, that is, read, select. There is not a letter, not a mark on the scrolls of the Law which is there by chance: to anyone who knows how to read, everything appears clear, every past, present and future enterprise, the formula and destiny of humanity and of every man, and of you, and those of all flesh, right down to the blind worm that pushes its path through the mud. Arié made his calculations, and found that the formula for the golem, as he wanted him, would not be such as to surpass human faculties. It was possible to write it down on thirty-nine pages,as many as his sons had been: the coincidence pleased him.

There remained the question of the prohibition against making images for oneself. As is known, one must 'put a hedge about the Law,' that is, it is prudent to interpret precepts and prohibitions in their broadest sense, because an error due to excessive diligence entails no harm, whereas a transgression can never be healed: expiation does not exist. Nevertheless, perhaps due to long coexistence with the gentiles , in the Prague ghetto a tolerant interpretation had prevailed. You shall not make yourself images of God, because God has no image, but why should you not make images for yourself of the world around you? Why should the raven's image tempt you to idolatry more than the raven itself, out there beyond your windowpanes, black and insolent amid the snow? Therefore, if your name is Wolf, it is permissible for you to draw a wolf on the door of your house, and if your name is Bear, a bear. If peradventure your name is Cohen, and you thus belong to the family of the blessers, why should you not have two blessing hands carved on your architrave, and (as late as possible) on your tombstone. And if, on the other hand, your are just any Fischbaum, you'll be content with a fish, upside down perhaps, trapped between the branches of a tree; or with an apple tree from which herrings hang instead of apples. If in fact you are an Arié, that is, a lion, becoming for you will be a shield on which is carved a small, disheveled lion that leaps at the sky as though to challenge it with gnashing mouth and unsheathed claws, similar in every detail to the innumerable lions the gentiles among whom you live choose for their insignia.

So Rabbi Arié-Lion began his work with a serene spirit, in the cellar of his house on Broad Street: the clay was brought to him at night by two disciples, together with water from the Moldau, and coal to feed the fire in the kiln. Day by day, actually night by night, the golem was taking shape. And it was ready in the year 1579 of the vulgar era, the 5,339th of the Creation; now, 5,339 is not really a prime number but it almost is, and it is the product of 19, which is the number of the sun and of gold, multiplied by 281, which is the number of the bones that compose our body.

He was a giant, and his figure was human from the waist up. There is a reason for this too: the waist is the frontier, only above the waist is man made in God's image, whereas below it he is a beast; because of this, the wise man must not forget to encircle it. Below the waist the golem was truly golem, that is, a fragment of chaos: underneath the suit of mail, which hung all the way to the ground like an apron, one could glimpse only a sturdy tangle of clay, metal and glass. His arms were gnarled and strong as oak branches; his hands nervous and bony, Arié had patterned them on his own. The face was not truly human, but rather leonine, because anyone bringing succor must inspire fear and because Arié had wanted to sign his name.

This then was the golem's figure, but the most remained to be done, for he was without a spirit. Arié hesitated a long time: should he give him blood, and with blood all the passions of beast and man? No, since his servant was incommensurably strong, the gift of blood would have been reckless; Arié wanted a trustworthy, not a rebellious servant. He denied him blood, and with blood he denied him will, Eve's curiosity, the desire for enterprise; but he infused in him other passions, and that came easy, because he only had to draw them from within himself. He endowed him with the ire of Moses and the Prophets, the obedience of Abraham, the arrogance of Cain, the courage of Joshua, and even with a bit of Ahab's madness; but not with Jacob's holy astuteness nor Solomon's wisdom nor Isaiah's light, because he did not want to create a rival for himself.

Therefore, at the decisive moment, when it became a matter of infusing into the servant's leonine skull the three principles of movement, which are the Nous, the Epithymia and the Thymos, Arié destroyed the letters of the first two and wrote on a parchment only those of the third; underneath he added, in large letters of fire, the symbols of God's ineffable name, rolled up the parchment and slipped it into a silver case. Thus the golem had no mind, but he had courage and strength, and the faculty of coming to life only when the case with the Name was slipped between his teeth.

When the time came for the first experiment, Arié's veins trembled as never before. He slipped the Name into place and the monster's eyes lit up and looked at him. He expected it to ask him, 'What do you want from me, oh master?' But instead he heard another question that wasn't new to him and that to him sounded full of anger, 'Why doth the impious prosper?' He then understood that the golem was his son and he experienced joy and at the same time fear before the Lord; because, as it is written, the joy of the Jew contains a crumb of fear.

Arié was not disappointed by his servant. When, deprived of the Name, he rested in the synagogue's caves, he was completely inert, a block of inanimate clay, and needed neither hay nor oats; when the Name called him back to life, he drew all of his strength from the Name and from the air around him: he did not need meat, bread or wine. Neither did he need the sight and the love of his master, on which the horse and dog are nourished: he was never sad or gay, but in his breast of clay hardened by fire burnt a taut anger, quiet and perennial, the same that had flashed in the question that had been his first living act. He did not undertake anything without Arié's command, but he did not undertake everything that Arié did command; the rabbi soon became aware of this and was at once happy and disquieted because of it. It was useless to ask the golem to go into the forest and cut wood, or to go to the fountain for water: he did indeed answer, 'It shall be done, oh master,' he ponderously turned around and left with his rumbling steps; but as soon as he was out of sight he slipped into his dark lair, spit out the Name, and lay rigid in his rocklike inertia. Instead, with a gay glint in his eyes, he accepted all the exploits that required courage and skill, and he performed them with a dark ingenuity all his own.

For many years he was a valid defender of the Prague community against high-handed injustice and violence. Several exploits of his are told: how, all by himself, he barred the way to a platoon of Turkoman warriors who intended to force the White Gate and plunder the ghetto; how he thwarted the plans for a slaughter by capturing the true perpetrator of a murder that the emperor's henchmen tried to disguise as a ritual murder; how, again by himself, he saved the store of grain in the warehouse from a sudden and disastrous flood of the Moldau river.

It is written: 'The seventh day is God's rest: on it you shall do no work whatsoever, you, your son, your servant, your ox, and the stranger within your gates.' Rabbi Arié meditated: the golem was not properly a servant but rather a machine moved by the Name's spirit; from this point of view it was similar to the windmills which are allowed to grind on the sabbath, and to sailboats, which can navigate. But then he remembered that one must put a hedge about the Law, and he decided to take the Name away from him every Friday evening at sunset, and this he did for many years.

Now there came a day (it was in fact a Friday) on which the rabbi had taken the golem into his own house, on the first floor of an ancient tenement on Broad Street, whose façade was black and corroded by time. He assigned to him a pile of small chunks of wood to chop, lifted one of his arms and put the axe into his hand. The golem, with the axe immobile in midair, slowly turned to him his inexpressive and ferocious mug and did not move. 'Come now, chop!' Arié ordered, and deep laughter tickled his heart without appearing on his face. The monster's laziness and disobedience flattered him because these are human, innate passions; he had not inspired them in him, the clay colossus had thought of them by himself: he was more human than Arié had meant him to be. 'Come now, to work,' Arié repeated.

The golem took two heavy steps toward the wood, holding the hatchet in front of him, his arm outstretched; he stopped; then he dropped the axe, which rang out against the granite slab. With his left hand he snatched up a first small log, placed it vertically on the block, brought down his right hand on it like an axe: the small log flew away in two chunks. He did the same with the second, the third and the others: two paces from the block to the pile, a half turn, two paces from the pile to the block, a slash of the naked clay hand, half a turn. Troubled and fascinated, Arié watched his servant's angry and mechanical work. Why had he refused the hatchet? He thought about it for a long time; his mind was accustomed to the interpretation of the Law and of sacred stories, which are made up of arduous questions and argumentative and witty answers, and yet for at least half an hour the solution eluded him. He persisted in his search: the golem was his work, his son, and it is a painful goad to discover in our children opinions and acts of will different from ours, distant, incomprehensible.

So: the golem was a servant who did not want to be a servant. The hatchet was for him a servile tool, a symbol of servitude, as the bit is for the horse and the yoke for the ox; not so the hand, which is part of you, and in whose palm is impressed your fate. He was pleased with this answer, he tarried to consider it and compare it to the texts, and he was satisfied with it. It was witty-acute, plausible and blessedly cheerful. He tarried so long that he did not notice that something was happening, indeed had already happened outside the window, in the air of Broad Street, in the hazy sky of Prague: the sun had set, the sabbath had begun.

When he did notice it, it was late. Arié tried in vain to stop his servant in order to extract the Name from his mouth: the golem eluded him, swept him away with hard arms, turned his back to him. The rabbi, who had never touched him before, came to know his inhuman weight, and a hardness like that of a rock: like a pendulum the golem swung back and forth in the small room and chopped wood on top of wood, so that the fragments sprayed all the way to the beams in the ceiling. Arié hoped and prayed that the golem's fury would cease when the pile of logs was finished; but at that point the giant bent over, creaking in all of his joints, picked up the hatchet, and with the hatchet he stormed away until dawn, shattering everything around him, the furniture, the drapes, the windows, the dividing walls, even the safe with the silver and the shelves of holy books.

Arié sought shelter under the staircase, and there he had the ease and time to meditate over a terrible truth: nothing brings one closer to madness than two contradictory orders. In the golem's stony brain was written, 'You shall faithfully serve your master: you shall obey him like a corpse'; but there was also written the entire Law of Moses, which had been transmitted to him with every letter of the message from which he had been born, because every letter of the Law contains all the Law. Thus in him was also written, 'You shall rest on the sabbath: you shall do no work whatsoever on it.' Arié understood his servant's madness and praised God for having understood, because whoever understands has gone more than halfway: he praised God despite the ruination of his house because he recognized that the guilt was his alone, neither God's nor the golem's.

When Saturday's dawn shone through the broken windows and there was nothing left to break in the rabbi's house, the golem stopped as though exhausted. Arié approached him fearfully, he reached out a hesitant hand and extracted from his mouth the silver capsule that contained the Name.

The monster's eyes darkened and did not light up again. When evening came, and the sad sabbath was over, Arié tried in vain to call him back to life so that he would help him, with the orderly strength of the past, and tidy up his devastated home. The golem remained immobile and inert, similar by now in everything to a forbidden and hateful idol, an obscene man-beast of reddish clay chipped here and there by his own frenzy. Arié touched him with one finger and the giant fell to the ground and was shattered. The rabbi collected the fragments and stored them in the attic of the house on Broad Street in Prague, already decrepit at that time, where, according to the story, they still remain.

Mutiny

To Mario Rigoni Stern

It is already ten years now that the Faragos cultivate the land adjacent to our garden, and from it has grown a rudimentary, summary and inarticulate friendship, as is typical of those established across a fence, or from bank to bank. The Faragos have been horticulturists forever, and we are filled with envy and admiration for them; they always know how to do the right thing in the right way and at the right moment, whereas we, who are dilettantes and citified, feed on errors. We devoutly follow their advice, the advice we solicit and the other bits that father Farago shouts to us through the fence when he sees us commit some enormity, or when the fruits of our enormities cry to high heaven; and yet despite this humility and docility of ours, our kerchief of land is filled with weeds and anthills, while their vegetable gardens, which are not less than two hectares, are clean, tidy and prosperous.

'You need an eye,' the Faragos say, or 'You need a hand.' Except for Clotilde, they do not like to come and see up close what we are doing: perhaps they do not want any responsibilities, or they realize that a greater intimacy and familiarity between them and us is neither possible nor desirable; or perhaps, indeed probably, they do not want to teach us too many things: for, you never know, one day we might get it into our heads to steal their trade. Advice, yes, but from a distance.

Clotilde is different. We've seen her grow from summer to summer like a poplar, and now she's eleven years old.

She's swarthy, slim, her hair is forever falling over her eyes, and she's full of mystery like all adolescent girls; but she was mysterious also before, when she was round, two feet tall, and covered with soil up to her eyes, and to all appearances was learning to speak and walk directly from the sky, or perhaps from the earth itself, with which she had an obvious but indecipherable relationship. At that time we would often see her stretched out between the furrows on the humid, tepid, recently turned-over soil: she smiled at the sky with closed eyes, intent on the palpitation of the butterflies that alighted on her as on a flower, motionless so as not to frighten them away. She held crickets and spiders in her hand, without revulsion and without harming them; she caressed them with her brown finger as one does with domestic animals, then she put them back on the ground: 'Go little beast, go on your way.'

Now that she has grown up, she too gives us advice and explanations, but of a different nature. She has explained to me that the bindweed is gentle but lazy; if you let it have its way, it invades the fields and chokes them – not to harm them, as we do, it is just too lazy to grow straight up. 'You see what it does? It too plants its root into the earth, but not very deep, because it does not feel like working hard and isn't very strong. Then it divides into threads, and every thread creeps along to look for something to eat, and they never cross: they're no fools, they agree beforehand, I go west and you go east. They make flowers, which are pretty enough and even a bit perfumed, and then these little balls, you see them? because they too think about the future.'

For weeds, on the contrary, she has no pity. 'It's useless for you to chop it to pieces with your hoe: every piece grows back anyhow later, like the dragons in the fairy tales. Indeed, the weed is a dragon: if you look carefully, you can see the teeth, the nails and scales. It kills all the other plants, and it never dies, because it stays underground; what you see outside is nothing, those small thin leaves with an innocent air, that almost look like grass. But the more you dig the more you find, and if you dig deep down you'll find a blackened, knotty skeleton, hard as iron and I don't know how old: there, that's the weed. Cows pass over it and trample it and it doesn't die: if you bury it in a tomb of stone, it cracks the stone and makes its way out. The only remedy is fire. I don't talk to the weed.'

I asked her whether she talks to other plants, and she told me of course. Her father and her mother do too, but she better than they: it isn't really a talking with the mouth, as we do, but it is clear that the plants give signs and make grimaces when they want something, and they understand ours; but one mustn't lose patience and one must try to make oneself understood, because in general plants are very slow, in understanding, in expressing themselves, and in moving. 'Do you see this?' she said to me, pointing to one of our lemon trees. 'He's complaining, he's been complaining for some time, and if you don't understand you don't notice, and meanwhile he suffers.'

'Complaining about what? He doesn't lack for water and we treat him exactly the same as the others.'

'I don't know, it's not always easy to understand. You can see that on this side his leaves are all shriveled up, so it's on this side that something is wrong. Maybe his roots are running into a rock: you can see that, still on the same side, there is an ugly fold in his trunk.'

According to Clotilde, everything that grows from the earth, and has green leaves, is 'people like us,' with whom one can find a way to get along; precisely because of this one mustn't keep plants and flowers in pots, because it is like locking up animals in a cage: they become either stupid or vicious, in short they are no longer the same, and it is selfish on our part to hem them in like that, simply for the pleasure of looking at them. Weeds, that is, crabgrass, are in fact the exception, because they do not come from the ground but from below ground, and that is the realm of treasures, dragons and the dead. In her opinion, the below-ground is a country as complicated as ours, only it is dark while here it is light: there are caves, tunnels, brooks, rivers and lakes, and in addition there are the veins of ores, which are poisonous and malignant save for iron, which within certain limits is man's friend. There are treasures too: some hidden by men in distant times, others that have lain down there forever, gold and diamonds. Here live the dead, but Clotilde does not like to speak of them. Last month, a bulldozer was at work in the property that borders theirs: pale and fascinated, Clotilde watched the machine's powerful work until the excavation was three meters deep, then she disappeared for several days and returned only after the machine had left, and we saw that in that big hole there were only earth and stone, puddles of still water and some exposed roots.

She also told me that not all plants are in agreement. There are those that are domesticated, like cows and chickens, and would not be able to get along without man, but there are others that protest, try to escape, and at times succeed. If you're not careful, pay attention, they go wild and no longer bear fruit, or bear fruit as they like and not the way we like: sour, hard, all pit. If it is not domesticated, a plant becomes homesick, especially if she lives in the vicinity of a wild wood. She would like to go back to the wood, and let only the bees take care of fertilizing her and the birds and wind spread her seed. She has shown me peaches from their orchard, and it was exactly as she said: the trees closest to the enclosure stretched their branches beyond it, like arms.

'Come with me: I must show you something.' She led me up the hill into a wood that almost no one knows, it is so dense with brushwood. And besides as though protected by a frame of old crumbling terraces, which are covered by a kind of thorny ivy whose name I don't know. It is beautiful to look at, with leaves shaped like spear tips, shiny, colored a brilliant green flecked with white; but the trunks, the twigs, and even the reverse side of the leaves themselves bristle with hooked thorns, barbed like arrowheads: if they merely graze the flesh, they penetrate it and tear away a piece of it.

On the way, while I had barely enough breath to direct my steps and voice a few syllables of assent, Clotilde went on talking. She was telling me that she had just picked up some important information and had learned it from a rosemary bush, who in fact is a peculiar type, man's friend but at a distance, a bit like cats; he likes to be independent, and that fine aromatic flavor that goes so well with roasted meat is an invention of his: men like it, but insects find it bitter. In short, it is a repellent that he invented thousands and thousands of years ago, when man didn't yet exist; and in fact you'll never see a rosemary chewed up by caterpillars or snails. Also his leaves, shaped like needles, are a good invention, but not the rosemary's. They were invented by the pine trees and firs, a long time before: they are a good defense, because tiny beasts who eat leaves always begin from the tip and if they find it woody and sharply pointed they soon lose their enthusiasm.

The rosemary had made certain gestures to make her understand that she must delve into that wood for a certain distance and in a certain direction and that she would find something important: she had already gone there a few days before, and it was really true, and she wanted to show it to me too. But she had been somewhat upset that the rosemary had given away a secret.

She showed me a path half buried by brambles, along which we managed to get into the wood without too many scratches: and there, at the centre of the wood, there was a small circular clearing that had never been there before. At that spot the ground was almost flat and the soil seemed smooth, pounded, without a single blade of grass and without a stone. There were, however, three or four stones at approximately a meter from the periphery, and Clotilde told me that she had put them there for reference, to verify what the rosemary had given her to understand: namely, that that was a tree school, a secret place where trees taught each other how to walk, in hatred of men and unbeknownst to them. She led me by the hand (she had a hand that was quite grown-up, rough and strong) around the circle, and she showed me many small, imperceptible things: that, around each trunk, the ground was loose, cracked, as though piled up on the outside, and hollowed out on the inside; that all the trunks were bent slightly outward, and that also the climbers ran radially outward. Obviously, I'm not at all sure that similar signs can be seen elsewhere in other clearings, or perhaps in all of them, and that they don't have a different meaning, or even none at all: but Clotilde was filled with excitement.

'There are intelligent and stupid ones, lazy and alert ones, and even the most clever don't really get that far. But this one, for example' – she pointed to a juniper – 'it's quite a while I've kept my eye on him, and I don't trust him.' That juniper she told me had moved at least one meter in four days. He had found the right way to do it: little by little he let all the roots on one side die and strengthened those on the other, and he wanted everybody to do the same. He was ambitious and patient – all plants are patient, that is their strength – but the fact was, he was also ambitious, and had been one of the first to understand that a plant that moves can conquer a country and free himself from men.

'They would all like to free themselves, but they don't know how, after so many years that we have given the orders. Some trees, like the olive trees, have been resigned for centuries, but they're ashamed, and it's quite clear from the way in which they grow, all contorted and desperate. Others, like the peach and almond trees, have surrendered and bear fruit, but even you know that as soon as they can they become wild again. As to others, I don't know yet – with chestnut trees and oaks it is difficult to understand what they want; perhaps they are too old and have too much wood, and by now they no longer want anything, as happens with old people: just that after summer should come winter, and after winter summer.'

There was also a wild cherry tree that spoke. It wasn't that he spoke Italian, but it was like when you have a conversation with the Dutch people who come to the seaside in July, whom in short you don't understand word for word, but by gestures and intonation you manage to find out pretty well what they're trying to say. That cherry tree spoke with the rustle of its leaves, which you could hear by pressing your ear against the trunk, and he said things with which Clotilde was not in agreement: that one mustn't make flowers because they are a flattery to man, nor fruits, which are a waste and an undeserved gift. One must fight man, no longer purify the air for him, pull up one's roots and leave, even at the cost of dying or becoming wild again. I too laid my ear against the trunk, but I caught only an indistinct murmur, even though it was a bit more sonorous than that produced by the other plants.

It had grown dark by now, and there was no moon. The lights of the village and of the beach gave us only a vague idea of the direction we should take in order to descend; in no time we were badly entangled in the brambles and the ruined terraces. We had to jump blindly from one to the next, trying to guess in the growing dark whether we would land on rocks or thorns, or solid ground. After an hour's descent we were both tired, scratched and dismayed, and the lights below were as distant as before.

Suddenly we heard a dog bark. We stopped: he was coming directly toward us, galloping horizontally along one of the terraces. This could be good or bad; from his voice he couldn't be a very large dog, but he barked with indignation and tenacity until he was out of breath, and then we could hear him gasp for air with a short convulsed rattle. In no time he was a few meters below us, and it became clear that he did not bark capriciously but out of duty: he did not intend to let us enter his territory. Clotilde asked his pardon for the invasion and she explained to him that we had lost our way and wanted nothing better than to leave; so he did well to bark, it was his business, but he would do better if he would show us the road that led to his house, and he would not be wasting any time and neither would we. She spoke in such a tranquil and persuasive voice that the dog immediately quieted down: we could make him out below us, like a vague white and black blotch. We descended a few steps, and felt under our feet the springy hardness of beaten-down earth; the dog set out to the right, parallel with the hill, every now and then making a small whining noise and stopping to see if we were following him. In this way after a quarter of an hour we reached the dog's house, welcomed by a tremulous chorus of goatish bleatings: from there, despite the darkness, we easily found a well-trodden trail that descended to the village.

Excellent is the Water

Boero was having a conversation with himself in the solitude of the laboratory, and he couldn't come to a conclusion. He had worked and studied hard for almost two years to win that position: he had also done things of which he was somewhat ashamed: he had courted Curti, for whom he had no respect whatsoever; he had even (calculatingly or naively? – this too he couldn't understand) in front of Curti cast doubt on the ability and preparation of two of his colleagues and rivals.

Now, he was there, he had made it, inside, with full title: he had a territory of his own, small but his, a stool, a desk, half a closet of glassware, a square meter of counter, a clothes-hanger and a smock. There he was, and it was not as splendid as he had expected; it wasn't even amusing, on the contrary it was very sad to think (a) that it was not enough to work in a laboratory, to feel mobilized, a soldier on the front line of science; (b) that he would have to, for at least a year, devote himself to diligent and idiotic work, diligent precisely because idiotic, work made up only of diligence, work already done by at least ten others, all of them obscure, all probably already dead, and dead without another name than the one lost among another thirty thousand, in the dizzying index by authors in Landolt's Tables.

Today, for example, he was supposed to verify the value of the viscosity coefficient of water. Yes, sir: of distilled water. Is it possible to imagine a more insipid job? A dishwasher's job, not a job befitting a young physicist: washing the viscosimeter twenty times a day.

The job of . . . an accountant, a nitpicker, an insect. And that's not all: the fact is that the values asertained today don't agree with those found yesterday; such things happen, but no one likes to admit them. There is a discrepancy, small but certain, obstinate as only facts know how to be: in any case it's a well-known business, it is the natural maliciousness of inanimate things. And so you repeat the washup of the apparatus, you distill the water for a fourth time, you check the thermostat for a sixth time, you whistle under your breath so as not to curse, and you repeat the measurements again.

He spent the entire afternoon repeating the measurements, but he did not do the calculations because he did not want to spoil his evening. He did them the following morning and, sure enough, the discrepancy was still there: not only that, it had even grown larger. Now you must know that the Landolt Tables are sacred, they are the Truth: one is asked to retake the measurements only out of sadism, Boero suspected, only to verify the fifth and fourth significant figure; but if the third does not correspond, and that was his case, what the hell are we going to do about it? You must know that doubting Landolt is far worse than doubting the Gospel: if you're wrong, you cover yourself with ridicule and compromise your career, and if you're right (which is improbable) you gain neither advantage nor glory but rather the reputation of being, precisely, an accountant, nitpicker and insect; and at most the grim joy of being right where another is wrong, a joy which lasts the space of a morning.

He went to talk about it with Curti, and Curti, as he could have foreseen, flew into a rage. He told him to do the measurements over again, he answered that he had already done them over many times and had them up to here, and Curti told him to change trades. Boero went down the stairs determined to change trades, but seriously, radically; let Curti go look for another slave. He did not return to the Institute for an entire week.

To mull over things is not very Christian, it is painful, boring, and in general yields no profit. He knew this, and yet for four days he had done nothing else: he tried all the variations, reviewed all the things he had done, heard and said, imagined the others that he could have said, heard or done, examined the causes and consequences of the first and of the second: he raved and haggled. He smoked one cigarette after another, stretched out on the gray sand of the Sangone, trying to calm down and retrieve the sense of reality. He asked himself whether he had truly burnt the bridges behind him, if he should really change trades, or if he should go back to Curti and come to an understanding, or whether it wouldn't have been even more sensible to go back to his job, tap the scale with his thumb and falsify the results.

Then the song of the cicadas distracted him, and he lost himself in contemplating the whirlpools at his feet. 'Excellent is the water' popped into his mind: who had said that? Pindar perhaps, or another of those fine fellows you study in *liceo*. And yet, looking more closely, it began to seem to him that something about that water was wrong. He had known that stream for many years, he had come to play there as a child, and later, precisely to that spot with a girl and then with another: well, the water looked strange. He touched it, tasted it: it was fresh, limpid, it had no taste, gave off the usual slight swampy odor, and yet it was strange. It gave the impression of being less mobile, less alive: the small cascades did not carry along bubbles of air, the surface was less rippled, also the rumble no longer seemed the same, it was more muffled, as though muted. He went down to the deep basin and threw a rock into it: the circular waves were slow and lazy, and died out before reaching the shore. At that he remembered that the pumping works of the municipal aqueduct were not far from that place, and suddenly his indolence evaporated, he felt as subtle and crafty as a snake. He had to take away a sample of that water: he rummaged through his pockets in vain, then he climbed the bank to where he had left his motorcycle. In one of the two bags he found a sheet of plastic that he sometimes used to protect the seat from the rain: with it he made a small bag, filled it with water and tied it tightly. Then he left in a whirlwind for the laboratory. That water was monstrous: thirteen hundred centipoise at 20 degrees Celsius, 30 percent more than the normal value.

The Sangone's water was viscous from its sources to where it flowed into the Po river: the water of all other streams and rivers was normal. Boero had made up with Curti; actually Curti, confronted by the onrush of facts, had made up with Boero. In furious haste they compiled a memorandum in both their names, but when it was in galleys they had to write another in even greater haste, because in the meantime also the water of Chisone and that of the Pellice had begun to turn viscous and that of the Sangone was up to a value of 1.45. These waters were not altered by distillation, dialysis and filtration through absorption columns; when subjected to electrolysis and recombining of hydrogen and oxygen, the water obtained was identical to the original; after a long electrolysis under high tensions the viscosity was further augmented.

That was in April, and in May the Po became abnormal too, at first in some of its stretches, then along the entire course all the way to its mouth. By now the water's viscosity was visible also to the untrained eye; the current flowed silent and murky, without a murmur, like a spill of depleted oil. The upper parts were clogged and tended to overflow, while the lower streams were drying up, and near Pavia and Mantua the stream's dead branches silted up in the span of a few weeks.

The suspended muds sedimented more slowly than usual: halfway through June, seen from the plains, the delta was surrounded by a yellowish haze for a radius of twenty kilometers. At the end of June it rained all over Europe: over northern Italy, Austria and Hungary the rain was viscous, drained off with difficulty and stagnated in the fields, which turned into swamps. On all the plains the harvests were destroyed, while in even slightly inclined areas the cultivations prospered more than usual.

The anomaly rapidly extended during the course of the summer, with a mechanism that defied all attempts at explanation: viscous rains were recorded in Montenegro, Denmark and Lithuania, while a second epicenter was showing up in the Atlantic, off the coast of Morocco. No instrument was needed to distinguish these from normal rains: the drops were heavy and large, like small blisters; they cut through the air with a thin hiss, and broke up against the ground with a particular splat. Drops weighing two to three grams were gathered; drenched by this water the asphalt became viscid, and it was impossible to drive on it with rubber-tired vehicles.

In the contaminated zone, almost all tall trunked trees died within a few months, and wild weeds and bushes sprung up in masses: this fact was attributed to the difficult ascent of viscous water through the trunks' capillary veins. In the cities civic life continued almost normally for a few months: only a reduction of pressure in all drinking-water pipes was observed, and also bathtubs and sinks took longer to empty. Washing machines became unusable: they filled up with foam the moment they were turned on, and the motors burnt out.

It seemed at the beginning that the animal world offered a protective barrier against the entry of viscous water into the human organism, but the hope was short-lived.

So, in less than a year, the present situation was established. The defenses have collapsed much sooner than feared: just like the water of the sea, the rivers and the clouds, so all the humors in our bodies have become denser and corrupt. The sick have died, and now we are all sick: our hearts, pitiful pumps planned for the water of another time, strain from dawn to dawn to introduce the viscous blood into the network of veins; we die at thirty or forty at the most, from edema, pure fatigue, fatigue at all hours, without mercy and without pause, a fatigue that weighs within us since the day of our birth, and impedes our every rapid and prolonged movement.

Just like the rivers, we too are torpid: the food we eat and the water we drink must wait hours before becoming part of us, and this makes us inert and sluggish. We do not weep: the lacrymal liquid dwells superfluous in our eyes, and it does not form in teardrops but oozes out like a serum that robs our weeping of dignity and relief. It is like this in all of Europe by now, and the evil caught us by surprise before we could understand it. Only now, in America and elsewhere, are they beginning to have an idea of the nature of water's alteration, but they are very far from knowing how to remedy it: meanwhile there have been reports that the level of the Great Lakes is rapidly increasing, that all of the Amazon is turning into a swamp, that the Hudson overflows and breaks all the dams along all its upper reaches, that Alaska's rivers and lakes form ice that is no longer fragile but as elastic and tenacious as steel. The Caribbean sea no longer has waves.

ABACUS